Buried Promises

Don't Call Me Hero
Book 7

Eliza Lentzski

Copyright © 2025 Eliza Lentzski
All rights reserved.

This is a work of fiction. All names, characters, places, and incidents are the products of the author's imagination or are used fictitiously. Any resemblance to events, locales, or real persons, living or dead, other than those in the public domain, is entirely coincidental.

No part of this book may be reproduced, re-sold, or transmitted electronically or otherwise, without written permission from the author.

ISBN: 9798284677254
Imprint: Independently published

Series by Eliza Lentzski

Don't Call Me Hero Series
Don't Call Me Hero
Damaged Goods
Cold Blooded Lover
One Little Secret
Grave Mistake
Stolen Hearts
Buried Promises

∾

Winter Jacket Series
Winter Jacket
Winter Jacket 2: New Beginnings
Winter Jacket 3: Finding Home
Winter Jacket 4: All In
Hunter

Standalone Novels

Half-Court Heat (forthcoming)

Hoops & Heartstrings

Lighthouse Keeper

Sour Grapes

The Woman in 3B

Sunscreen & Coconuts

The Final Rose

Bittersweet Homecoming

Fragmented

Apophis: A Love Story for the End of the World

Second Chances

Date Night

Love, Lust, & Other Mistakes

Diary of a Human

∽

Works as E.L. Blaisdell

Drained: The Lucid (with Nica Curt)

To C

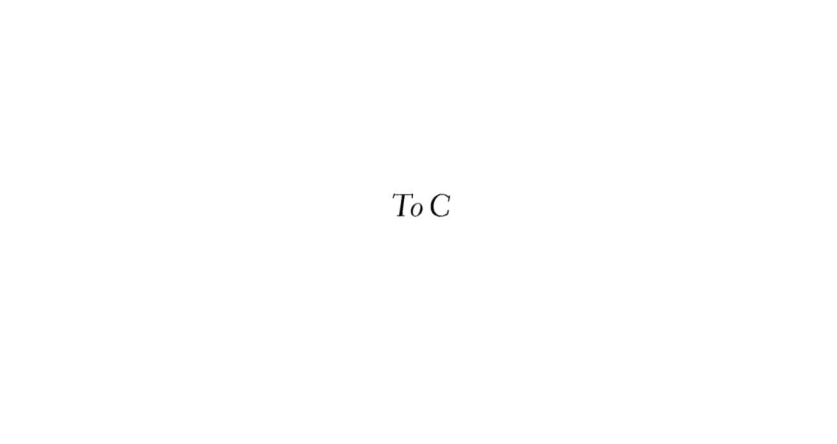

Chapter One

I heard the sharp *clickclack* of her designer heels before I actually saw her. The punctuated sound rose above the din of the busy stadium. Or maybe it only seemed that way—maybe it was only my quickened pulse. Nearly a year of dating, and she still made my heart race.

Because, seriously—who wore red bottom shoes to a basketball game?

Julia appeared at the edge of the crowd, the refined silhouette of her tailored pantsuit standing out against a sea of jerseys and graphic t-shirts. The pinched look on her face softened when she spotted me by an elevated cocktail table.

I wiped my palms on my jeans, feeling every bit as casual as I looked in my player jersey and sneakers. I'd had time after work to swing by Julia's condo to change clothes, but she had presumably come directly from her office. The remnants of a greasy slice of pepperoni pizza sat on a paper plate in front of me—one of my less glamorous moments.

Julia didn't seem to care. She closed the distance between us, her hands sliding over my hips as she leaned in. We were close—close enough that I could smell her skin and the spicy scent of her sandalwood shampoo.

She tugged lightly at the bottom hem of my jersey, a teasing smile on her lips. "You always have such team spirit."

I grinned. "We could grab you something at the Team Store?" I suggested. "Maybe a foam finger?"

Her laugh was soft. Tired. "How about you get me something to drink instead?"

"Rough day?" My smile turned sympathetic. "We can go home if you want to."

Her days lately had stretched beyond typical working hours as she continued to get acclimated to her new job as a *pro bono* lawyer for one of the Twin Cities' most ruthless criminal defense law firms. Her position had been created to give back to the community—to show that even the most cut-throat team of litigators had heart.

Julia's mood shifted and she purposefully brightened. "That's not necessary, darling. I'll be fine."

She looped her arm through mine and allowed me to guide her in the direction of the closest beverage vendor. Not long after, I was balancing an oversized beer in one hand and a plastic bucket of buttery popcorn in the other while Julia sipped her wine.

We made our way down to the courtside seats—a perk

of Julia's new job. My excitement grew the closer we descended to the court. Courtside wasn't a bad way to watch a game. I could already anticipate being disappointed with anything less.

"This is so cool," I enthused. "I've never sat this close before."

I'd been to several pro and semi-pro Minnesota-based sporting events, mostly with my dad growing up. But he'd never splurged on tickets. We tended to sit in the nosebleed seats, the highest level of the arena, so far away that the athletes had looked like miniature action figures.

I tried to imagine surprising him with courtside seats. He'd bristle at the extravagance and once at the game he'd feign disinterest as if watching a game only a few feet from the action was an everyday occurrence.

What was it that made Midwesterners so hard to impress? So reluctant to show emotion?

Julia, predictably, maintained a cool and unaffected exterior, although I suspected her nonchalance stemmed from something else. She gestured toward the giant men taking warm-up shots. "How hard is it to make a basket when you're seven feet tall? That hardly seems like a skill to me."

I smirked. "You're a tough woman to impress."

We settled into our respective cushioned seats close to the court's edge. "We should get tickets to a women's game next season," I suggested. "If you want to see skill and pure basketball game play—that's where it's at." I popped a few pieces of buttery popcorn into my mouth and smiled around the addictive artificial flavor. "I could even buy you your own jersey."

"I doubt I could pull off that look as well as you do, darling," Julia resisted.

"Maybe not layered over your power suit," I teased, "but think about the statement it would make at your office."

Julia tilted her head, her lips curving. "What, that I'm approachable?" she huffed. "That's already the PR campaign for my position at the firm. *Pro bono* queen. Champion of the underdog."

"It's not the worst title." I leaned back in my seat and shoveled more popcorn into my open mouth.

Julia gave a knowing hum, her expression guarded. "Although behind closed doors, I'm sure the nicknames are far less generous. Forcing culture change at an established business isn't the key to making friends." She straightened in her chair and seemed to roll her shoulders. "But that's fine. I'm not there to be liked or make friends."

I frowned and lowered the popcorn bucket. "That sounds pretty lonely."

Julia met my gaze, her eyes softening. "It's not lonely when I get to come home to someone who reminds me why I do it. Someone who believes in me even when the rest of the room doesn't."

My cheeks warmed, and I looked away, pretending to focus on the players still getting limber on the court. "I'm just saying, they should be giving you a parade, not the cold shoulder."

Julia smiled faintly. "You're very kind to say so, Cassidy."

I reached for her hand, curling my fingers around hers. She didn't pull away despite the lingering, buttery grease that coated my fingertips. "And I plan to keep saying so. Motivational texts. Daily affirmations?"

Her laugh was soft, but it reached her eyes this time. "Chronically online memes?"

I beamed. "Memes are modern wisdom, babe."

She shook her head, visibly amused, and settled back into her seat. The game was moments away from starting, players gathering at center court for the opening tip-off, but I wasn't thinking about the court or the players or the cheering fans that surrounded us. My thoughts only had room for the beautiful woman seated beside me, her hand resting lightly on my knee.

The buzzer sounded, signaling halftime, and the players jogged off the court to polite applause. Around us, the crowd began to buzz with conversation or stood from their seats for a bathroom break and a concession stand visit.

I turned to Julia and caught her consulting her watch.

"You ready to call it?" I asked.

Her lips twitched into a half-smile. "Would you mind terribly? I don't want to rob you of the experience, but I have another long day tomorrow."

I immediately sprang to my feet and grabbed my leather jacket from the back of my chair. "Say no more."

As we walked toward the exit, I kept close, shielding Julia from the jostling crowd. Minnesota Nice had apparently given way to more carnal impulses in the desire for beer refills and getting to the front of the bathroom line. I led the way, half a step in front of Julia. Old instincts—it didn't matter that this wasn't a combat zone. Julia's hand brushed my arm, a small reminder that she didn't need protection, but she didn't push me away either.

"So, what now?" she asked once we hit the chilly night air. Her breath puffed out in delicate clouds, the outside temperature a sharp contrast to the warmth of the stadium. "Back home? Or is this the part where you try to tempt me with greasy fast food?"

I shoved my hands into my jacket pockets, my breath forming a foggy trail in front of me. "Depends. Have you ever tried one of those cheese curd burgers from Murphy's on Hennepin? Life changing."

Her look was pointed but amused. "I've managed to go my entire life without cheese curds. Somehow I think I'll survive."

∼

Julia stood before the vanity in the condo's en-suite bathroom, carefully removing her makeup with gentle swipes of a cotton pad. The soft lighting in the master bathroom cast her features in a warm glow, making her look more relaxed than she had all evening. I leaned against the doorframe, brushing my teeth and watching her. It was a quiet ritual, one I never tired of.

"You've got a full day tomorrow," I said, rinsing my mouth. "Anything I can help with?"

She glanced at me through the mirror, her expression soft but inscrutable. "It's nothing you need to worry about."

"I'm already worrying."

Julia set the cotton pad down and turned to face me. "I'm visiting my mother in the morning." Her tone was carefully measured. "And then I have an appointment with my doctor in the afternoon for my first hormone injection."

I swallowed. "Oh. That's ... big."

Her smile was faint, almost rueful. "It is."

"Do you want me to come with you? To either one?"

"You don't have to do that. I know your plate is just as full as mine."

I reached for her hand, threading my fingers through hers. "That doesn't mean I don't want to be there if you need me."

Julia had finally settled on a new assisted-living facility for her mother just before the Christmas holiday. The suburban location wasn't necessarily convenient to her St. Paul condo, but she'd preferred the spread out footprint of the suburban site to any of the smaller facilities we'd toured in the Twin Cities.

I tried not to get jealous about the stolen time. It was her mother, after all, not Julia going to a bar after work to get drunk with her friends. I hadn't accompanied her on any visits since her mother's rehoming, but I knew I should make more of an effort. I'd never liked healthcare facilities, however, and old people made me nervous.

Julia's shoulders relaxed a fraction, the tension easing out of her posture. "Visiting my mother … it's not always pleasant."

I nodded and squeezed her hand. "Still. I'm happy to go if it would help you."

"And the doctor?" she asked, her voice quieter.

This was to be the first of many injections. From what I'd learned since Julia had first revealed that she wanted to freeze her eggs, hormone shots and ultrasounds would take place over the next ten to fourteen days, followed by the actual retrieval procedure. The hormone shots would trick her body into producing multiple eggs at once to be harvested and stored until the timing was right.

"That, too," I said. "Whatever you need."

For a moment, she said nothing—she only studied our joined hands. Then she leaned in, her lips brushing against my temple. "Thank you. I'll let you know."

"You'd better."

My tone was teasing, but my chest felt tight. Julia carried so much, always with poise and precision, but sometimes I wondered how much she let herself feel.

Julia pulled back and met my gaze. Her smile softened into something real. "You're a perfect partner, Cassidy."

"Just trying to keep up with you," I said, letting myself smile back.

. . .

By the time we climbed into bed, the condo was quiet except for the occasional hum of traffic from the street below. Julia had already dimmed the lights, casting the room in soft shadows. She slid under the covers with her usual grace, her bare legs brushing against mine as I settled in beside her.

I shifted closer, wrapping an arm around her waist and resting my head on her shoulder. She didn't protest; her hand lightly trailed down my forearm in a way that felt both reassuring and grounding.

"That's an awfully nice ring," she murmured. "Someone has exquisite taste."

My gaze lowered to the flashing diamond on my left ring finger. Rather than admiring the engagement ring, I experienced a pang of guilt. I still wanted to get a ring for Julia, but the prospect intimidated me. What if I chose something she hated? Would she second-guess her own proposal that I knew her so little to buy her something so ugly?

"Have you thought about a sperm donor?" I asked.

"Is this a serious conversation?" she returned.

"Would you want to know the guy? Or do you think you'll go to a bank and get a stranger's sperm?" I wondered. "Do they still call them banks? Like, making a *deposit* sounds really gross. There's got to be another term for that by now, right?"

I heard her quiet puff of air. "I guess we *are* having this conversation."

"I was only curious if you'd thought about the next step, that's all," I insisted. "No pressure."

"No pressure indeed." She let out a quiet, exasperated sigh, but her hand resumed its slow, absentminded movements on my arm. "In truth, I wish I could eliminate the necessity of a man altogether, but unfortunately science doesn't work that way yet."

"I kind of envy straight couples," I thought aloud. "They don't have to go through this."

"Fertility complications are more common than you'd think," Julia observed. "Many couples, even opposite-sex partners, often need a little boost from a doctor."

"Yeah, sure, but you know when couples are like *'we're trying to have a baby'* and it's just polite-speak for having a lot of sex? It sounds kind of fun."

Julia quietly chuckled. "I don't think we've ever needed an excuse to be intimate."

"I'm just saying, if you want my opinion on potential donors, I'm here for that, too."

Julia's head tilted toward me. "Darling, you're impossible sometimes."

"And yet you still love me."

She didn't respond immediately, but her hand moved to cradle my cheek. Her thumb brushed softly against my skin. "I do," she said quietly, almost as if it were a confession.

I leaned into her touch, closing my eyes and letting the moment settle over us. Julia's walls could be formidable, but every now and then, she let me peek behind them.

I felt subtle movements beside me. The bedsheets rustled and the queen-sized mattress shifted. Julia's reposed figure pressed tight against my own. Strong, feminine fingers curled around the waistband of my flannel sleep shorts while fingers from a second hand slid up my upper thigh and beneath the leg hole of my shorts.

"What are you doing?" Suspicion crept into my tone.

"If we're going to have a baby, I don't want you missing out on all of that *fun sex* while we're trying to conceive."

Julia's voice was remarkably matter-of-fact, as though her fingertips weren't tracing the outline of my naked pussy with a gentle, teasing touch.

I swallowed hard and barely resisted canting into her hand. "What-what happened to having an early morning?"

I wasn't really complaining or concerned, but it felt like the noble thing to do—to give her an out.

Julia's laughter was low and husky. "Cassidy, be a dear and just enjoy this."

My voice was barely audible over the sound of my own ragged breathing: "Yes, ma'am."

The bedroom was dark, seemingly heightening my other senses. The scent of Julia's spicy, earthy perfume. Her warm breath tickling against my neck. Her voice in my ear.

"You like this, don't you, dear?" she said in that smoky, low burr. "You like being touched. Being teased. Being made to feel like you're the only thing that matters."

Julia continued to tease me beneath my shorts. Her fingers traced light circles around my entrance; my hips instinctively arched to meet her touch. When her fingers grazed my clit, my entire body convulsed.

Her fingers never stopped moving. She circled my clit and tapped against my entrance. I felt my hips arching up, my legs spreading wider as I invited her to touch me more.

"I can feel how wet you are. So ready," Julia approved, her voice still a murmur in my ear. "I can feel your pussy trembling, desperate for my fingers." Her lips moved against my ear when she spoke: "But if you want my fingers, you'll have to do it yourself."

Julia's words were a challenge—a dare to take what I wanted. I hesitated, only briefly, before reaching beneath the blankets that covered us. I lifted my backside off the mattress and pushed my shorts down my legs. The fabric bunched around my thighs as I exposed myself to her.

I continued to blindly seek her out. I found her hand, despite the darkness, and guided her fingers to where I needed her the most.

Julia let out a soft hum of approval, first one finger and then two, slipping inside me with ease.

"That's my good girl."

I groaned, my body responding to her words as much as her touch.

Julia began to move her fingers in a slow, deliberate rhythm. All the way in. All the way out.

"You're so beautiful like this," she murmured, her voice full of praise. Her lips brushed against my ear. "You're so sensitive, so receptive. It's like your body was made for me to fuck."

"God, Julia," I wheezed.

Her free hand snaked up to my neck. Her fingers tangled in my hair, which I'd pulled back in a high ponytail. She wrapped the end of my ponytail around her palm and tugged. "Show me how much you love being fucked."

My hand found its way to her wrist. I held her in place and shamelessly ground against her. The friction from her fingers mashed against my clit pulled a greedy whimper from my mouth.

Julia's fingers reached impossibly deeper. "You're almost there, aren't you, dear?" she seemed to taunt. "You're almost ready to come for me."

I exhaled sharply and my stomach muscles coiled. "Uh huh."

Julia's fingers moved faster, her touch more insistent. "That's it, darling. Come for me." Her voice was quiet, but urgent. "Come all over my fingers."

When her thumb pressed down on my clit, I could only respond with a strangled cry. Suddenly, Julia's mouth was on mine, her lips claiming me in a fierce kiss. Our tongues tangled, and I felt like I was drowning.

I came hard, my body convulsing around her fingers, as I cried out into her mouth. Julia's kiss swallowed my sounds. Her lips were gentle as she rode out my orgasm with me.

"I think ... I think we're getting the hang of this baby-making thing," I said, my voice shaky and my breathing labored.

Julia chuckled darkly, her fingers still buried inside me. "I don't know ... I think we're going to need more practice."

Her fingers flexed, letting me know she wasn't done with me yet.

I rolled my hips, forcing her deeper again. "Happy to oblige." A quiet groan vibrated in my throat. "After all, practice makes perfect."

Chapter Two

"Sweet nectar of the gods," I breathed into my cardboard coffee cup, "please do your thing."

I inhaled the coffee's rich aroma and sighed. My alarm had gone off far too early that morning. I could already predict needing an IV of caffeine to get through the day.

I fished my cell phone out of the pocket of my leather jacket as I let myself into the basement office of the Minneapolis Police Department's Cold Case Division. I juggled my To-Go coffee cup as I shot off a cheeky text.

> Sorry I kept you up past your bedtime last night.

Julia had already left by the time I'd woken up. It was expected, however, since I knew she planned on visiting her mom before her work day started.

> I'll somehow survive, but I appreciate your concern.

I flipped on the overhead lights as I walked into the empty office. There was a delayed response before the halogen lightbulbs buzzed, flickered, and finally turned on. I routinely walked to my colleague Sarah Conrad's desk and turned on the small space heater she'd brought in a few weeks ago.

I couldn't recall if she was expected in the office that morning—she divided her time between Cold Case and a Victims' Advocate office across town. Either way, the extra heat boost was necessary. The basement office stayed cool during the summer months, but those frigid temperatures remained and deepened during winter.

I'd only had time to hang my jacket on the back of my chair and sit down when my phone buzzed on my desk with new messages.

> How are you doing?
>
> Can you still feel me?

I stared at the phone and read the texts again as if I'd misread them the first time around.

Was Julia Desjardin sexting me?

An unexpected voice interrupted my thoughts: "Hey, Miller. Happy New Year."

I hastily flipped my phone over so the screen faced down.

"Happy New Year," I recited back.

I'd returned the greeting without actually identifying my well-wisher. With my cell phone's screen out of sight, but not necessarily out of mind, I focused on the silhouette that walked through the open office door.

Jason Ryan, a detective from MPD's Homicide division grinned his boyish smile. We'd worked together a few months back to discover the circumstances behind a young woman who'd been found in her abandoned car—a bullet in her stomach. Kennedy Petersik had deliberately shot herself, and in doing so, had ensnared her childhood friend, Landon Tauer. It had taken employing Julia as the young man's defense lawyer to evade a wrongful conviction.

I'd been suspicious of Detective Ryan from the start. His trendy, youthful haircut, manscaped stubble, and fitted suits had rubbed me the wrong way. We'd butted heads a few times in the course of solving the case, but I held no ill-will towards the man. We were friendly enough to grab a beer after work, but not close enough that I'd ever really confide in him.

I leaned back in my office chair. "Jason Ryan. What brings you to our modest little dungeon? Was the oxygen too good up in Homicide?"

Ryan's grin widened. "Maybe I missed our witty repertoire, Miller. Seems a damn shame MPD's got a good cop like you hidden down here. Damn shame indeed."

Like the Island of Misfit Toys.

I snorted. "Out with it. I know you didn't come down here just to blow smoke up my ass."

Ryan made an apologetic gesture. "You got me. Homicide just unearthed a shit show. *Literally* unearthed."

I arched an eyebrow, curious. "Something buried?"

"It was actually a few months ago," he corrected, "but the shit just keeps piling up, deeper and higher. And I thought to myself, you know who loves this kind of stuff? Cold Case."

"It's related to one of ours?" I asked.

"It's not ... technically," he admitted. "But you guys are really good at research."

I saw through his empty compliment.

"Dusty archival boxes."

He snapped his fingers. "Bingo."

"I'm not your research assistant, Ryan."

Jason Ryan looked around the admittedly empty room. "You got a better use of your time right now?"

The division had recently closed a case involving a missing indigenous woman: Danika Laroque. Her on-and-off again boyfriend had struck her with a car one snowy night, thirty years prior, inadvertently or otherwise. He'd dumped her body into a lake popular for ice fishing.

Since wrapping up the Laroque case, the phones had gone quiet. I was still expected to sit behind a desk from 8:00 a.m. to 4:00 p.m. while my colleagues Sarah Conrad and Stanley Harris split time between the basement of the Fourth Precinct and another location—Sarah at the Victim's Advocate office and Stanley at the cross-town facility where the majority of the division's material evidence was stored.

Until we received a tip that warranted revisiting an old case, we were under strict instructions from our amateur taxidermist supervisor, Captain Forrester, not to waste departmental resources chasing after ghosts.

"What's the case?" I reluctantly asked.

Ryan grinned broadly like Tom Sawyer convincing some stooge to paint his aunt's fence in his place.

"A local developer broke ground on a new high-rise a few months ago near Sumner Field Park. The demolition team found human remains. And those remains need names," he continued. "We've sent them to the lab for processing, but I doubt we'll get any hits."

"And they can't continue construction until police determine who the bones belong to?" I guessed.

Ryan made an obnoxious noise like a shrill siren. "And the lady wins a prize."

"What did the initial forensic report say?"

Ryan's smile was smug as he produced a slim manila folder. "I knew you'd be interested."

"Not interested," I stubbornly denied. "But maybe you've piqued my curiosity."

Ryan held out the folder, but pulled it back at the last second like a game of Keep-A-Way. "This stays between us. It's an active police investigation."

I gave him an incredulous look. "Who am I gonna tell?"

Ryan hummed. "Rumor has it, you're pretty chummy with a podcaster."

"Melody Sternbridge was a means to an end," I said flatly.

"Ouch," Ryan hissed. "You really put the *cold* in Cold Case, Miller."

I curled my fingers, already impatient with the ridiculous conversation. "Forensics. Please."

Ryan finally handed over the official paperwork.

"Where'd you hear about that podcast thing anyway?" I wanted to know.

"I'm a regular listener to *Lost Girls*," Ryan admitted. "Imagine my surprise to hear the sound of your mellifluous voice during my morning commute."

I wrinkled my nose. "God damn it."

Melody Sternbridge, the local host of a true crime podcast, had been a pain in my ass during the Danika Laroque case. She'd been the one to initially draw our attention to the thirty-year-old case, and she'd had a few smart ideas along the way, but for the most part she'd been an annoyance.

The episodes about the Laroque case were going to be published soon or whatever podcasters called new releases. Melody had given me a curtesy phone call as a heads up in case the new episodes brought with it unwanted attention.

"You're gonna be a star, Miller," Ryan grinned. "I'm going to get to say *I knew you when*."

"Can't wait," I grumbled.

I shifted my attention to the paperwork I held in my

hands. My eyes scanned the generic form in search of what the initial forensics report had discovered. The recovered bones were old, but not so old to be archaeological remains. The developer hadn't stumbled upon an indigenous burial ground à la *Poltergeist*.

"No signs of trauma," I read aloud. "No evidence of foul play. Just bones. Intact skeletons."

"Uh huh," Ryan confirmed.

"So why is Homicide involved?"

Ryan cleared his throat and looked uncharacteristically uncomfortable. He shifted his weight from one shiny leather loafer to the other. "They're ... small. The bones."

I exhaled. "Kids."

Jason Ryan grimaced. "Yeah. Maybe even babies."

A sour sensation settled in my stomach. "What do you need from us?"

"We're kind of in limbo until the lab comes back with DNA profiles. I'm guessing we won't get a match, so in the meantime, I was thinking of checking out rental agreements or census data to figure out who used to live in those apartments. To be honest," he frowned, "I'm feeling out of my league. This isn't the kind of detective work I'm used to."

I nodded in sympathy. When I'd first been assigned to Cold Case, I'd been wildly unsure of my role. I'd been a beat cop before—writing tickets and responding to citizen complaints. What did I know about research and databases and solving crimes older than myself? I still routinely felt like a fish out of water, but that disequilibrium was becoming more routine.

"I'll start out with missing persons in our database and focus on the area surrounding the location where your bodies were found. It's a long shot," I conceded, "but maybe your victims overlap with one of our cases."

Ryan's body language seemed to relax where he stood. "Thanks. And I'll let you know what the lab finds as soon as we get those results back. Even if we don't get a DNA match, the crime lab should be able to carbon date the bones so we at least know the time period we're dealing with."

"Probably looking at a few months at least?" I guessed.

Minneapolis was large enough to have its own forensics lab, but I knew that the crime lab in City Hall didn't process human remains. That work was typically sent to the Bureau of Criminal Apprehension where there tended to be a lengthy backup for processing evidence.

Ryan hollowed out his cheeks. "Might not be that long; our bones are apparently getting the VIP treatment. I'm guessing the property developer is leaning on the Mayor's office to make this go away."

"Lucky you," I remarked with a chuckle.

I wasn't really envious; I liked my under-the-radar department just fine. I'd had one run-in with a local senator while working a case, and I was in no hurry to bump heads with any other politicians while I tried to do my job.

"Nuh uh," Jason Ryan said with that annoyingly cocky smile. "Lucky *us*, Miller."

∽

The sun had long set by the time I returned to Julia's condo at the end of the workday.

My brain was tired. It was a different kind of exhaustion than what I'd experienced in the Marines or as a beat cop, where my feet or lower back might ache from being physically active. The only workout I got on the job these days was walking back and forth to the departmental coffee pot.

It was the mental strain that got to me now—the endless files, the dead ends, the constant need to think three steps ahead of people who had managed to bury their sins for decades.

I'd caught Stanley up on the directive from Jason Ryan and Homicide, and we'd spent the day trying to find some overlap between the bodies recovered from Sumner Field Park and any of our unsolved cases. Our searches had come up empty, but it had made the day go by more quickly with a discernible task. Until the crime lab came back with concrete data on the recovered remains, we'd have to be creative with our police work. I didn't mind putting in the effort, but I hated the waiting.

When I stepped inside the condo, the scent of soy sauce, sesame oil, and fresh fish hit me before I even spotted the plastic delivery bag on the dining room table.

"Takeout?" I asked, shedding my coat and hanging it in the front foyer.

Julia appeared from the hallway, her dark hair tied back in a loose bun, dressed in a navy crewneck sweatshirt and running tights. She looked effortlessly elegant, even in loungewear.

"I wasn't in the mood to cook tonight," she admitted. Her voice was soft, tinged with the kind of weariness I knew all too well.

"Not criticizing at all, babe."

I kissed her cheek as I passed by, my fingers skimming over the small of her back. She leaned into my touch, her body warm, and I could feel just a hint of tension lingering there.

"How was your day?" I asked, pulling out a chair.

With the exception of the curiously suggestive texts she'd sent earlier, I hadn't heard from her. That wasn't unusual, however; we weren't the kind of couple glued to our phones who chatted throughout the day.

"Long. Exhausting." She sighed and stretched her arms overhead before dropping into the dining room chair beside me. "It felt like I was running from one side of the city to the other all day."

"Rub your feet?" I offered.

She gave me a look of pure appreciation. "You're a dream."

I reached for her ankle, resting her foot in my lap as I started kneading slow, firm circles into the arch. She exhaled, melting into the chair, and I made a mental note to do this more often.

"How was your mom?" I asked, keeping my voice gentle.

Julia's expression faltered slightly. "A little irritable, if I'm being honest. I understand, though. She's not in her home. She doesn't even have Joy around. Nothing is familiar, barely even me."

That hit me in the chest. I squeezed her ankle lightly. "I'm sorry."

She nodded, but her lips pressed together, like she was holding something back. Finally, she admitted something I hadn't expected: "I haven't told her about freezing my eggs."

I frowned. "Why not?"

"I don't want to get either of our hopes up. My doctor has been very upfront that the chances of a live birth are well under fifty percent, even if I go through egg retrieval several times."

"Fifty percent?"

That seemed so low. I hadn't thought much about fertility before, but I knew Julia—knew how methodical she was, how much she researched. She wouldn't have gone into this lightly.

Julia nodded. "The chances of a viable pregnancy go up the younger you are when you freeze your eggs. I may have waited too long."

I swallowed, my fingers still working gently over her foot.

All of that effort. All of that money. And it might not even work?

I glanced up at her, trying to read the emotions in her face. She wasn't just tired—there was something heavier in her expression, something bordering on resignation.

"How-how many more shots to supercharge your eggs?" I asked, attempting to keep my tone light.

"They're stimulating them," she gently corrected.

"I don't stimulate you enough on my own?"

I was reaching. I was being corny. But I only wanted to bring a little levity. I just wanted to make her smile.

She exhaled and rubbed a hand over her thigh. "I'll do the shots myself at home for the next two weeks. I have a few appointments for blood work and ultrasounds to track my progress—to make sure the eggs are maturing properly. And then I'll have the egg retrieval procedure."

"Do you have a date for when that'll happen?"

"Yes. The fourteenth."

"Of February?" I asked.

"That would be the one."

I made a noise. "Huh."

Recognition colored Julia's features. "Oh. I didn't even realize." She shook her head. "The doctor's assistant said the earliest date and time, so I took it. I'll have her reschedule."

"Why?"

"It's Valentine's Day."

"So?"

I could see the frustration settle on her bones.

I shrugged. "Babe, it's just a day on the calendar. Every day can be Valentine's Day if you work at it."

She rolled her eyes, resistant to my attempt to be charming.

"Hey! I thought that was pretty smooth," I protested. "I came up with it on the spot."

"Yes, you're very clever, darling."

A hint of a smile ticked at the corners of her lips. Her stubbornness was crumbling.

"Would you be able to accompany me to that appointment?" she asked after a pause. "I don't know if I'll be in any condition to drive afterward, and I don't particularly relish the idea of poring myself into a ride-share vehicle."

"I'll put in my PTO request first thing tomorrow," I vowed, squeezing her foot lightly before letting it go.

"Thank you." Her shoulders seemed to relax.

I knew how difficult it was for her to ask for help—even from me. She must have really been nervous about the procedure.

"Do you want some company on any of your other appointments?" I offered.

"No. Those are fairly quick and routine," she rejected. "I'm fine to go alone."

The phrasing of her reassurances was anything but reassuring.

"You never have to do it alone," I insisted. "We're a team, remember?"

Julia met my gaze, something shifting behind her caramel-colored eyes. Then she reached for my hand and laced our fingers together, squeezing tightly.

"Yes. We are."

Chapter Three

I hadn't expected to see protesters at the crime scene.

A handful of onlookers, all bundled up to fend off the worst of the early morning chill, had gathered on the curb outside of the fenced-off construction site. The chainlink fence around the property would normally offer little privacy from prying eyes on the street, but the construction company had wrapped the fence with promotional banners boasting promises like "coming soon" and "units still available" for the future high-rise complex.

The crowd was no more than a dozen or so, but their presence concerned me. They remained relatively docile on the sidewalk with their hand-painted signs whose messaging all seemed to indicate their displeasure that a portion of the neighborhood park was being turned into luxury accommodations. The driver of a passing vehicle honked their car horn, activating the group to cheer and collectively raise their homemade placards.

I nodded at Detective Jason Ryan as I approached.

"What's up with the audience?" I asked, keeping my tone low.

"They were here when we first investigated the site," Ryan remarked. "Neighbors upset with the developers, I guess. I don't get the sense that they know about the bodies, though."

"Let's keep it that way, eh?"

"Agreed," he nodded.

Stanley Harris, my Cold Case division co-worker, coughed beside me. The crowd of protesters had rattled me so much that I'd apparently forgotten about him.

"Ryan, you remember my colleague, Stanley Harris," I reintroduced.

The three of us had worked on the same case a few months prior, but Ryan didn't strike me as the kind of guy who remembered ancillary characters. He had decidedly Main Character energy.

Ryan gave Stanley a nod. "Glad to have you on board, Stanley. We need all the help we can get. City Hall has been leaning hard on Homicide to wrap this thing up so construction can continue."

"Does that happen a lot?" I asked.

"Not with great regularity, no," Ryan said. "There's always internal pressure to clear cases, but City Hall usually stays out of it. I imagine the developer must be a generous donor to a few re-election campaigns to be getting this kind of VIP treatment."

"Great," I grumbled.

Ryan strode toward the chainlink fence that surrounded the construction site. He opened a squeaking gate and motioned for me to enter. "Ladies first."

I resisted the urge to retort with something snarky about chivalry not being dead. Instead, I raised an eyebrow and kept the comment to myself. It wasn't the time for playful banter.

Sentient construction machines sat motionless and abandoned on the other side of the privacy fence. Limited work had occurred on the condo. The grass had been dug up and the topsoil flattened. In other places, deep holes had been excavated; unearthed boulders sat beside the earth that had produced them, waiting to be hauled away. No foundations had been poured, however, no steel beams had been welded, and no rebar had been installed.

"The bodies were discovered over here," Ryan spoke up. He lengthened his stride and led Stanley and me toward a large dirt pile.

Yellow police tape had been employed to create a perimeter around one of the deeper holes. I peered down into the crater-sized hole, but it was just a hole. Nothing else to see or look at.

Stanley pulled an iPad out of the messenger bag slung across his chest. He held up the device to the horizon and tapped the screen until the camera app activated. Instead of only seeing what was in front of us, however, a black and white photograph layered over the screen.

Ryan leaned a little closer. "That's the old housing project, right?"

Stanley nodded. "I found some historical images from the public library's digital collections. I thought it might be useful to see what the crime scene used to look like."

"Good thinking," Ryan complimented in earnest.

"The building was constructed in 1938," Stanley recited. "It was the first public housing development in the city. Forty-four two-story row houses and four three-story apartment buildings. It was razed in the late nineties and has been vacant ever since."

I peered over Stanley's shoulder to see the photo on the tablet. I looked back and forth between the historic image and what the landscape currently looked like.

I gestured toward the excavated earth. "It looks like our burial ground was right behind one of the larger apartments."

I heard Ryan's sharp exhale. "Shit." He ran his fingers through his perfectly coiffed hair. "What if there's *more* bodies?"

"We can get a scan of the property to confirm if you found them all," I suggested. "We just worked with a professor at U of M who does ground penetrating radar. It's like archaeology without digging."

"You did that for the Larocque case?" Ryan asked.

"You heard about that?" Stanley questioned.

"Only from my favorite true crime podcast," Ryan admitted. He smiled brightly. "I keep telling Miller that she's about to become a celebrity. Did you get interviewed, too, Stanley?"

"No," he stated flatly.

Stanley's lack of affect wasn't from disappointment that he hadn't gotten his fifteen minutes of fame. He was actually disgusted with the work Melody Sternbridge did on her true crime podcast. Stanley hadn't held back, telling the woman exactly what he thought of her and how she commercialized the trauma of others.

"Think your podcaster friend might be interested in this case?" Detective Ryan proposed.

I shot him a sharp look. "Absolutely not."

I didn't know much about the man, but Detective Jason Ryan had long given me the impression of someone who was always looking for an angle, preoccupied with prestige and notoriety. He was relatively young to have already worked his way up to the rank of detective. It made me wonder about his ultimate career goals. My own title was a bit of a fluke due to my unorthodox employment record.

Ryan held up his hands in easy defeat. "I was only asking," he seemed to apologize.

I turned our attention back to the case. "How many bodies were recovered?"

"It's hard to say," Ryan said. "Five?" he guessed. "Six? The bodies were buried without coffins and the excavators damaged some of the remains when they broke ground. The coroner tried to reassemble the body parts, but it was a bit of a jigsaw puzzle."

"Body parts?" I echoed. "Like, flesh still intact?"

"No, sorry. I misspoke," Ryan clarified. "Only bones."

"No hair either?" I pushed.

"Not that I can remember," he said.

I turned to my partner. "Stanley, how long does it take for a body to decompose when it's been buried?"

Stanley had gone to school to be a medical examiner, but he'd ended up in Cold Case instead of the Coroner's office.

"Without a coffin, a body typically skeletonizes underground within five years," he said.

"Only five?" I hadn't realized it was so quick. "Has Homicide considered this case might not be that old?" My latter question was for Jason Ryan.

Ryan shrugged. "Seems unlikely someone would be able to bury so many bodies in a public park without anyone noticing."

"But behind an apartment complex seems more likely?" I questioned.

Ryan shrugged again. "Maybe someone *did* notice back then, but they didn't tell anyone. That's why I got Cold Case involved. You guys are good at this kind of stuff, right? Interviewing old people?"

I sighed but didn't respond to what was surely a rhetorical question.

"I'll contact Professor Washington about scanning the property at his earliest convenience. And you," I said, pointing at Jason Ryan, "you let us know when those lab results come in."

We hadn't had much of a reason to stick around the construction site, so Stanley and I returned to our basement office while Jason Ryan went to harass some lab techs. The crime lab in City Hall didn't deal with human remains, so I wasn't going to be able to use Stanley Harris to sweet talk our local connection, Celeste Rivers.

I made a phone call to Professor Washington at the university to officially request he scan the construction site for underground anomalies while Stanley continued to scour our missing persons database for any open cases that overlapped with the Sumner Field neighborhood.

I was getting used to our cases better resembling a wild goose chase—searching for needles in a haystack—but the unearthed bodies at Sumner Field felt more directionless than usual. Ryan had turned over the original medical examiner's reports for our perusal. We had detailed notes and photography of the recovered bones, but it made me wish we'd been brought in on the case before the remains had been sent to be processed.

It was after six by the time I looked up from the stack of case files and printouts scattered across my desk. The overhead light buzzed softly, casting a sterile glow over the basement office, but I barely noticed it anymore. Stanley had long gone quiet, headphones in as he scrolled through decades-old reports.

I leaned back in my chair and rubbed my eyes. The unearthed bodies weren't telling us much—not yet. Just bones and silence and questions no one had answers to. No timeline. No identities. No real way to know if the victims had even gone missing in the traditional sense. They'd been forgotten long before we ever knew to look.

It felt like trying to solve a puzzle with half of the pieces lost forever.

Outside, the Minneapolis cold was jarring, like waking up too quickly from a bad dream. I was well acquainted with that feeling.

I pulled up the collar of my leather jacket and walked briskly to the bus stop, breath fogging the air in front of me. The sky had that overcast, monochromatic look it wore for most of winter—gray on gray, without even the decency of snow to brighten it.

The weather was still incompatible with riding a motorcycle, so I took public transit from the Fourth Precinct to Julia's condo at the end of the work day. My Harley was in storage, leaving me without reliable transportation until the last of the snow melted, which might not happen for a few months more. I didn't mind the bus, but I suspected Julia might start dropping hints about me getting a proper car.

As I sat on the bus and watched the city crawl past, I let my head rest against the window. Even the glass was freezing. I thought about Julia, probably already home. Probably changed out of her lawyer attire and into something soft and expensive. I thought about the quiet of her condo, the warmth of it, the way she always had the lights set low and the air lightly perfumed with something that made the place feel like a real sanctuary.

I didn't have a word for what I was feeling. Not tired, exactly. Not sad. Just ... adrift. Listless.

The front of the condo was empty when I got home, but Julia's leather work bag was on the dining room table. The kitchen was similarly vacant, lights dimmed, leaving only the master bedroom and bathroom to be explored. I found Julia's outfit from the day laid out on the mattress, her high heels discarded on the floor. I touched my fingertips to the expensive blouse and pencil skirt, half-expecting the clothes to still hold her warmth.

I looked up sharply when I heard a sound—like a bathroom cabinet opening and closing.

"Babe?" I called out.

Julia's voice called to me from the *en suite*. "In here."

I knocked lightly on the bathroom door before entering.

And then stopped.

Julia stood in front of the bathroom mirror in only her bra and underwear. The light beige set nearly disappeared into her skin. For a second, I forgot to breathe. You'd think I'd be used to the sight of her, but somehow, I never was.

I leaned against the doorframe, taking her in. "What's going on in here?"

She exhaled. "I'm trying to psych myself up. The nurse made it look so easy yesterday. Doing it myself feels ..." She made a face. "Different."

Only then did I register the small pharmacy sprawled

across the bathroom countertop: syringes, vials, cotton swabs. I straightened instinctively.

Julia had chewed off most of the lipstick on her bottom lip. "The nurse said it should go into a fatty area."

"So I guess that rules you out," I said with a faint smile.

Julia gave me a look. "Funny."

She picked up a syringe and hesitated. "I might need your help."

"Of course," I said immediately. I had no clue what I was doing, but if she needed me, I was in.

Julia waited for me to wash my hands before handing me the narrow syringe. Her words were quiet, betraying her anxiety. "The stomach, I think."

I nodded, feeling the gravity of the situation. Julia's lower abdomen was smooth and flat, but I managed to take purchase of her skin between my thumb and forefinger.

"Just a little pinch," I said, repeating what the VA nurses used to tell me before sticking in IVs.

When I was done, I kissed near the injection spot and looked up at her. "You okay?"

Julia exhaled through her nose. "Yes. Thank you, dear."

I lingered in the doorway while she packed everything up, methodical and silent. She pulled on a thin robe over the matching bra and underwear. Still effortless. Still stunning.

"Do you want to have a baby in the condo?" I asked.

Julia wrinkled her nose as she tied the sash around her

waist. "God, no. Do I seem like the water birth and doula kind of woman to you?"

"Not actually *have* the kid here," I clarified. "I mean like raise one here."

"Oh." Julia blinked several times. "I actually hadn't considered that. It's only the one bedroom."

"And lugging up grocery bags in the elevator is hard enough without a pallet of diapers, too," I pointed out.

Julia swallowed. "Diapers."

"Uh oh," I said, lightly teasing. "I broke you."

"I plan everything. *Everything*, Cassidy. How could I have overlooked such a massive detail?"

She was unraveling—her version of it, anyway. She didn't pace the length of the bathroom or raise her voice, but I could see it in the way her forehead crinkled and how her normally precise posture slumped, ever so slightly.

"Did you plan on falling in love with me?"

"Of course not," she huffed.

"That turned out pretty okay, right?"

Julia made a disgruntled noise. "Passable."

I smiled despite her stubbornness. "Then this will be fine, too."

She didn't respond right away. Instead, she stood before me, her fingers toying with the buckle of my belt. It was a nervous, anxious movement, not one meant to seduce me.

"You're so good with me," she murmured. "I don't know how you do it or how you even put up with me."

I leaned back against the bathroom counter and

grinned when her body seemed to magnetically tilt toward me to keep our torsos close. "Those Oxford shirts that show *just* the right amount of cleavage certainly help."

She smiled knowingly—a genuine smile, not something forced or pained.

I nudged the next idea forward: "We could move closer to your mom? Somewhere with more space. No elevators. No condo association telling you a Christmas tree is a fire hazard."

She raised an eyebrow. "You'd want to move to the suburbs?"

I shrugged. "It could be nice. A real backyard. Baby's first snowman. Hell, you could even get one of those concrete geese for the front porch. A new outfit for each holiday."

I watched her face as I made my next suggestion, trying to keep it light. "Or maybe we move to Embarrass? Rumor has it, you've got a lot of real estate there."

Julia's features didn't change.

"You've only just started your new job," I said gently. "Maybe it's not what you'd imagined. Maybe you go back to Embarrass and be a lawyer there." I paused. "Or—hear me out—become the mayor?"

She hollowed out her cheeks. "In another life, maybe."

"Why not this life?" I posed.

Julia looked at me carefully. "Cassidy." She said my name with such tenderness that it felt like both a caress and a warning. "We were back in Embarrass for only a short time and your nightmares were worse than I'd ever seen them."

"Oh."

I looked down at my hands. My fingers had curled into fists without me noticing. I wanted to cry. I wanted to scream. I wanted her to be wrong, even though I knew she wasn't.

Julia was very quiet before she spoke again. "I like the Twin Cities just fine."

I nodded, but my chest felt too tight to speak. I wasn't sure if it was grief or guilt or just the ache of wanting things to be simple when they never really were.

Chapter Four

"What's on your finger?"

I looked down at my hands, convinced that maybe remnants from that morning's breakfast still clung to me.

"Jesus, Miller," my colleague Sarah exclaimed from her side of the office. "Are you *engaged*?"

With the whirlwind of the holidays and vacation time away, I realized Sarah and I hadn't seen each other in at least a few weeks.

I ran the pad of my thumb across the diamond-studded band, making it spin. "Oh. Yeah. Over New Years."

Sarah snapped her fingers with impatience. "Let me see the ring."

I grunted as I stood from my desk. I shuffled across the asbestos tiled basement floor to reach Sarah's work station.

I held out my hand, feeling a little like livestock at the County Fair.

Sarah grabbed my wrist and tugged my hand closer for inspection. I heard her low whistle. "Dang, that's classy," she approved. "She did the proposing, I'm guessing?"

"Uh huh."

Sarah snorted. "And I bet that's eating you up."

"You aren't wrong," I huffed.

"Do you have a date?" she pressed. "I'm expecting an invite to the wedding."

"No. No date. We haven't discussed that yet."

Unprompted, a school-yard rhyme popped into my head. *First comes love, then comes marriage, then comes a baby in the baby carriage.*

Julia and I had the love part down—in spades. Everything else was out of order, though. All of our conversations lately had been about babies and eggs and hormone shots. But did the order matter? Maybe we worked best when things weren't orthodox. After all, I'd fallen in love with her well before our first official date.

I didn't have an opportunity to dwell on the chronology of my relationship with Julia before Stanley strode through the office door, a folded up newspaper under one arm.

"Stanley," Sarah barked out, "did you know Cassidy got engaged?"

Stanley jolted to a stop in the entryway like he'd been caught with his hand in the cookie jar. "No. Should I have?"

"Yes," Sarah snapped before I could jump in. "But she hid it from us."

"I wasn't *hiding* anything," I insisted.

Sharing news about a major life event with the people with whom I worked had honestly never crossed my mind. I'd never made friends easily, and that had only gotten worse with my PTSD. If I limited the people with whom I was close, it kept small the circle of people who knew about my condition.

"Stanley, any word from the crime lab or from Professor Washington?" I asked.

Stanley hadn't moved from the doorway, still frozen from Sarah's and my back-and-forth. He confirmed what I already knew: "Nothing from either."

"What can we do in the meantime?" I probed.

"Pick out your wedding dress?" Sarah proposed. "Actually, you're probably wearing a suit, right?"

"I wear dresses!" I defended, my voice lifting up. I stopped myself before I got sucked into Sarah's trap. "Anyway—*Stanley*—did you find any results for missing persons in the Sumner Field area? Do any victims from our unsolved cases connect back to that area?"

"I'm still looking," he admitted. "My search would be more efficient if we knew what time period those recovered bodies came from. But we won't know that until the labs come back."

"Do they, like, carbon date the dirt or something?" I asked.

With each new case my knowledge base was expanding, but this was still new territory for me.

"Close," Stanley confirmed. "They'll analyze the state

of decomposition, and if the bones are old enough they can use radiocarbon dating to more precisely estimate their age using a process called post-mortem interval estimation."

"And they'll be able to determine the age of the person, too, right?"

He nodded. "Right. Skeletal features, dental development, and pubic symphysis will tell us the age range for the deceased individuals."

"What about finding rental agreements for the old apartments?" I questioned, thinking aloud.

Jason Ryan hadn't been wrong about us needing to interview a bunch of old folks. Once we had a relative range for when those bodies had gone into the ground, we would need to round up former Sumner Field residents. The big problem, however, was I had no idea how to find them.

I heard Sarah's loud, exaggerated sigh.

"What's wrong?" I asked.

"You two," she complained. "All work and no play."

"We can plan your Barbie dream wedding later," I said.

Sarah rolled her eyes. "Fine. But don't think you're getting off easy, Miller. If I don't get to witness a cake tasting or force you into half a dozen dress options that make you cry, I'll be personally offended."

"I'll pencil you in for emotional turmoil," I muttered.

Stanley cleared his throat, noticeably uncomfortable with our banter. "I'll keep digging through the missing persons reports and see if I can narrow it down based on last known addresses in the Sumner Field vicinity."

"That would be really helpful, thank you," I said, settling back into my chair.

My engagement ring caught the overhead light. The diamonds sparkled even under the unflattering halogen lamps. I stared at it longer than I meant to. I still needed to get Julia a ring of her own.

"You're doing that thing," Sarah chuckled.

My head snapped up. "What thing?"

"That newly-engaged, starry-eyed, daydreamy thing," she said. "It's honestly gross."

I gave her the finger—not the one with a ring on it.

∼

It had taken some time to identify where the city's historical land deeds were archived. Even then, we'd only been able to find property deeds for home ownership, not rental agreements, but it was better than nothing—we had to start somewhere.

The city's historical society oversaw the searchable databases, but when I'd spoken with one of the staff archivists about the details of my inquiry, she'd asked if I'd spoken to Charlotte Cunningham yet. When I reached out to an administrator for Hennepin County's Registrar of Land Titles, he'd said the same thing: go talk to Charlotte Cunningham.

Curiosity had me seeking out this person who seemed

to be top of mind of every archivist, librarian, and executive assistant with whom I'd spoken. More internet sleuthing produced the biography and contact info for one Charlotte P. Cunningham.

She was a professor at the state university. The area of academic study listed on her faculty bio didn't particularly strike me as useful to our investigation, but I still reached out to her, and we made plans to meet in the map room at one of the university's libraries.

Professor Cunningham looked to be in her late forties or early fifties. Her features were fair and Scandinavian like my own. She wore her blonde hair in a sensible yet conservative bob that reminded me of an on-camera news anchor.

Her handshake was delicate, a noticeable contrast to her broad-shouldered frame. Even in flats she was several inches taller than myself, maybe 5'10" or taller.

"Charlotte Cunningham," she introduced herself. "How can I help you, Detective?"

I'd been stingy with the details over the phone.

"I was kind of hoping you'd be able to tell me," I admitted. "Everyone I've spoken with who is even tangentially connected to the city's historical land deeds recommended I speak with you."

Professor Cunningham gave a knowing hum. "That's probably because of the racial covenants."

"The what?"

"I'm the project lead for a long-running digital history project," she said. "Our map of racial restrictions in

Hennepin County was the first-ever comprehensive visualization of racial covenants for an American city. To date we've mapped 42,000 covenants."

I shook my head. "I'm sorry. I'm just a humble cop. Can we start at the beginning?"

I had intended my words to lighten the conversation, but my self-deprecation only produced a deep frown.

"They were called housing covenants," she said. "Legal clauses in property deeds that blocked people of color from buying homes in certain neighborhoods. The first one in Minneapolis showed up in 1910. After that, it spread fast."

She leaned back slightly, eyes steady. "Say you're a young couple in the 1940s, looking to buy your first home. If you're Black, the developer won't sell to you. If you're white, you get the house—along with a contract that says you can never resell to someone who isn't white."

"That's—seriously?"

"It happened. A lot. People think of segregation as a Southern thing—Jim Crow, water fountains, bus seats," she ticked off. "But up here? We had our own systems. These covenants didn't get outlawed until the Fair Housing Act in 1968. And the fallout is still with us."

She didn't wait for me to respond. "Add in redlining—banks refusing mortgages in so-called 'high-risk' neighborhoods, which usually meant Black neighborhoods—and the problem got worse. Or if someone did get a loan, the terms were often predatory."

"So people couldn't buy homes."

"Exactly," she nodded. "So they rented. For generations. No equity. No safety net. And if you lived in public housing, you risked losing everything the moment someone decided the land would be better used for a luxury condo or a football stadium."

"Jesus." I rubbed a hand over my face. "Why haven't I heard about any of this before?"

She looked at me for a hard moment. "Why do *you* think, Detective?"

I frowned.

Her expression softened. "Do you have time for a road trip?"

I closely followed the taillights of Charlotte Cunningham's sensible SUV. We left campus and crossed downtown via the Interstate and continued to drive south for several miles. As we drove farther away from downtown, I began second-guessing my decision to let this woman lead the way while I blindly tagged along.

Eventually, she took an exit ramp towards South Minneapolis. From there her vehicle drove slowly through a quaint neighborhood whose streets were lined with modest-sized bungalows. She drove for a few more minutes until her right blinker signaled that I should pull over.

I waited in the warmth of the Crown Vic until the red of her taillights dimmed and she exited the vehicle. I similarly shut off my car and joined her on the curb.

Professor Cunningham turned to face a house on a corner lot.

"Arthur and Edith Lee bought this home in 1931," she said. "They were Black. There was no racial covenant restricting their right to purchase this home, and yet a mob of over 4,000 white people was waiting for them on the day they moved in. They yelled and threatened the Lees. They threw rocks at their home. They even killed their dog." She paused for a beat. "The Lees held out in this home for two years, but eventually they moved to another neighborhood."

She gestured to a column that stuck out of the yard. I hadn't noticed it before; the light stone material blended in with the snowbank on the corner.

"This historical marker was placed here in 2014 when the Lee's home was added to the National Registry of Historic Places," she said. "You'll see yard signs for *Hate Has No Home Here* scattered around the neighborhood, but that wasn't always the case."

I swallowed, feeling dizzy from the history lesson.

"What do you know about Sumner Field?" I asked.

"Let's go get a coffee."

~

Professor Cunningham blew across the top of a plain white coffee mug. We'd relocated to a small coffee shop not far from the Lees' historic home. It was late enough in the afternoon that we were the only customers. We sat at a table for two near the back of the café.

"Are you from the Twin Cities originally?" she asked me.

"No. St. Cloud," I said. "But I've lived here, on and off, for the past three years."

She nodded, distracted, her eyes on her coffee.

"I grew up in Minneapolis. I went away for school, but then I got hired by the university not long after getting my doctorate. I was so excited to bring my husband here. To raise our children in the same city that raised me."

I didn't interject when she paused and continued to fiddle with her coffee cup. Charlotte Cunningham seemed to be building toward something.

"We bought a house. Our first one, in fact. I'd only been a renter before. It was adorable. Nothing too fancy, but in a great neighborhood. Great schools for our kids." She pushed her hair away from her face and I saw the wistful smile. "I was cleaning out some things the previous owners had left behind when I found the home's original blueprints and title information. Being a historian, I was excited to be in possession of the home's original paperwork."

She stopped to open a sugar packet and stirred slowly.

"I was in bed, reading over the documents, when I saw the covenant. Nestled between a statement about what kind of material the roof could be made out of and another declaration that prohibited fences over five feet tall was another statement that prohibited the sale of the house to a person of color. It was so …" She searched for the word. "…

casual. Like saying you can't park an RV in your driveway. No Blacks allowed."

I leaned in without meaning to, caught in her words.

She sighed. "I'd known about racial covenants, of course. But it had always felt academic—something buried in archives or textbooks. Seeing it in the context of my home …" She trailed off and sighed. "It rewired something in me. Changed the way I looked at this city. *My* city."

"So that's when you started the mapping project," I guessed.

She nodded, but her frown remained. "Those discriminatory words impacted real people, Detective. And they're still impacting them today. Minneapolis has the highest housing gap between Black & white residents in the *country*. Only twenty-three percent of housing units are owned by Black residents, while seventy-five percent are owned by whites. And where you live affects what resources and opportunities you have access to: jobs, food, health care, and education."

Speaking with the professor was a lot like brainstorming with Stanley, only instead of carbon-dating bones, she knew the backstory of our crime scene.

"We found bodies where the Sumner Field projects used to be located," I told her. "It doesn't look like a mass grave—more like an unmarked cemetery. Any idea why someone would be buried on-site instead of in a proper graveyard? Were cemeteries segregated, too?"

She considered my question. "In places like Mankato and Rochester, yes. Some cities refused to integrate their cemeteries. But not the Twin Cities, at least not officially. Still, it's possible the families didn't know that. A lot of those original tenants came from the South—part of the Great Migration. They may have assumed the same restrictions applied here. Or maybe they just wanted their loved ones close. It could have even been financial—burials are expensive."

"Have you reached out to former residents?" she asked.

"No. We're still trying to track down old rental agreements. But I don't know if they even exist anymore."

"They probably don't," she anticipated. "Wood rots. Metal rusts. Paper disintegrates. The historical record is uneven and wildly unfair."

I took a breath. "Will you help us?" I asked. "We've been consulting old photos, but to be honest, we haven't had much success figuring out what we're looking at."

She looked surprised by my request. "I'm not ... I'm not law enforcement," she resisted. "I'm an educator."

"Then come educate us," I coaxed.

Professor Cunningham stared at me for a long moment. Her fingers still rested on the coffee spoon, but they'd gone still. Behind her, the barista laughed at something on their phone, the sound distant and incongruous in the quiet hum of the café.

I could see the gears turning behind her eyes, her internal calculus running through every possible reason to say no. But something shifted in her face as she wrapped her hands around the coffee mug like she was drawing warmth from it. She wasn't just thinking about her old house anymore.

"I suppose," she said slowly, "there are worse things than being asked to teach someone who actually wants to learn."

I smiled, but it faded just as quickly. "We're trying to identify the victims. The sooner we can figure out who was buried there, the better the chance of notifying any living family. If there even is any family left."

Charlotte's mouth pressed into a tight line. "Do you know how many people came up North thinking they were escaping danger only to find a quieter version of the same hate?" She shook her head. "They built lives here anyway. And if someone dumped their remains like garbage …"

She didn't finish her sentence. She didn't have to.

"I'll help," she said finally, reaching into her coat pocket and pulling out a sleek leather planner. She flipped to a blank page. "You'll need photographs—historical ones, preferably aerial shots if they exist. Blueprints. Census records. And the address of every known building in and around the project, ideally broken down by decade. I can start cross-referencing those with property records and oral histories."

I blinked at her sudden pivot to action. "You have access to all that?"

"I do," she said matter-of-factly. "And what I don't have, I usually know where to find."

I was quiet, watching her scribble notes like a woman on a mission.

Charlotte didn't look up. "You'd be amazed how much trauma hides behind property lines and zoning codes." She finally glanced up, meeting my gaze. "People think history is dead and done. But it's not. It's just underground, waiting for someone to start digging."

"Do you want to see the site?" I asked her.

Charlotte snapped her planner shut. "Not want. Need."

We stood up together, gathering our things, and as I held the door open for her, I felt the cold air rush in—and with it, something else. A shift. Like maybe this case was no longer just about bones in the ground. Maybe it never had been.

We stepped outside. We had a lot of work to do.

Chapter Five

Professor Cunningham pulled her coat tighter as a brisk wind swirled around us. "I used to walk by this neighborhood with my kids on the way to the park. We'd count squirrels and guess what kind of trees we were passing."

She looked at me, something sharper in her expression. "I never thought to wonder what was beneath our feet."

I didn't say anything. Because I hadn't either.

But we were about to find out.

The criminal lab had returned its results from testing the human remains recovered from the construction site. As predicted, they hadn't been able to identify the victims, but they had aged the bones and surrounding environments to the 1960s.

It was a group outing that day. Professor Washington had brought his ground-penetrating radar equipment to the construction site and I planned on giving Professor

Cunningham a tour of the crime scene. Detective Jason Ryan had joined us, but I was the only representative from Cold Case. Stanley was at the evidence warehouse and Sarah had remained behind in the Fourth Precinct basement office to field phone calls.

Charlotte Cunningham's eyes passed over my face and then Jason Ryan's. "Ready for your history lesson?"

Ryan produced the slim spiral notebook that he always seemed to have tucked away in his designer suits. "Yes, ma'am."

"We're about a mile north of downtown Minneapolis right now—the Near Northside," Charlotte began. "Back in the early 1900s, this was a tight-knit working-class neighborhood until the federal government knocked it all down. This was during the Great Depression; the government wanted to solve a housing shortage and end unemployment. They used eminent domain and slum clearance to condemn this entire area, raze whatever was here before, and replace it with the Sumner Field housing project. Single-family homes were replaced by multi-family units."

She paused and wet her lips. "It created new construction jobs, but it also started the trend of concentrating public housing in North Minneapolis, which favored homeownership for whites and rental units for people of color. And because of redlining, Black families who lived in the projects had little to no chance of ever leaving."

"Redlining?" Ryan echoed.

Professor Cunningham took a breath. "Do you know how an FHA loan works?"

"The government insures the loan so it can be offered at a lower interest rate, right?" he replied.

"And they also lower the amount needed for a down payment or even make loans accessible for people with less than perfect credit scores," Charlotte added. "All of that started during the Great Depression. The FHA wanted to avoid insuring risky mortgages. So they rated neighborhoods in every major city with a color-coded system. Green was safe and red was hazardous. And guess who lived in the red-coded neighborhoods?"

My stomach twisted uncomfortably. "People of color."

Charlotte nodded grimly. "It made it nearly impossible for Black residents to obtain FHA loans. People of color, regardless of their financial status, were classified as 'too risky.'"

"So we've got racial covenants keeping Black families from buying houses in so-called white neighborhoods and redlining making sure they can't get a mortgage in the only neighborhoods where they were allowed," I said, pulling it all together.

Charlotte offered me a sad-looking smile. "You're an A-plus student, Detective Miller."

My brain continued to work through the details of our case. "The housing project was built in the 1930s, but our bodies are from the 1960s. Any ideas on the timing of that?"

Professor Cunningham nodded. "I did some digging. The blocks just west of here were combined into a superblock in the Sixties. It cut off street access between the housing projects and the surrounding neighborhood. That kind of isolation led to deeper poverty, rising crime, and even more entrenched segregation."

Her expression turned grave. "We know from city records that tenants could be relocated without much warning. Sometimes people disappeared, and no one asked questions. Evictions. Displacement," she ticked off. "In a neighborhood this isolated, in an era like that ..."

The Sixties. Civil Rights. Redlining. Urban renewal. The Twin Cities trying to rebrand itself, one razed neighborhood at a time.

"We've got to find out who they were," I said, more to myself than to either of them.

"Any ideas on how we do that, Professor?" Ryan asked.

"You could start with tenant records," Charlotte replied. "The Housing Authority would have kept rosters of residents, even back then. They're public records, so you can request them under the Minnesota Government Data Practices Act."

One detail continued to scratch at my brain. The skeletal remains had shown no signs of trauma, leading the medical examiner to believe our victims had died of natural causes.

"But why not use a cemetery?" I thought out loud.

Charlotte looked at me for a long moment, her breath visible in the cold air. "People bury the forgotten where they think no one will look."

The silence that followed was heavy. Even Professor Washington had paused in his scanning, the soft hum of the ground-penetrating radar equipment the only sound as he swept its arm in careful arcs over the nearly frozen soil.

Ryan flipped his notebook closed. "So our victims might not have even lived here."

My stomach dropped. Our impossible case was becoming even more impossible.

"Jesus," I murmured.

We'd just stepped off the hard-packed dirt of the Sumner Field construction site when the shouting started.

"Shame on you!"

I blinked into the winter sunlight when we reached the chain-link fence separating the construction zone from the sidewalk. A small but vocal group had gathered again, their signs bobbing in the cold air.

STOP THE CONDOS
NO MORE LUXURY ON STOLEN LAND
YOU CAN'T EVICT A COMMUNITY
AFFORDABLE HOUSING IS A RIGHT

Detective Ryan cursed under his breath as he stepped in front of Charlotte Cunningham and myself, instinctively shielding us from the increasingly agitated crowd.

"Sellouts!" someone yelled.

"Affordable housing *now*!" came another angry voice. "Not granite countertops!"

"Don't engage," Ryan said quietly, eyes scanning for anything that might escalate. "We're not here for this."

"You're with the city?" a woman shouted at us, her voice hoarse from the cold or shouting or both.

"We're with MPD," Ryan said.

Wrong answer.

A ripple of anger surged through the protestors like someone had flipped a switch.

"Of *course* you are."

"Cops show up and suddenly they care about the Northside?"

Charlotte tensed beside me. Her hands were buried in the pockets of her wool coat, her expression unreadable, mouth set in a hard line. She didn't speak, didn't move. She stood there taking it all in, eyes sweeping the faces of the people shouting us down.

A younger man stepped forward, holding his phone like he was already live streaming. "Y'all gonna protect the developers or the people who used to live here?"

"We're just here for a site inspection," Ryan said, but no one was listening anymore. "We're not here to stop your protest. We're not the enemy here."

A woman near the front of the protesters crossed her arms. "Sure looks like you are."

She pushed closer to the fence, and a few others followed. Jason Ryan stepped forward instinctively, his hand brushing his coat where I knew his badge and service weapon were tucked away.

I stayed close to Charlotte's side.

Ryan raised his voice but kept it even. "We're not in charge of what happens to this land."

"Then who is?" a man with a bullhorn demanded. "Because it sure looks like the city is more interested in building luxury apartments than giving people a place to live."

"They're not even luxury," someone else shouted. "They're mediocre with quartz countertops."

A small laugh rippled through the crowd, but the anger remained.

Charlotte was still silent. Her face was pale now, drained in a way that had nothing to do with the cold. She looked at the signs and the people holding them, not with disdain, but with something closer to guilt.

"This is public land!" the man with the megaphone shouted. "Where's our vote in this? Where's the community input?"

"Let's go," Ryan muttered.

The crowd didn't part so much as shift, letting us slide sideways down the sidewalk in a bubble of barely-contained rage.

"Go ahead and pretend you're not part of it," someone called after us. "That's what the police are good at, right? Pretending justice is blind."

Ryan was tight-lipped until we reached his unmarked squad car. He pulled open the rear passenger door, then paused when he saw Charlotte wasn't moving.

"You okay, Professor?"

She blinked at him. "Y-Yes."

Ryan didn't notice her unease. He rounded the front of

the car, already pulling out his phone to update someone at the precinct.

Charlotte stared at me, still standing on the curb. "I thought coming here meant doing something important. Something good. But now ..."

Her voice trailed off. She didn't finish the sentence.

She didn't have to.

∽

I came home that night to discover Julia on the edge of the bed in a camisole and pajama shorts, the silk bunched up slightly where her hand rested against her thigh. A slim white box of syringes lay open beside her, along with alcohol swabs, a sharps container, and a folded sheet of instructions she didn't need anymore.

I stood in the doorway for a second, watching her. Her shoulders were rigid, her expression blank. It wasn't the mask she wore at work, but the kind that came from too many emotions stacking up all at once.

"Hey," I said quietly.

Julia looked up and tried to smile. "I was just about to do it."

"Want me to help?"

She hesitated, her fingers curling around the alcohol swab. "You don't have to."

"I know," I said. "But do you want me to?"

She bit down on her lower lip. After a moment, she nodded.

I washed my hands and joined her on the bed. She passed me the syringe she'd already prepped, the one with the tiny, sharp needle and the magic formula that would trick her body into producing more eggs. I took it from her carefully, like it was something fragile.

"Where do you want it tonight?" I asked.

She shifted slightly and pulled the waistband of her shorts down over one hip, exposing the smooth, pale curve of her lower abdomen. "Left side."

I nodded and wiped the spot with alcohol. Her skin was warm under my fingertips.

"Okay," I said. "Ready?"

She didn't answer right away, just gave a tiny nod. I could feel her hold her breath.

I pressed the needle in gently, watching her face the whole time. She didn't flinch. I injected the medication slowly, then slid the needle back out and pressed a gauze pad to the spot.

"All good," I murmured.

I tossed the syringe into the sharps container and set the gauze aside.

"How's the patient tonight?"

Julia exhaled and let her head tilt forward slightly, her hair falling into her face. "Tired. Overwhelmed. It's not the shots, though. It's everything."

"I know."

I moved closer, close enough that our knees touched. She leaned her head against my shoulder. No makeup. No expensive power suit. No armor. Just Julia.

"Thank you," she whispered.

I kissed the top of her head. "Always."

We sat in silence for a few seconds. I could hear the faint hum of the heater kicking on, the occasional whoosh of a car outside on the wet pavement.

"How was your day?" she asked. "You toured the construction site with the history professor, right?"

I looked at her for a long moment—at the woman who was letting me in even when everything in her wanted to retreat. I thought about children's skeletons buried under playgrounds, about protests stretching across decades, about the weight of history pressing up through the semi-frozen ground.

But I also thought about this—about showing up every day for each other.

I gave her hand a squeeze.

"I'll tell you," I said. "But maybe after you lie down. You look like you've been holding up the whole world."

That earned me a soft, tired smile.

"Maybe just half of it," she said.

She leaned into me, and for the first time all day, I felt like maybe I could breathe, too.

Chapter Six

I received an unexpected text message not long after arriving to the office that morning.

> Are you busy?

> I'm at work?

Julia's response was immediate.

> That's not what I asked.

I frowned, tapping my fingers against my desk. Julia rarely texted me during the workday. Something about her message made my pulse quicken.

> Everything okay?

A pause. It was too long for my liking.

> Just tell me if you're busy.

That was enough for me. I was already grabbing my jacket.

> I can be there in twenty.

~

I made good time getting to Julia's office building. The sleek glass doors of the downtown high-rise reflected the overcast sky as I stepped inside. The ground-level lobby was all wood and polished marble, the kind of place that made you lower your voice without thinking about it.

After a brief elevator ride, I explained myself to the receptionist who held court at the entrance to Grisham & Stein. I assured her I knew the way, although I'd only been to Julia's office once—a very memorable holiday party the previous month.

"Hi, Cassidy!"

I stopped short and stared. "Alice?"

The pretty office manager from Julia's former employer as a public defender smiled and waved from a bank of short-walled cubicles just outside of Julia's office door.

Alice stood from her chair to greet me. She tugged at the bottom of her pencil skirt to straighten the hemline. "Ms. Desjardin gave me an offer I couldn't refuse," she explained with an easy shrug.

"I bet she did."

The intonation of my words caused an attractive blush to reach the young woman's normally pale features. "I just mean the *pro bono* work," she explained away. "Wrongful convictions."

"I'm yanking your chain, Alice," I assured her with a grin. "I'm sure it's a great help for Julia to have a familiar face at her new place of work."

Alice bobbed her head. "Is she expecting you? Do you want me to tell her you're here?"

I lifted a hand. "It's okay. I can tell her myself."

Alice's body language took on a protective yet apprehensive stance that I'd come to recognize from her. It was clear that Alice respected and probably even worshiped Julia. There was a protocol to someone wanting to see her boss, and Alice took that responsibility seriously.

"I'll tell her you tried to tackle me, but I was too quick," I promised with a playful wink.

Alice laughed and ruefully shook her head. "It's nice to know that the new office space hasn't changed you either."

I knocked sharply on Julia's closed office door. I smiled, not for the first time, to see her name engraved on a placard just beside the door.

"Come in," I heard her melodic voice.

I eased the door open and stuck my head inside. Julia sat behind a formidable desk. Her framed college and law school diplomas hung on the wall behind her. The room was light and bright, a far cry from the faux wooden paneled walls, stained carpet, and cheaply constructed furniture at her last place of employment.

"Poaching the competition's talent?" I teased. "Alice said you made her an offer she couldn't refuse."

"That makes me sound like a mob boss," Julia sniffed. "If you mean higher pay, benefits, and a work environment that doesn't consistently smell like burned coffee and maple syrup, then yes, she would be correct."

I stepped inside and shut the door behind me. "I'm surprised you didn't say anything about it."

It wasn't really a big deal, but we always talked about our respective days at dinner or in bed at the end of the night. I was a little surprised she hadn't told me about the familiar hire.

Julia stood from her office chair in one fluid motion. "I'm sorry. I suppose it slipped my mind."

I nodded. It checked out. Things had been busier than usual.

"Any luck on putting together the rest of your team?" I asked.

Julia pointedly stared. "Well, I made one offer to a potential private investigator, but she apparently *was* able to refuse my offer."

"Hey!"

"I'm only teasing, darling." Julia rested a placating hand on my forearm. "I know you're finding your way with Cold Case; it was unfair of me to expect you to give that up. Besides, you said yes to the most important question of all."

"Breakfast for dinner?" I joked.

Julia didn't get distracted. She took my left hand in hers and lifted my fingers to her mouth. She gently kissed the skin between my lower knuckle and the engagement band.

"I have to admit—seeing you with this ring on your finger—knowing that I'm the one who put it there. It does something to me."

I swallowed with difficulty. She was standing so close. Her spicy, earthy perfume overpowered the sterile scents of a new office building. Her proximity, her breath caressing my knuckles, the low burn of her voice, made it hard to remember that we were in public—her fancy lawyer office—with her new co-workers only on the other side of her office door.

I closed my eyes and released an uneven breath.

"So what's, uh, what's with the S.O.S. message?"

"Super-ovulation has made me super horny." She wet her lips and let the declaration hang in the air for a moment before continuing. "The estrogen boost from the shots," she explained. "I can hardly concentrate. And I *need* to focus. I have a meeting with the partners later today to update them on my progress."

"Oh, uh ... that-that's bad timing, huh."

Julia tucked her lower lip into her mouth. "I'm terribly turned on. To the point of distraction. I need you to fuck me."

Heat flickered in my stomach and slid lower. "Here?"

I was surprised my voice hadn't cracked.

"This is no time to play coy, Detective," she censured. "Or should I take matters into my own hands instead?"

Her voice was all challenge, like a game of chicken. I had no doubt her hands were more than up to the task. But she'd summoned me for the job. I had no intention of letting her down.

"That won't be necessary." I said, straightening my spine. "Why don't you take a seat?"

Julia's painted smile curved with victory.

I turned the lock on the office door. Alice would never barge in without Julia's permission, but I was less confident about her other co-workers. I shed my leather jacket and carefully hung it over the back of one of her extra office chairs.

It was only then that I realized Julia's private office wasn't at all private. The partition that separated us from the rest of her colleagues was entirely transparent. The front-facing wall was made of clear glass.

"Should we, uh, take this somewhere else?" I proposed.

"That won't be necessary."

She reached for something on her desk and pressed a button. The glass wall instantly frosted over, turning from clear to opaque in a slow ripple of shifting light.

"Electrochromic glass," she explained. "A necessity when you're working with high-profile clients whose privacy is paramount."

I cleared my throat. "Neat trick."

Julia pulled her office chair away from her desk. It glided on its wheels across the thin carpet. She maintained eye contact as she sat down. One elegant leg crossed over the other. She rested her hands on the arms of her chair and quirked an expectant eyebrow.

I made a big show of stretching out my arms and turning my head and neck this way and that like an elite athlete getting loose before a competition. My antics pulled an amused smile to Julia's painted lips.

She lifted her hand from the arm of her chair and curled her finger, beckoning me to come closer. I knew we didn't have all day—I *did* have to return to work at some point and Julia had meetings.

I stalked closer until I stood directly in front of her. She uncrossed her legs and let her thighs fall wantonly open so I could stand even closer.

I rested my hands on top of hers, anchoring her to the arms of the office chair. I bent and placed a light, fleeting kiss to her mouth. Julia tilted her head toward me, leaning into the kiss as much as her seated position allowed. She sighed against my moving lips, content in the knowledge that her needs would soon be met.

I slid my palms down her arms and marveled at the limber strength she possessed. She was more than capable in every way, so when she let me in—let me help—even if it was only an orgasm, I basked in the moment.

I moved from her mouth to the shell of her ear. "You know you'll have to be quiet." I flicked my tongue against her ear. I licked a short line along the outer shell. "Alice will hear. She probably already knows what's happening in here. Why else would you have activated your secret agent office wall?"

Julia's caramel eyes shifted from my eyes to my mouth. "You assume you have the ability to make me loud, dear."

I straightened with an incredulous laugh bubbling up my throat.

Julia elongated her spine where she sat, proud defiance rolling off her shoulders.

I pinned her with a stern stare. "You're going to come on my mouth, Julia. And every time you sit in that chair, you're going to remember what I did to you."

I took delight in the widening of her eyes as the truth in my words resonated with her. The office space, just like her job, was relatively new. She hadn't had time to fill the space with knickknacks or memories just yet. Whatever we did in this moment would linger for a very long time.

I stood before her, somewhat towering over her seated form. I reached for the first button of her blouse and smiled as she exhaled, long and expectant. I pursed my lips before deciding on my first command.

"Play with your nipples."

Julia's silk shirt was thinly constructed, similar to the flimsy lace bra that I knew she wore underneath. She had no need to unfasten additional buttons.

Her fingertips skimmed over the tops of her breasts through her shirt. Trim, polished nails ghosted over the expensive material. The touch was deft and delicate like the woman herself. Her movements detoured to lower real estate until she was openly pinching and flicking at her nipples, coaxing them to stiff peaks through her bra. Her lower body began to squirm where she sat, yet her stare never left my face, a silent challenge that she was ready for more.

I dropped to my knees and inelegantly rucked her pencil skirt up her thighs. I heard the perceptible hitch in her breath. I might have been the one on my knees, but we both knew I was the one in control.

My mouth watered at the thigh-high stockings and garters she wore beneath the professional layers. It was one of the sexiest things I'd ever seen—professional, serious, stoical Julia—and the naughty, sexy underthings hidden beneath the wool, cotton, and silk.

I slipped her high heels from her nyloned feet, not that I didn't love when her stilettos dug into my back or ass when I went down on her. I wanted her as stripped down as I dared in the middle of the workday.

She willfully raised her backside so I could remove the lace and silk panties. I balled them up and tucked them into my pants pocket—out of the way but not forgotten.

I maneuvered her lower body so one leg hung over my shoulder and the other draped over the arm of her office chair, spread as wide as her hips would allow. I pressed gently on her inner thighs to test if she could open for me any wider.

"You look so fucking hot like this," I roughly whispered. "So fucking wide open for me."

"Cassidy," she whimpered.

The cockiness, the icy aloofness from before, was gone.

I stroked my fingertips down her molten center. Her clit slipped through my fingers like I couldn't catch it.

"Babe. You're so wet." I inspected my fingertips, glistening with her juices. My eyebrows rocketed up. "You've been like this all day?"

She whimpered again in lieu of a proper response.

"Don't worry, baby." I slid my palms beneath her naked thighs and lowered my mouth to her pussy. "I've got you."

Julia let out a soft, stifled gasp when my tongue made first contact. Her eyes fluttered shut in response to the sensation of my mouth pressed against her most sensitive skin. I hummed in the negative, and her eyes snapped open again. She knew, without me having to vocalize a single syllable, that I wanted her to watch me.

I tongued her clit, up and down, applying gentle pressure. Julia grasped the arms of her office chair, holding tight as she arched her back. Her hips shifted beneath me, seeking more contact.

I spread her pussy lips with my fingers, giving me better access to her clit. Her inner flesh was flushed a beautiful pink ombre. When I sucked on her clit, pulling it into my mouth, Julia made a small, strangled noise in the back of her throat.

I pulled back, not wanting to overstimulate her too soon. I feathered my tongue across her clit and swirled the tip of my tongue against her clenching opening. Her hips bucked against me slightly, pushing her pussy harder against my mouth.

Julia exhaled her demand: "Inside."

I obediently pushed my tongue into her pussy. Julia's mouth opened slightly, and I heard the tiny gasp of air. I could feel her body tremble from the effort to stay quiet and the impossibility of it. My tongue moved rapidly as I worked to push her toward the edge.

"Fingers," came her next strangled command.

I replaced my tongue with my middle and index fingers. My fingers slid easily into her molten core. Julia's pussy walls contracted around me, like she was trying to pull me deeper, to suck my fingers further into her.

I withdrew my index and middle finger and slowly added a third. Julia's eyes widened; she looked down to where my fingers connected with her sex with a mixture of surprise and awe.

I moved gently, giving her time to adjust. The sensation of having three fingers inside of her was almost overwhelming. I could feel every contour of her pussy, every curve and texture. The feeling was intense; Julia might have been the one getting a workout, but I was finding it difficult to breath.

I bit down on my lower lip. I could feel my own heat growing between my thighs as I worked to bring Julia to orgasm.

"You're so beautiful," I quietly praised.

As I continued to finger her, Julia's body began to tremble. First, her lower abdomen clenched. Then, her thighs began to shake. Her hands, still grasping the arms of the chair, tightened as she arched her back, pushing her hips further into my touch.

My three fingers kept moving, plunging into her pussy with deep, even strokes as I pushed her towards climax.

I leaned in, my face inches from her pussy. "Do it. Come for me."

I added a slight twist to my fingers, curling them upward. Julia's eyes went wide and her mouth opened in a silent scream.

Her body suddenly went stiff in the chair, and she let out a tiny whimper of pleasure. It was a soft sound—barely audible—but it told me everything I needed to know.

I settled back on my haunches to give my knees some respite from the solid floor. Eventually, Julia's eyes began to focus more sharply on me. She reached out a languid hand and brushed it against my cheekbone before letting it fall away.

"Again," she murmured.

I chuckled low in my throat at the demand hidden behind that single word.

"Greedy," I teased back.

Julia's thighs parted slightly wider apart—an invitation that needed no further explanation.

∼

I returned to the office later that afternoon with a bounce in my step and a slightly sore jaw. The buoyancy drained from my limbs, however, the moment a sharp voice cut through the air.

"Where were you?" Sarah demanded.

I'd lingered longer at Julia's office than what was probably appropriate for the middle of the workday, but there was no pressing need for me to be chained to my desk.

"Why? Phones ringing off the hook?" I deflected with a joke.

Strangely, one of the landlines in the office—the phone on my desk—chose that moment to ring.

I heard Sarah's annoyed huff as she stood from her desk. She crossed the open-floor office space and snatched the phone from its receiver. Instead of speaking with the caller, however, she forcefully returned the phone to its cradle, hanging up.

"Sarah!" I squeaked.

"I'm sure they'll call back."

As if on cue, the phone rang again.

"What the hell is going on?" I demanded.

Sarah's features were unreadable. "Detective Cassidy Miller has apparently gone viral."

I shut my eyes and cursed: "Mother fucker."

∼

I rang the doorbell and immediately heard a loud bark, followed by Melody Sternbridge's exasperated voice: "Brady!"

A second too late, I remembered her giant black lab

lost his mind at the sound of the doorbell. On any other day, I might have felt bad for setting him off. Today, I was too annoyed with the canine's human to care.

Smirking despite my sour mood, I rang the bell again. Another deep bark was followed by the sound of claws scratching against wood. I pictured Melody Sternbridge on the other side of the door, wrestling with her overexcited dog.

The door swung open, and I braced for impact.

"Oh! It's you!"

Melody held her dog by the collar, struggling to keep him from launching at me. The black lab whined and strained, not in pain—just desperate to get outside.

I hollowed out my cheeks. "We need to talk."

"Sure!" She sounded out of breath. "But come inside before Brady yanks my arm off."

I stepped inside the perpetually warm house and instinctively scanned the interior. The decor was a distinct BoHo chic, cluttered with vintage knickknacks and antique furniture. Melody looked at home in the space with her high-waisted jeans and crewneck sweatshirt, the arms pulled up to her elbows.

Before I could launch into the reason for my unsolicited visit, Melody's dog escaped her grasp and nearly bowled me over. Its snout struck me solidly in the pelvic bone, and I doubled over.

"Jesus," I gasped.

"Brady, down!" Melody shrieked. She grabbed the

dog's collar and yanked him back. "Sorry, he loves a broody woman in distress."

"I'm not in distress," I scowled. I righted myself with some difficulty. *God, that had hurt.* "The phones at Cold Case won't stop ringing. Reporters—all asking for a damn interview. We've had to forward every call to voicemail just for a little peace."

The last time I'd found myself in a similar position was when Grace Kelly Donovan had published a story about me in the local Embarrass newspaper. I'd been annoyed to find my life story was front page news, but it hadn't produced anywhere close to the kind of attention I was currently getting.

Detective Cassidy Miller, reluctant hero, local celebrity. I'd never hated a phrase more in my life.

Melody busied herself with kenneling Brady. "And what exactly do you want me to do? Tell the world to stop being obsessed with you? I don't have that kind of power."

I clenched my jaw. "You're the reason they're calling. You got them worked up. You can get them to back off."

Melody hummed. "Or ... and hear me out ... you could use this. People clearly love you. You're the badass ex-Marine-turned-detective who cracks cold cases." She grinned. "Hell, if you really leaned into it, I could probably get you a book deal."

"You're not helping," I grumbled.

Melody looked pensive. "You're really that freaked out about some attention?"

I exhaled sharply. "I don't like it. I don't want it. I just want to do my job."

Melody folded her arms across her chest. She tapped manicured fingernails against her bare forearms while she considered my words. "Okay. So you *don't* want to do more interviews."

"No."

"But," she continued, dragging out the word, "what if you weren't talking about yourself? What if you were talking about the cases you're working on? Think of all the extra ears we'd get."

I narrowed my eyes. "*We?*"

She shrugged. "If the goal is to solve these unsolvable cases, why not use the attention? My audience is massive. Someone out there might know something."

I hated that she had a point.

Melody grinned like she could read my mind. "I'm not asking you to become a podcast personality. Just … think about it."

I sighed and rubbed my temples. Either the heat of the house or the situation itself was starting to give me a headache.

"I hate you."

"No, you don't." She bounced on her toes. "You just hate that I'm right."

Chapter Seven

I had never hated my reflection more than I did sitting in that chair, under the hot lights of a makeshift studio in the Channel 5 Newsroom. They'd tried to "soften my image," whatever the hell that meant. A touch of powder to kill the shine on my face. A little gel to tame what my hair apparently did "naturally," which—according to a production assistant—was "too aggressive" for the camera.

I wasn't sure if I or my curls should be more offended.

"You're gonna be great," a different PA chirped as she attached a microphone to the front of my button-down. She was maybe twenty, with a ring through one nostril.

"I'm not trying to be great," I muttered. "I'm trying to get this over with."

She just smiled and patted my shoulder like I was a nervous golden retriever.

Buried Promises

I took a breath, deep and slow. I was sweaty. Uncomfortably so.

My thighs were already starting to stick to the plastic of the chair. I had half a mind to stand up and leave. But Melody had all but begged me to take the interview, arguing that even if I hated it, it would "shift the narrative" and put the spotlight back on Danika and other missing women like her.

That was the only reason I was there.

"Two minutes," someone called out.

I focused on my hands. They were resting in my lap, fingers loosely tangled. I frowned at the calluses across my knuckles and the scars whose origins were too old to recall. They looked like the hands of someone who knew how to hit a man squarely across the jaw. They weren't the polished, manicured hands of someone who belonged on television.

But then again, Danika Laroque hadn't belonged in that lake, either.

I snorted to myself. If only Grace Kelly Donovan could see me now. But this wasn't a front-page feature in the local Embarrass newspaper.

"Detective Miller," a voice called.

I looked up and saw the reporter—Dawn LeClaire—walking toward me with a practiced smile. She was older than I expected, maybe in her fifties, dressed in a tailored blazer with dark glasses perched atop her head.

"I'm Dawn." She introduced herself as though I didn't

see her face plastered on every bus stop around the city. "It's nice to meet you."

I tried to smile, but my lips were dry and stuck together.

"We'll be live-to-tape," she said, "so if you need a moment, just let me know. We can cut and edit as needed."

I nodded once.

"Nervous?" she asked.

"Yup."

She smiled a little wider, like she hadn't expected my honesty.

"Alright. Let's do this."

The lights clicked on. I hadn't realized they could go even brighter. The red camera light blinked. Someone yelled a command in the background. We were rolling.

"Welcome back to *Northwoods Today*. I'm Dawn LeClaire. With me in the studio today is Detective Cassidy Miller of the Minneapolis Police Department's Cold Case Division. You might know her as the investigator who recently solved the thirty-year-old disappearance of Danika Laroque—a case that has haunted the region for decades. Detective Miller, thank you for being here."

I stared at her for a beat too long before nodding. "Yeah. Thanks."

Awesome start.

Dawn didn't miss a beat. "I know you don't normally speak to the media. Why the change of heart?"

I inhaled through my nose and exhaled. "I didn't come here to talk about myself. This case wasn't about me. It was about Danika and about the people who didn't stop looking for her. The people who knew she didn't just run away."

"And yet, for thirty years, that's what many assumed," Dawn said gently. "Runaway. Troubled. Another statistic."

I felt the twist in my gut. "She was twenty-four. Restless. Angry, maybe. But she didn't run away."

"No," Dawn agreed. "She didn't. What she did was vanish. Until you came along."

I looked down at my hands again. "I picked up where other people left off. That's all. There were records, witnesses who'd never been thoroughly interviewed. Physical evidence that hadn't been re-tested. I didn't do anything special—I just didn't stop."

"But that's the point, isn't it?" Dawn leaned forward and her tone softened. "You didn't stop. Even when other people did. And in doing so, you brought Danika's remains home. You gave her family answers."

That part caught in my throat. I pictured Danika's mother in her snowflake patterned sweater. The sound she had made when I confirmed what she'd long suspected. Danika hadn't run away. Danika had never left.

"She should have had justice a long time ago," I said quietly. "It shouldn't have taken this long."

"Why do you think it did?" Dawn asked. She tilted her head, the journalist's version of pulling a trigger.

I hesitated. The truth. I was there to tell the truth.

"Because she was Indigenous," I said finally. "Because the people who were supposed to care didn't."

Dawn nodded slowly. "You spoke about systemic failures on Melody Sternbridge's popular podcast. About how missing Indigenous women are often overlooked by law enforcement, especially in rural areas. *Lost Girls* has drawn national attention to the case," she continued. "What's it been like to suddenly be at the center of that?"

I exhaled hard. "It sucks."

She chuckled.

I met her gaze squarely. "Look, I didn't ask for any of this. I didn't solve this case for the press or the praise. I did my job—a job that should have been done three decades ago. That doesn't make me special. It just makes me late."

There was a long pause. I took another breath.

"But," I added, "if my face is what it takes to keep people from forgetting about people like Danika, then fine. Put me on a billboard. Just don't make it about me. Make it about them."

Dawn leaned back slightly, switching gears. "You're an ex-Marine. You returned to Minneapolis and became a police officer, eventually specializing in cold cases. What drew you to them?"

Fuck. Why had I agreed to do this? I couldn't very well reveal that I was too dangerous to be on the streets with a gun so they'd stashed me behind a desk.

"I want ..." I took a necessary breath. The air in the studio was too warm, heightened by the unforgiving bright lights. "I want everyone to have a name. I want families to get answers. When you solve a new case, you feel good. You solve a cold case, someone gets a voice again for the first time in years."

Dawn smiled. "That's poetic, Detective."

I shrugged. "It's not poetic. It's necessary."

There was another stretch of dead air. It was the kind of pause I was sure they taught you to embrace in journalism school. Dawn LeClaire was a professional. She let that silence linger before leaning forward again.

"If there's one thing you'd want the people watching to take away from this—just one thing—what would it be?"

I stared at the camera, into the red blinking light.

"Danika mattered. Her family knew that. Her community knew that. The system didn't." I cleared my throat. "So if there's one thing to take away from this—don't wait thirty years to give a damn."

Dawn sat back and smiled. "I don't think I could have said it better myself."

The camera light blinked off.

I remained in my seat until receiving the all clear. I didn't want to make a mistake and find out we needed to do the whole damn thing all over again.

Dawn LeClaire removed her glasses and slid them back in her hair. "That was powerful," she said.

I shook my head. "I didn't mean to get dramatic."

"It wasn't dramatic," she denied. "It was honest. Raw. People will respond to that."

I exhaled, still trying to control the rapid beat of my heart. "Do me a favor?"

"Of course."

"Make sure Danika's name is the headline. Not mine."

Dawn nodded. "Done."

I stepped off set, blinking against the sudden dimness of the backstage area. I heard the sound of a slow clap before my eyes adjusted to the darkness.

"Hey," I said.

Julia stood just beyond the curtain. "Only one curse word," she observed. "I'm proud of you."

"That makes two of us."

She reached up to brush a bit of powder off my cheekbone. "Want to get out of here?"

"Desperately."

"There's a diner down the street that's supposed to have good pie."

I arched an eyebrow. "Pie? You want pie?"

"I didn't say it was for me," she corrected. "You did something hard today. You spoke for someone who couldn't. I think that deserves something."

I stared at her, disoriented in the best way. "So you're offering me pie?"

"I'm offering you twenty-eight minutes of sanctioned sugar and caffeine, Miss Miller. Don't ruin it."

A laugh escaped before I could stop it. "This is a trap, right?"

"This is a limited time offer. You should accept the deal before I change my mind."

I smiled, feeling the equilibrium return to my body just from her presence. "Thank you for coming today," I said softly. "I know you're a busy woman."

She wrapped her arms around my waist and leaned in until our noses touched. "I wouldn't want to be anywhere else."

∼

The local media blitz continued to be relentless over the next few days. I'd been naive about the popularity of Melody Sternbridge's podcast and the resulting chaos of being featured on a local news program. I checked in with Danika Laroque's family to be sure they were being left alone. No one in the family had agreed to an interview with Melody, however, so for the time being it seemed like they'd escaped the spotlight.

I, however, was not that lucky. Calls to our basement office—all requests to interview me—had to be rerouted to a central police dispatcher until the frenzy died down. I had wrongly assumed that agreeing to do one local interview would satisfy the wolves, but it only seemed to drum up more interest.

I experienced a feeling of dread each time my cell phone buzzed with an incoming text, worried that some local news anchor had gotten ahold of my personal number. By the end of the week, I was relieved to receive a text from Rich that our group of friends was meeting at the local cop bar for a drink after work.

Spencer's was the same as it had always been—dimly lit and occasionally boisterous when something happened in whatever sporting event was playing on the small TV over the bar. The noxious combination of beer, fried everything, and cleaning fluids assailed my nostrils.

I spotted my friends at our usual table. Brent, as massive as a modern-day Viking, was wildly gesturing with a beer in one hand as he told some tall tale. Angie sat next to him, unimpressed but still listening. And Rich—Rich just looked at me with raised eyebrows as if he wasn't sure I was real.

"Well, well, well," he clucked as I approached. "Look who finally remembered she has friends."

Brent let out a rumbling, deep chuckle. "Thought you went all Hollywood on us, Cass."

I scowled and slid across the bench to sit beside Rich. "Yeah, right. I haven't even watched the damn thing."

"You should," Rich said, tilting his glass at me. "The part where Dawn LeClaire calls you a reluctant hero is real cute."

I curled my lip and signaled a server to get a beer. "I'm sorry I've been MIA. Things have been busy," came my weak ass explanation. "All of this attention is temporary, though. Something new will come along, and then I'll be old news."

"That's not what I've been hearing," Rich hummed.

I turned sharp eyes on my friend. "What's that supposed to mean?"

"Only that I hear you're working on another high

profile case," he explained. "They're not going to be able to keep you in that basement for long, Rookie."

Frustrated, I tapped at my forehead. "You forget my busted brain. MPD is more than okay with stashing me in the basement."

"Wait. What high profile case?" Angie questioned. "Second shift's got me totally out of the loop."

I opened my mouth to fill in my friend on the new case, but before I could, Angie's eyebrows shot up. "Uh, hold up. What the hell is that?"

I followed her line of sight and realized she was staring at my hand. More specifically, my left hand. Fourth finger.

Shit.

The platinum band with its multiple inlaid diamonds had caught the bar's neon lights just enough to damn me.

"Cass," she said slowly. "Is there something you want to tell us?"

I grabbed Rich's pint glass and took a long sip to stall. "Where's that server? I'm spitting tacks over here."

"No, no, no," Angie said, cutting through the deflection. "Out with it."

I swallowed and sighed. "Yeah. Uh. I'm engaged."

Our waitress chose that exact moment to return, setting a beer in front of me. No one spoke. The bar suddenly felt too quiet.

Angie was the first to recover. "*Engaged?* As in wedding vows, until death do you part?"

"Last time I checked," I muttered. I dutifully began peeling the paper label from my beer bottle.

"To Julia?" Brent asked, as if there was another possible answer.

I sighed, already exhausted with the conversation. "No, to my side piece. *Yes*, obviously to Julia."

Rich only chuckled. "I knew she'd civilize you eventually."

Angie still looked a mix of shocked and betrayed. "And when exactly were you planning on telling us? After the honeymoon?"

I frowned, a guilty feeling rolling around in my stomach. "It's not like I kept it from you on purpose. It just—it happened fast."

Rich gave me a knowing look. "Is that why you asked if I'd leave IA to work for Julia?"

Angie snorted. "Damn. Not only did you get engaged without telling us, but now you're poaching our guy?"

"*Trying* to," Rich corrected. "I haven't said yes."

Brent was still processing, stroking his handlebar mustache. "Cass got engaged." He huffed out a laugh. "Poor Julia."

Brent's verbal musings seemed to break the tension at the table. Angie snorted, and even I smirked.

"Alright, well," Rich said, raising his glass. "Guess we gotta toast to the lucky lady."

Angie lifted her drink. "And to our girl Cassidy, for finding someone who puts up with her ass."

I rolled my eyes but clinked my bottle with everyone's drink. "Yeah, yeah. Love you guys, too."

As we made the celebratory toast, I felt the knot in my

chest loosen. They were giving me shit, sure, but they were my people.

Brent set his beer down with a grin. "So—who's planning the bachelorette party?"

I nearly choked on a mouthful beer. I sputtered and wiped my hand across my mouth. "Absolutely not."

Chapter Eight

I was halfway through my first cup of coffee when Detective Ryan swooped through the door of the Cold Case office.

"Morning," he greeted. "I've got something you're gonna hate."

"Awesome," I deadpanned, leaning back in my chair. "Hit me."

He waved the manila folder he held in his hand. "You know that list of former Sumner Field tenants we requested from the Housing Authority?"

An excited, eager feeling washed over me. "They sent them already?"

"Kind of. Turns out the original paper records were boxed up before they tore down the apartments. But before they could be digitized, they were destroyed in a warehouse flood."

My excitement turned to disbelief. "You're kidding."

"I wish I was." He dropped the envelope onto my desk. "There's a single scanned spreadsheet from the late 'Eighties that someone found on an old zip drive. Half the names are missing or corrupted, though. I printed what I could."

I slipped the computer paper out of the envelope for inspection. The top half of the spreadsheet was intact, but most of it was gibberish—symbols, broken characters, entire addresses replaced with ##REF.

I stared at the paper like I could will it into making sense.

"They didn't keep backup files?" I asked.

"Nope."

I let out a slow breath. "So all we have is a destroyed archive, a half-corrupted zip drive, and the assumption that no one thought preserving the residential records of one of the city's most historically marginalized communities might be, I don't know, important?"

"That about sums it up," Ryan confirmed.

I pinched the bridge of my nose. A headache had started to bloom behind my eyes. "How are we going to find them?" I lamented.

"Social media posts?" Ryan proposed with a shrug. "A call-to-action for former residents?"

"From MPD's Homicide Division?" I dismissively snorted. "We need someone who can reach people who don't want to be found. Or who don't even know they might have seen something important."

Sarah piped up from her desk. "What about a popular, local podcaster?"

I shot a look in her direction. "What about her?"

"She's got reach," Sarah reasoned. "And her listeners aren't just True Crime fans—they're people from around here, too. People who might've grown up in Sumner Field or had relatives there."

The headache had spread to my forehead.

I dropped my head and sighed. "She's going to fucking love this."

∽

I went alone. I didn't need Jason Ryan fanboying over the narrator of his favorite podcast.

I lightly knocked on Melody Sternberg's front door rather than activating her black lab with the doorbell. When the door swung open, I braced myself for impact.

Melody stood in the doorway, her red hair pulled up in a messy bun. She frowned and pushed oversized glasses up her narrow nose.

"What did I do this time?"

I frowned at her reaction. Maybe I'd been a little hard on her.

"What's the reach of your social media following?" I asked.

"More than the Minnesota Vikings."

I had no idea what those numbers were, but it sounded impressive.

"Would you make a post for us? For Cold Case?" I clarified.

I could tell she wasn't overly excited by my unsolicited appearance, but her innate curiosity would be too much to turn me away.

"Come in."

I took a quick step inside on the off-chance she changed her mind.

I scanned the small foyer, alert as always for the giant Labrador who'd once tackled me in the snow.

"He's in the basement," she told me. "I just came up for a quick break from editing when I heard your knock."

I nodded, but I continued to look around the space, a lingering habit from both my time in the military and as uniformed police.

"New episode?" I asked conversationally.

"Uh huh. But don't worry. You're not in it."

Melody folded her arms across her chest, the time for pleasantries and small talk having come to an end.

"So what's up?" she asked.

"Do you want to sit?" I proposed.

"Not really," she rejected. "Sitting is the new smoking."

"O-okay," I breathed.

An awkward, tense moment passed before she unexpectedly laughed.

I bristled. "What?"

"You."

Melody turned on her bare heel and left me for the

kitchen. She didn't have to go far. The arts and crafts bungalow-style house had a small but open floor plan. She reached into her fridge and pulled out a slim aluminum can of sparkling water. She cracked it open and took a quick sip.

"You show up at my door, obviously needing my help, but you're too stubborn and proud to actually ask."

"I'm not asking you to solve a case," I grunted.

She grinned. "No?"

I heaved another great sigh. "Fine! We've recovered human remains from an old housing project that date back to the 1960s. We haven't been able to identify the bodies. I thought maybe you could do a social media post to have people who used to live in the Sumner Field area get in contact with us."

Melody's features immediately brightened. "I can do you one better, Detective."

She motioned for me to follow her downstairs where I knew her recording equipment was located.

"I'm *not* doing an interview," I resisted.

Melody snorted. "Duh. Like I'd make that same mistake again."

She disappeared down the basement stairs, leaving me no other option but to follow behind.

Brady, her black lab, slept under her standing desk. Melody bent to affectionately pat the slumbering giant. When she righted herself, she applied a shiny layer of chapstick. She rubbed her lips together with an audible pop.

"Sumner Field in the 1960s, right?" she asked.

The confirming words got caught in my throat, so I nodded instead.

Melody pulled on a pair of heavy-duty headphones.

I stood a few feet away, arms crossed, as she adjusted an expensive-looking microphone and hit record.

"Hey fam," she said into the mic, her voice shifting into that smooth, charismatic podcast cadence. "It's Melody Sternbridge, and today we're shifting gears from hauntings and heartbreak to history—real, local, buried history. Literally."

She glanced at me, then continued, "I've been working with the Minneapolis PD on an ongoing Cold Case investigation. Human remains were found under what used to be the Sumner Field housing project. We believe these people might have lived—and died—there in the 1960s. But we don't know their names. We don't know who they were. And maybe, just maybe, you do."

She leaned in, voice low and earnest. "If you—or someone you love—lived in the Sumner Field projects, we want to hear from you. We're not here to reopen old wounds. We're here to remember. To honor. To find the truth."

Melody clicked a button on her laptop and music kicked in. It was soft, thoughtful, and a tad melodramatic. She turned back to me with a raised eyebrow and a particularly smug smile.

"Boom goes the dynamite."

I heard the *clickclack* of stilettos in the hallway outside of the Cold Case office, but the sound didn't really register with me until she was standing in front of my desk.

"I'm here to take you home," Julia announced.

I blinked up at her, taking in the elegant silhouette of her wool trench coat and the careful application of her makeup.

"Oh! Really?"

"Unless you'd rather take the bus?" she posed.

I hopped up from my office chair so fast it scraped against the floor. "No, no bus," I said, grabbing my leather jacket off the back of the chair.

Julia's gaze swept the room as I shrugged into my coat. She had never been to my office before, and it showed in the way her eyes lingered on the scuffed linoleum floors, the cracked ceiling tiles, and the dented filing cabinets stacked along the walls.

"This is ... cozy," she said diplomatically.

"It's a dungeon," I muttered.

She smiled, a small, private thing, until her attention caught on the only other living soul in the room.

"Hello, Stanley," Julia greeted. "It's good to see you." Her voice was warm, but there was something about the way she carried herself that always made people a little nervous.

Stanley had never needed much of an excuse to be nervous around pretty women.

"H-Hi," he stammered. They had met before, when we'd hosted Thanksgiving, but he still looked like he wasn't sure whether to salute her or faint.

"Are you keeping Cassidy in line down here?" she teased gently.

Stanley laughed a little too loudly and flashed me a panicked look, like he wasn't sure if it was a real question.

"See you tomorrow, Stan," I said quickly, steering Julia toward the door before he could combust.

Julia chuckled under her breath as we stepped out into the hallway. Her hand brushed lightly against mine, just enough to make my chest ache in that good, dangerous way.

The heavy door groaned behind us as we stepped outside the building. The walkway leading away from the Fourth Precinct was slick with patches of old, stubborn ice. February's darkness seemed to cling to everything.

Julia slipped her arm through mine, casual and easy.

"This is a nice surprise," I remarked.

"My schedule is starting to get more routine," she explained, "so we could make this a regular thing if you'd like. At least until I officially decide on my inaugural case."

"Getting any closer on that?"

"Not until my entire team is assembled," she said. "I've hired new paralegals, but I'm not ready to pull the trigger on a P.I. just yet." Her gloved fingers tightened around my bicep. "I suppose I'm stubbornly hoping you'll change your mind. But now that I've seen your office," she teased, "it's no wonder you won't come work with me."

"You'd get sick of me," I anticipated. "Us being around each other all of the time?"

Julia's hum was thoughtful. "Doesn't sound like the worst thing to me."

We were nearly to her black Mercedes when I heard it: "Miller! Hey, Miller! Cassidy ... Cassidy Miller!"

I froze for a long moment, my heart jamming into my throat.

Monica Hernandez was leaning against a light pole outside of the Fourth Precinct, her coat too thin for the weather, a backpack dropped at her feet.

I turned instinctively toward Julia.

"Can you wait here?" My voice was thinner than I meant it to be. It felt like every molecule in my body was vibrating at the wrong frequency. "I'll just be a second."

Julia nodded once, her gaze sharp but patient.

I walked toward Monica, my boots crunching over the dirty snow and scattered salt. I tried to steady my breathing.

She grinned when I got close. That same old smirk. That same mouth.

"You look like you've seen a ghost, Miller." Her voice had always been a little low and scratchy from too many cigarettes. She seemed proud of herself for rattling me.

I glanced over my shoulder at Julia. She was watching, too far away to hear anything, but close enough that I could feel her attention.

"I can't talk right now," I said quickly, keeping my voice quiet. "I'm late for something."

The lie came out easily.

"Tomorrow," Monica said. "Coffee."

I hesitated. I should have said no. I should have said *hell no*.

"Coffee. Yeah. I can do that."

Her smile widened like she'd won something.

I turned back toward Julia, my legs stiff. She was already opening the driver's side door.

"Who was that, dear?" Her voice was smooth but curious.

I swallowed the lump in my throat. "My, uh, my girlfriend?"

∽

Afghanistan, 2010

The slip of paper I discovered in my foot locker had indicated the location and time where she wanted to meet.

I check the hallway for traffic before slipping unobtrusively into the cramped supply closet. The door is always unlocked. I don't know how she manages that detail, and I'm half afraid to ask. Like most things with the armed forces, it's probably better that I don't know.

It's stuffy inside. It's not like the forward operating base has the best HVAC systems, but they seem to have bypassed this closet entirely.

The dim fluorescent light overhead casts eerie shadows on her heart-shaped face. No pleasantries are exchanged. We don't speak for fear of being discovered. It's a risk every time we meet like this, but we can't seem to help ourselves.

My hands roam over her body, tracing patterns on her hips and thighs through the fabric of her canvas pants. I can feel her warmth, her skin radiating heat through our clothes. We don't dare undress—not here, not ever—but we make do with what little privacy we have. I squeeze her ass, feeling the generous curve of her backside beneath my searching fingers.

Her lips meet mine in a fierce kiss, tongues tangling. The closet is small, but we make use of every square inch. Our bodies entwine as we shift and press together. Around us, boxes and bins creak in protest as we move.

My hands slide up under her military-issued t-shirt, tracing the swell of her full breasts through her sports bra. She moans softly, quietly, into my mouth as I cup them in my hands and gently squeeze. Her nipples harden beneath my touch, and I pinch them lightly between two fingers.

She's soaking by the time I shove my hand down the front of her pants. My fingers slice into her wet pussy; her heat envelopes me as I slide inside. My thumb finds her clit, and I start to rub it in slow circles.

She sucks on the fingers of my free hand, trying to stifle her moans as I work her over. Her mouth is hot and wet, and I can feel her tongue wrapping around my digits as she tries to keep quiet. But it's hard—she's getting louder, her breathing getting more ragged, as I push her closer to the edge.

I curl my fingers inside her, feeling for that sweet spot that will make her lose control. She gasps around my fingers, her eyes flashing up to meet mine as I hit it just right. Her body starts to tremble, her legs shaking as she tries to hold back.

But I'm not having it. I press down on her clit as I finger fuck her faster. She's sucking on my fingers so hard it's almost painful, but I don't care; I'm too busy watching her come apart.

She bites down on the meat of my palm, trying to muffle her cries, as she grinds herself down on my fingers. Her strategy to keep quiet—her teeth digging into my skin nearly causes me to make noises of my own. I can feel her orgasm building, feel it rising up like a tidal wave, before it finally crashes over her.

For a moment, we're both still—me with my hand buried in her pussy, and her with my fingers stuffed in her mouth. Then she sags against me, panting and trembling as she tries to catch her breath.

The sound of footsteps outside of the supply closet causes me to freeze. The heavy footsteps get closer, and I can hear a muffled voice on the other side of the door. My heart drops along with the front zipper of my pants. Her hazel eyes lock with mine while a mischievous hand dips beneath the waistband of my underwear.

She's reckless. She's going to get us caught. But all I

can do is hold my breath and widen my stance when searching fingertips dance across my clit.

I gasped into the darkened bedroom. The pungent scent of cleaning supplies left my nostrils, and the fabric softener Julia used on the sheets took its place.

A sleep-heavy hand crossed the expanse of the bed and rested on my chest. Julia's voice was tired but concerned: "Nightmare?"

I pressed the pads of my fingers into my left palm. It ached with phantom pain from Lance Corporal Monica Hernandez's teeth.

"Not exactly."

Chapter Nine

I chose a café close to the Fourth Precinct. I'd purposely avoided the coffee spot in Julia's neighborhood. Even though I'd told Julia all of the details the previous night, it still made me uncomfortable to be meeting up with Monica. There were too many unanswered questions. Too much unfinished business.

Monica looked unimpressed as I approached the small table where she sat.

"You came."

I dropped down into the empty chair across from her. "You didn't think I would?"

"Truth?" She shrugged. "I thought you might be too chicken shit."

I rolled my shoulders and tried to not let her words affect me. "Well, I didn't chicken out. I'm here."

"Yeah, you're here." She let out a short, humorless laugh. "Big hero move."

I opened my mouth, then closed it again. There was no winning with Monica—there never had been. She had a way of twisting everything, like a knife she didn't mind sinking just a little deeper.

"So..." she drawled. "Are we actually gonna talk? Or are you just gonna sit there looking like you've got someplace better to be?"

I stiffened. I *did* have someplace better to be. With Julia. With the life I'd managed to patch together despite everything I'd been through. Still, guilt sat in my stomach like a heavy stone.

"I'm here," I repeated, softer this time.

Monica leaned forward suddenly, reaching across the small table. Her fingers brushed mine—cold and dry—before curling around my wrist.

Something akin to panic ripped up my arm. I hopped to my feet so quickly that my chair screeched against the floor.

"What are you having? I got it." I worked to keep my tone neutral like this was only a casual meetup between old friends.

Monica stared up at me. There was no way she couldn't tell that I was spooked. She made no comment on it though. "Flat white. Almond milk."

I nodded, already backing away.

I turned and quickened my step towards the front counter. The line wasn't long, but it gave me time to breathe, to settle my nerves. Maybe I wasn't actually ready for this. Maybe I should have chickened out.

The line, thankfully, moved slowly. I alternated my attention between the person in front of me who couldn't decide if they wanted their bagel toasted or not and the ghost from my past seated a few feet away.

Three years. It didn't seem like that long until I really looked at her. She was thinner than I remembered, not in a deliberate way, but in the way people got when life wore them out. It was like someone had taken a file to her edges and kept grinding them down.

I'd been too frazzled the previous day to really take in her appearance, but I was almost certain she was wearing the same outfit as before. Her clothes hung wrong on her frame, a second-hand coat too thin for February in Minnesota. The sleeves were frayed at the cuffs, and the zipper looked like it hadn't worked in a while. It was the kind of jacket you grabbed from a Lost & Found bin because it was better than nothing.

She tucked a strand of dark hair behind her ear as she glanced around the busy coffee shop. I watched her stuff a few sugar packets from the table into her jacket pocket like she couldn't help herself.

It twisted something in my gut. Not pity, exactly. Something messier. Sadder.

When I finally reached the front of the line, I ordered a black coffee for myself and whatever fancy beverage Monica had requested.

The bored-looking girl behind the cash register barely looked up at me. "Anything else?"

I hesitated and glanced once more in Monica's direction. "Yeah. A blueberry muffin."

I carefully balanced our drinks and a small ceramic plate upon which a fresh blueberry muffin sat. I set the drinks between us with the muffin closer to her side of the table like it was part of her order and not some half-assed apology I didn't know how to say out loud.

"Where are you staying these days?" I asked, returning to my seat.

"I'm just passing through," she evaded. "Thought I'd look up my old pal, Cassidy Miller."

The way she said my name sounded almost musical, like I wasn't real.

"How did you find me?"

I mentally cringed at my own question. I hadn't intended on sounding like I was in hiding.

She picked up the muffin and tore a chunk off the top. "The Internet. It wasn't hard."

I exhaled. "I guess IT finally got around to updating the departmental web page."

"No, it was a podcast. *Lost Girls?*"

I stiffened, a wave of annoyance rising in my chest. "Not you, too."

"Huh?"

"It's nothing," I quickly dismissed. "I just didn't expect so many people to hear those episodes."

"Oh, I don't listen," Monica clarified. "But there was a transcript online. The narrator chick said you worked for Minneapolis' Cold Case division. And the internet told me where to find the Cold Case office."

"Quite the detective yourself," I tried to crack.

My joke didn't land.

"You look good," she approved. "Civilian life is treating you well." She made a small humming noise. "That's quite the ring, too."

I dropped my left hand into my lap.

"H-how have you been?" I asked, desperate to shift the conversation.

Monica sipped from her coffee before wiping at her mouth with the back of her hand. "We can skip the small talk, Miller. You're not really interested. You would have looked me up if that had been the case."

I bit the inside of my cheek. Monica had always had a chip on her shoulder. I'd thought she was a brat when we'd first met. Time had passed, but apparently that hadn't changed.

"No one on the FOB would tell me what had happened to you," she said. "I wasn't family, so I had no business knowing if you were dead or alive."

"How long did you stay enlisted?" I asked.

She tapped fingernails that had been chewed down to nothing against the porcelain coffee cup. "I separated a few months after you left. I had a change of heart about if I was really doing any good over there."

"What are you up to now?" I asked.

God, I hated the sound of my voice. The robotic questions like I was a cop interviewing a suspect.

She shrugged like it didn't matter. "A little bit of this, a little bit of that. I've tried a lot of things," she said, "but nothing really sticks."

I nodded slowly, letting the words hang between us. I didn't ask for more. I didn't offer anything back. I just sipped my coffee and waited.

Monica peeled back the muffin wrapper and took a small, almost absentminded bite. The act of eating seemed more automatic than satisfying.

She wiped her fingers on a crumpled napkin. "Detective Miller, Cold Case. I bet you're good at it." Her words fell someplace in between a compliment and an accusation.

I didn't answer. I wasn't sure she actually wanted me to.

For a minute, we sat in a fragile kind of silence, the noise of the café—the hiss of the espresso machine, the low murmur of other conversations—filling the space between us.

Monica drummed her fingers on the table, glancing toward the window like she was already halfway out the door. She stuffed a few more sugar packets into her pocket, like it was just another habit she couldn't break.

"Listen," she said. "I should go. I just—" She broke off and exhaled hard through her nose. "Forget it."

She stood and pulled the too-thin jacket tighter around

her frame and tugged her hood up over her dark, uneven hair.

I stayed seated, hands wrapped around my coffee cup. I squeezed a little harder and let the platinum band around my left ring finger bite into my skin.

"Take care of yourself, Miller," she tossed over her shoulder.

"You, too," I returned. I wasn't sure she heard me.

I stared out the glass plate window for a long moment after she disappeared through the coffee shop door. A familiar ache settled into my chest—the one that said some things couldn't be fixed, no matter how much you tried.

Not three years ago. Not today.

∽

I didn't go directly to work after my brief meet up with Monica. I was only around the corner from the Fourth Precinct, but I lingered only long enough to grab the departmental car from the employee parking lot. I didn't take the aging Crown Vic on any official business. My immediate supervisor, Captain Forrester, would have probably called it an abuse of departmental resources, but that was honestly the furthest thing from my mind.

I knocked on the doorframe to Julia's open office door. "Do you have a minute?"

Julia looked away from her computer monitor. "Of course, darling. Come in."

I shut the door behind me and sank into one of the

semi-rigid conference chairs opposite of her desk. Julia remained in her own office chair—the same chair where I had efficiently dismantled her only a few days prior. I wondered if the same thought passed her mind; the apples of her cheeks seemed to flush as she removed her readers, but perhaps that was only my imagination.

"I had coffee with Monica."

"Yes, I know. You told me that was happening."

I chewed on my lower lip. "It was just coffee. I bought her a muffin, too." I took a breath. "She looked a little …"

"Homeless?" Julia finished for me.

I deflated where I sat. "Yeah."

Julia stood and rounded her expensive desk. I expected her to sit at the edge of the desk or in the vacant seat beside mine. Instead, she compelled me to uncross my legs so she could sit delicately on my lap. Her long, lean arms went around my shoulders and neck.

"What do you want to do?" she asked me.

"Is there anything *to* do?"

"I know you feel very deeply," she started. "And I know you carry an immense amount of guilt for how your life has turned out compared to others with whom you served. The men in your unit. Terrance. Geoff Reilly."

I exhaled. "Yeah."

"You've worked hard to get where you are, Cassidy. Nothing has come to you unearned. Even me," she smiled softly.

"*Especially* you," I laughed.

Julia toyed with the lapel of my leather jacket. "Would money help her?"

"She'd never accept a handout."

"I didn't think so." Julia paused, silent with her thoughts. "Is she staying at a local shelter?"

"She didn't say." I made a face. "And I didn't ask."

"Don't beat yourself up about it, dear. It's not an easy situation."

"Uh huh," I sighed.

Julia's words were reassuring, but I couldn't help feeling like I should have asked more questions, probed a little more. Instead, I'd wanted to get through the meeting quickly with as little carnage as possible.

"Do you have plans to see her again?" Julia asked.

"We didn't exchange numbers or anything." I busied myself with the reading glasses that hung from a chain around Julia's neck. "But she tracked me down at work, so I guess she knows where to find me if she needs to get a hold of me again."

"Are you having second-thoughts?" Julia asked.

"About?"

She twisted her head to stare at something on the far wall. Her voice grew so quiet that I nearly missed her words: "About ... me."

My arms tightened around her waist. "You're joking, right?"

Julia flicked her fingers through her hair. "I wouldn't want to assume anything."

"Babe, you're not getting rid of me that easily. Just because someone I fooled around with for a few years suddenly shows up, that doesn't mean—"

She interrupted my reassurances: "A few *years*?"

"I was in the desert for a very long time," I said with an easy shrug. "It was never official though. Just when one of us got horny enough and had an itch to scratch."

"You can spare me the details."

"You sure?" I teased.

"Positive," she deadpanned.

"Not even the time we—"

"*Cassidy*."

"Okay, okay." I held up my hands in mock surrender, then settled them back on her hips. "You know I don't want anyone but you."

Her expression softened, and she leaned in a little, just enough for me to catch her scent—spicy and earthy and expensive.

I tilted my face toward hers. "I mean it."

Her lips were close, her breath sweet and warm. "Show me."

So I did.

I closed the distance and kissed her, slow and tender, and without hesitation. Her mouth met mine with a practiced precision that told me she'd been waiting for this. Not the kiss itself—we kissed all the time. But *this* one. The one that said *I'm right here. I choose you.*

Julia deepened the kiss with a sigh, her fingers tightening against the back of my neck. I lost myself for a long, breathless moment until finally, reluctantly, I pulled back just enough to rest my forehead against hers.

"I love you, Julia."

"I know, darling." Her lips brushed against mine again. "But it's always nice to hear."

Chapter Ten

Melody Sternbridge called the office just after nine o'clock in the morning. "I've decided to start an oral history podcast series."

"Careful. You can't just go around saying 'oral,'" I joked.

I heard her scoff. "Very mature, Detective Miller."

"So you're giving up the True Crime series?" I asked.

"No. Even better," she chirped. "I'm expanding my brand. And I have *you* to thank."

I tightened my grip around the phone's receiver. "Oh, this oughta be interesting."

"Once I put the call out for families who'd lived at the Sumner Field projects, the emails and DMs started rolling in," she said. "People want to share their stories. No one had ever asked them about their experiences before. I have my first one-on-one tomorrow morning, and I want you to come with."

"To hold your mic?" I deadpanned.

"To be another set of ears," she said. "Isn't that why you asked for my help in the first place?"

I could think of a million other things I'd rather do with a million other people, but she was right; this was what I'd asked her to do. She'd put the call to action out there and people had responded. Now I needed to make myself available to speak with these potential witnesses.

"Yeah. Okay," I agreed. "Give me an address and I'll be there."

"Great." Melody went quiet. "Just ... just don't go in there like a cop, okay?"

"Like a cop?" I echoed.

"Don't play dumb; you know what I mean," she chastised. "Deep voice. Swagger walk. Leading with your gun."

I *did* know what she meant. Every cop I knew talked that way—walked that way. I guess I hadn't realized I still did that, even without the bulletproof vest and gun belt.

"So I'm not a cop," I played along. "Who am I instead?"

Melody's voice was matter-of-fact: "You're my assistant."

My upper lip curled at the request.

"She won't talk to you if she thinks you're a cop," she warned. "No offense, but MPD doesn't have the best relationship with this community."

I closed my eyes and sighed. "Fine. I'll see you tomorrow."

Melody gave me an address and a name: Ms. Margerie Price. Eighty-six years old. Lived in a senior co-op near the river. Used to be a seamstress. Raised five kids in Sumner Field before the superblock cut her street off from the rest of the neighborhood.

Ms. Price's apartment was on the third floor. I wasn't there to be a cop, but I still took everything in: floral carpet, a plastic runner in the hallway, and a wreath on her door that read *Bless This Mess*.

I met Melody in the hallway.

Her smile was too much. "So! Are you ready to be my assistant?"

I gave her a mock salute. "Sure thing, boss."

I noticed the white box in her hands. "Sweetening up the witness?"

Melody looked down to where my attention had strayed. "This isn't my first rodeo, Detective. You of all people should know that a donut goes a long way."

She didn't wait for my reply. She knocked briskly on the door, and we waited.

"You still look like a cop," she quipped, not looking at me.

I glanced down at my outfit: jeans and an unadorned crewneck sweater.

"It's just how I look," I defended.

The door opened and a small Black woman stood in

the threshold. Ms. Margerie Price wore a purple cardigan and a look that said she didn't trust us.

"You're the podcaster?" she asked, squinting into the hallway.

"I am, ma'am," Melody spoke up. She turned slightly toward me. "And this is my assistant, Cassidy Miller. We brought pastries."

Ms. Price stepped aside and nodded toward the living room. "You can put them on the coffee table. Don't sit in the recliner though. That's for my bad hip."

I eased onto the edge of a floral loveseat and waited while Ms. Price shuffled into the back kitchenette. She moved slowly, but her steps were remarkably light. She returned, moments later, with two coffee mugs.

"You take cream?" she asked.

Melody spoke for the two of us: "That would be great, thank you."

"Too bad. I only have oat milk." Ms. Price gave me a half-smile and an unexpected wink. "Gotta keep the cholesterol down."

We sat in silence for a moment, donuts untouched, the coffee warm in my hands. I heard music coming from somewhere in the apartment, playing something quiet and sad.

Ms. Price sighed, deep and low. "I hadn't thought about that place in a very long time."

I vocalized the obvious: "Sumner Field?"

She pursed her lips and nodded. "My youngest—she listens to your podcast. I didn't even know what that was until just recently. She said to me, 'Mama, isn't that where you lived?'" Ms. Price took a small sip from the ceramic mug sitting on an end table beside her recliner. "Not quite sure why anyone would be interested in that old place."

I glanced in Melody's direction, unsure of how to proceed. Did we tell her about the bodies? Or was this only a fact-finding mission? I wish we'd devised a plan of action earlier so no one's time would be wasted.

I cleared my throat and leaned forward just slightly, enough to show I was serious but not about to interrogate her. *Don't be a cop.*

"Ms. Price," I said, "we're looking into something that happened a long time ago. Near Sumner Field. They found ..." I hesitated, and then decided to just say it. "They found human remains. Buried where some of the old buildings used to be."

Ms. Prince didn't flinch. "People?" she shrewdly asked. "Or *children?*"

Melody and I exchanged a glance. It wasn't the kind of question someone asked if they didn't already suspect something.

"We're not sure yet," I said. "That's why we're here. We're hoping maybe you could help us understand what that neighborhood was like back then."

Ms. Price set her mug down, hands steady in a way that belied her age. "You want to know what it was like? It was like trying to raise babies in a house that could barely hold the wind out. It was knowing the cops wouldn't come if you called and being afraid that they *would* if you did."

She looked directly at me—past Melody and past the box of donuts. "You think this is the first time someone's gone missing from Sumner Field?"

"Did anyone report it?" Melody asked.

"Back then?" Her laugh was humorless. "Nobody came looking for poor Black children. You know how many mothers cried in those hallways? It was just part of the noise."

I swallowed hard. "Ms. Price, do you remember who went missing?"

Ms. Price fell silent.

"There was a girl," she started. "Used to live three doors down from us. Her name was Linda. Pretty thing. Always wore pink barrettes, even when they didn't match her clothes. Her mama worked nights at the hospital. I don't know what happened to her daddy. People didn't ask too many questions back then."

Melody leaned forward, but was careful not to interrupt. I didn't have to worry about her. This was what she did—interviewed people who didn't necessarily want to talk.

"She was ten," Ms. Price said. "Maybe eleven. One day, she didn't come home from school. The police showed up two days later. Said she probably ran off." She sighed, a low, sorrowful sound. "They always said that back then—like little Black girls were just out there taking off on cross-country adventures with no shoes and no money."

Her voice hardened for a moment.

"I remember her mother standing in the courtyard,

screaming her name like she could drag her home by willpower alone. You ever hear a woman scream like that?" She didn't wait for an answer. "You don't forget it. Not for the rest of your life."

Melody reached for her notebook. "Do you remember Linda's last name?"

Ms. Price nodded slowly like the memories were shifting back into focus. "Walker. Linda Walker. We lit candles for her that first week."

My chest tightened. We had a name.

Chapter Eleven

Olivia Desjardin was having a bad day. That's what the staff at her assisted living facility called it when a memory slipped through the crevasses of her mind or when she didn't recognize her own reflection or wandered into a room that wasn't hers.

I'd received the frantic call from Julia earlier that day. She was at her doctor's for a routine ultrasound—one of the monitoring check-ins leading up to egg retrieval—and her mom was having a bad day.

I didn't hesitate when Julia asked if I could go check on her mom until she could get there herself. The facility and old people and Olivia Desjardin made me wildly uncomfortable, but Julia had enough on her plate without worrying about whether her mother was safe.

The facility was quiet when I arrived. It was mid-morning, after breakfast but before lunch, when the common room smelled faintly of instant oatmeal and scrambled eggs.

Mrs. Desjardin was sitting in a chair by the window, her back straight, her hair pinned in soft, wispy rolls like she'd once been a woman who never left the house without lipstick. She was watching the world beyond the window, but I wasn't sure if she was really looking at anything.

I pulled up a chair and sat beside her.

For a while, we didn't speak. Her fingers moved along the top of a knitted blanket, tapping out an invisible pattern. My own mother had once been a piano teacher. I wondered if Olivia Desjardin had ever played an instrument.

"I used to predict when it was going to snow," she said suddenly. "Not like they do now, watching the forecast on TV. I could smell it coming."

"You grew up in Embarrass, right?" The words caught in my throat.

She smiled faintly. "The Cold Spot. That's what the sign says."

"Sounds like a brag and a threat," I remarked.

Olivia gave a soft chuckle. "It's not so bad when you're young. We'd build tunnels through the drifts. One year, it snowed so high you could walk from the porch roof to the apple tree."

I smiled with her. "I bet your mother loved that."

"She did not," Olivia said, a trace of pride in her voice. "But she let us do it anyway."

She lapsed into silence again. Her hands stopped moving.

After a minute, she turned to me. "Have you known my daughter for very long?"

I grew very still. I'd met Mrs. Desjardin on several occasions, but I was usually in the peripheral. She'd once confused me for one of Julia's childhood friends. Julia had told me it was because of my blonde hair.

I swallowed before speaking. "Not long."

It hadn't even been a year, and yet I couldn't imagine my life without her.

"She always was so serious, even as a child. Wild, but serious. There was a fire in her," she carefully described. "She doesn't let people see it. Too worried about seeming fragile." She turned back to the window. "She always thought that made her mother weak."

I didn't respond. Not out of discomfort, but because I didn't want to interrupt.

Olivia went on. "I wish ... I wish ..." She seemed to be losing momentum, like a clock in need of winding or a runner just short of the finish line.

"What's that, Mrs. Desjardin?" I urged her to continue.

"I don't think we're meant to go through this life alone."

Emotions crept up my throat. Julia still hadn't told her mother about me.

I was trying to respect that decision. Hell, I hadn't even told my parents about our relationship until over the

Christmas holiday. But if we were really going to get married and start a family, it seemed pretty crucial that her mother be let into that. But I would have to be patient. Julia would tell her mother about me or not.

Olivia turned away from the window. She regarded me as though I hadn't been sitting there the whole time. Her eyes were so like her daughter's. If I squinted, I could see Julia's future.

"Where's my daughter?" she asked. "She was supposed to bring me my scarf."

"She'll be here soon," I assured her. "She's just at a doctor's appointment."

Olivia frowned, trying to place the puzzle piece.

I reached out and lightly covered her hand with mine. "I'll stay with you until she gets here."

She looked at our joined hands, then back at the window.

"I could smell it." She spoke quietly, almost to herself. "Right before it snowed. The whole sky would change."

∽

I heard the familiar click of heels before I saw her. Julia entered the common room in a rush, still in her wool trench coat, hair half-tucked behind one ear. She looked tired in a way that had nothing to do with sleep.

She saw me sitting with her mother and stopped short.

"Hey," I said quietly.

Her painted mouth trembled. She pressed a clenched fist to her lips, as if holding something in.

"She's been okay," I offered gently. "She remembered the snow in Embarrass."

Julia gave a choked laugh, but it came out like a sob. She crossed the room in two strides and crouched in front of her mother.

She clasped Olivia's hands in her own. "I'm sorry I wasn't here sooner."

"She knew you were coming," I said. "I told her."

Julia nodded. She didn't take her eyes off her mom.

We stood in the hallway, just outside of the common room. Olivia was with a nurse, getting a round of medication. I had to get back to work.

Julia leaned against a wall, eyes closed but breathing.

"How'd the appointment go?" I asked.

She didn't open her eyes. "The follicles are responding, but not as fast as they want. They might push the retrieval date. Or cancel it altogether."

I didn't say anything. I didn't know what I *could* say. "Sorry" felt inadequate for the moment.

"I don't know what I'm doing, Cassidy." Her eyes finally opened, shining and damp. "I'm trying to take care of her. To build a career. To do this one impossible thing with my body. And I—" Her voice broke. "I can't possibly have it all."

I reached across the distance that separated us—physically, at least. I held onto her fingertips. It was a precarious hold, as if she might slip from my grasp entirely.

"You don't have to do it. Not all at once."

Julia sniffed and blinked hard, like she was trying to shove the tears back in. "Like eating an elephant."

She repeated my words from when we'd been in Embarrass for her father's funeral. There'd been so much to take care of in a short amount of time.

"And you don't need to be perfect," I added. "You can only do your best."

"And if my best isn't good enough?" I heard the fearfulness in her tone.

I shifted my grip and held her hand tighter. "It will be."

Julia walked me out to the parking lot. She kissed my cheek and squeezed my hand like she didn't want to let go.

I brought her hand up to my mouth and kissed her knuckles. "I'll see you tonight."

She nodded, almost imperceptibly.

I watched her disappear through the automatic doors of the assisted living facility before heading to the beat-up Crown Vic. The car's interior was warm from the sun, but I didn't start the engine right away.

Instead, I pulled out my phone. I scrolled to the contact I needed, tapped, and held the phone to my ear.

One ring. Two.

"Hey," came the voice on the other end. She didn't sound surprised, almost like she'd been waiting for my call.

Outside, a school bus rumbled down the side street, churning up loose dust in its wake.

"Hey," I returned. "Can you set up another meeting with Ms. Price?"

∼

The rec room at the senior center smelled like coffee and lemon-scented wood polish. The well-used card table creaked every time Ms. Price shuffled the deck of cards. Around her, three others—Mr. Earl, Ms. Ruby, and a wiry man named Leon—ribbed each other with the kind of fondness that only came from decades of shared history.

They'd lived at Sumner Field once, before it had been bulldozed in the name of urban renewal. Their jokes were sharp, but so were their memories.

I didn't ask questions; I wasn't there to interrogate anyone. I was content to sit on the periphery and soak it all in—these stories, these memories, this community that had been scattered and displaced, yet somehow still found their way back to one another.

Melody buzzed around the perimeter of the room, testing sound levels, I guessed. "Just pretend like we're not even here," she directed.

Ms. Price snapped the cards against the table. "Tell me again what we're supposed to be doing?"

"We're just here to listen, ma'am," I remarked. "Whatever you might remember from back then."

"Any interesting characters or happenings," Melody chimed in.

"Remember the Nelsons?" Ms. Ruby asked, tilting her head toward Mr. Earl.

He nodded. "Oh yeah. Lived in the corner unit, across from the laundry building. Real quiet people."

"They had that little boy," Ms. Price added, eyes narrowing like she was trying to pull the memory into focus. "Skinny thing. Always humming to himself."

Leon chuckled. "That wasn't just humming. That boy had music in him even back then."

He used his cane to tap out a beat that was vaguely familiar, but I couldn't quite place it.

Ms. Ruby hummed a wordless tune along with the stilted beat. It, too, was somehow familiar.

Mr. Earl caught my eye. "You know why they were called the Sumner Field projects, right?"

I sat a little more erect like speaking with a commanding officer. Even in a Marvin Gaye t-shirt, Mr. Earl carried himself with gravitas. I wondered if he'd been a soldier himself.

"No, sir."

"Charles Sumner."

"I'm sorry, I don't ..."

My ignorance was humbling.

"Massachusetts Senator before the Civil War," he said. "He was a vocal opponent of slavery, which led to his vicious beating right on the Senate floor. South Carolina's Preston Brooks whipped him with his cane. It nearly killed Sumner."

Ms. Ruby clucked. "Oh, don't be boring these girls with your history books, Earl."

"It's not boring," I defended the man. "Thank you for telling me, sir."

He nodded, curt but perceptible.

Ms. Ruby sipped her hot tea. "We used to pick wild rhubarb behind the rec center. You remember that, Margerie?"

Ms. Price nodded. "I do. And your mama made the best pies."

"And the bonfires in the summer," Leon added. "Old man Davis would bring his radio out and all the kids would dance."

"They used to call it the Circle," Ms. Price said, almost to herself. "That patch of grass beside Building Nine. Always something going on."

I committed the detail to memory: the Circle. Building Nine. I wondered at its location relative to where the bodies had been recovered.

Around the card table, another round of trash talk had begun. Leon accused Ms. Price of reneging; she responded by showing him her hand and daring him to prove it.

Melody touched her fingertips to my elbow. "I didn't realize the time," she said apologetically. "I've got to let Brady out."

I glanced back at the table. Ms. Ruby was reshuffling. Leon was demanding a rematch.

"Okay," I said. "Let's go."

We stepped out into the late afternoon, the screen door creaking closed behind us. The air was heavy with the smell of laundry detergent from an exterior vent nearby. Cars lined the cracked asphalt of the senior living center's parking lot, most of them past their prime, my unit's Crown Vic included.

Melody slowed her pace to match mine. "I wasn't expecting your call," she said. "What prompted that?"

I hesitated with the truth. "My future mother-in-law has dementia. I guess I wanted to make sure someone heard their memories before they're gone."

Melody's step faltered, just a little. "Wow. I didn't know you had it in you."

I stared at my feet, at the horizon, at cars in the parking lot—anything to avoid her curious gaze. I didn't know why I'd been so forthcoming.

"You know, I don't think they'd mind you asking questions," she remarked. "You might actually get someplace with them next time."

I glanced sideways at her. "Yeah?"

Melody hummed. "You realize who they were talking about, right? The Nelson family?"

"No. Should I?"

"Prince Rogers Nelson."

It was the second unfamiliar name of the short day. I shook my head.

Melody's voice lilted in disbelief. "Prince. As in *the* Prince? *Purple Rain* Prince? He's only, like, the most famous Minnesotan. He grew up in the Sumner Field projects."

"Ohh." The name finally clicked. "That's cool."

"My God, you're hard to impress," Melody scowled.

I shrugged. "I've never been that into celebrities."

"I suppose you wouldn't be when you're practically a celebrity yourself," she said, teasing.

I shoved my hands into the pockets of my leather jacket and forced out a humorless laugh. "Right. That's me—local legend."

"So, any new leads?"

Melody raised her hands when I shot her a warning look. "I'm only making conversation! God forbid you actually let me help."

I sighed at her dramatics. "Thank you for putting me in contact with Ms. Price again. We don't have anything new, but I'll let you know if something comes up."

Melody made a noise like she didn't quite believe me.

"We actually had that professor from the university use his ground-penetrating radar out at the park," I said, throwing her a bone. "He hasn't reported his findings yet though."

It had been Melody who'd introduced me to the idea of GPR when I'd been working the Danika Laroque case. The local tribal leader had refused to let us disturb the ground in search of the missing woman. Melody's suggestion hadn't produced Danika herself, but when we realized she wasn't in the ground, it had prompted me to dredge the area lakes instead.

"Oh, really?" Melody looked unabashedly smug.

"Yeah," I snorted. "Turns out you're the gift that keeps giving."

"Careful, Detective." She batted her long eyelashes. "Keep sweet-talking like that and people will think we're in love."

Chapter Twelve

I came home from work later that day to find Julia already there.

She was sitting at the dining room table, still in her work clothes, her posture too perfect, her hands clasped tightly in front of her. She wasn't reading, wasn't looking at her phone—she only sat there, eyes cast down like she'd been rehearsing something for hours.

"Hey," I said, setting my keys down slowly. "Everything okay?"

She looked up at me; the expression on her face made my stomach clench. She looked solemn—morose, almost.

My mind jumped to the worst case scenario. Her mother. More bad news from the fertility clinic. Something she'd been keeping from me altogether.

"What's wrong?" I asked, crossing the room. "Did something happen?"

Her throat bobbed as she swallowed. "The strap-on," she said quietly. "Would you mind terribly?"

My body relaxed with the request. "Jesus, Julia," I breathed. "You scared the shit out of me. I thought someone had died."

"I'm sorry," she murmured, visibly embarrassed. "I don't mean to be dramatic. The hormone shots are doing unexpected *things* to me."

"You have nothing to be embarrassed about," I assured her. "It's biology. Besides," I added with a smile, "I don't think anyone in the history of the world has asked to be strapped so politely."

Julia's nostrils seemed to flare. "Too much talking. Not enough fucking."

The pink dildo and its nylon harness resided in a shoebox in Julia's walk-in closet. We didn't normally bring toys into the bedroom, with the exception of Julia's birthday the previous year. The strap-on had remained in its box, untouched, since then.

I carefully removed my own outer shell, first my work pants and then the button-up shirt. I fastened the harness around my hips and thighs, the nylon straps digging into my skin as I adjusted the fit. The pink dildo protruded lewdly from the harness, its smooth surface glinting in the dim light of the bedroom.

Julia made no complaint when I tugged the hem of her blouse from the waistband of her tailored pants. I unfastened small, careful buttons until the expensive fabric hung loose in the front. She shrugged the shirt off, letting it drift to the bedroom floor. Her bra quickly followed, unclasped with practiced ease, to join the blouse in a pile at her feet.

Her nipples were already tight. I leaned in and took one into my mouth, swirling my tongue around the peak until her breath hitched and her fingers threaded through my hair.

"I need all of you tonight," she murmured. "Don't go easy on me."

I wouldn't.

I dropped to my knees and pressed hot kisses down her stomach. I hooked my fingers into the waistband of her wool trousers. I found the hidden clasp and then the narrow zipper. She held onto the top of my shoulders as she stepped out of her pants and then her underwear. I kissed just above the tidy, trim curls at the apex of her sex. She was already wet.

I held onto the backs of her thighs and looked up at her. "On the bed."

Julia backed up and laid down, legs parting in silent invitation. Her voice, low and breathy, made my stomach tighten. "Hurry, Cassidy. Please."

This wasn't about romance, but efficiency. It was a means to an end.

I climbed onto the bed and happily obliged. I pressed the tip of the dildo against her opening and slowly pushed forward. I held my breath, transfixed by the erotic sight.

First the tapered end, then one inch after another. Pale pink entered a deeper blush.

I took my time, gently working the toy in and out, despite her assurances that she was ready for all of me. She gasped when I bottomed out. I stilled, not wanting to overwhelm her, but she arched beneath me, hands gripping my thighs.

I kissed her neck, her jaw, and sucked at the spot beneath her ear until she whimpered. I began to move—deeper, harder—her body meeting mine in a desperate rhythm.

"You feel so good," I whispered, one hand anchored at her hip, holding her steady as I thrust.

Julia clawed at my back. "Don't stop. Please, don't stop."

The sounds of our bodies—wet, slick, insistent—filled the room, joined by the faint creak of the mattress and Julia's soft cries.

She wrapped her legs around my waist, heels digging in and forcing me deeper. She opened to me, her tongue tangling with mine, breath hot and uneven. Her hips met each thrust with matching desperation, her body hungry and unashamed.

With each thrust of the dildo, Julia's body responded more urgently. She clawed at my skin with frantic fingers, pulling me deeper into her heat.

"More, Cassidy," she begged. "Give me more."

I grabbed the headboard for leverage and gave her everything she asked for. No holding back. Everything I had was all for her. My biceps burned and my lower back ached, but I didn't give in to fatigue.

"Fuck me, Cassidy," she urged. "Don't stop fucking me."

I could feel how close she was—her body twitching, every muscle taut. I reached between us and pressed two fingers to her clit, circling in time with each thrust. Her body jerked in response.

She gasped my name like it was the only word she remembered. I didn't stop moving until she sagged beneath me, liquid and spent.

I slowed, then stilled, and brushed the hair back from her flushed face.

Her eyes fluttered open. "Jesus."

I leaned in and kissed her gently. "You okay?"

She nodded, breathless. "Better than okay."

"Still embarrassed?"

Her knees tightened at my ribs. "Not even a little."

I pulled the duvet over both of us and felt her tuck herself into me. Her face pressed against my neck and her bare legs tangled with mine. For a while, we just breathed. My palm found the small of her back, where I drew idle circles.

Julia nuzzled closer. "Next time," she stated quietly, "I'm returning the favor."

"Next time can be right now, if you want."

She pulled back just enough to meet my eyes. "Is that so?"

My cheeks warmed. "I mean … if you're not too tired."

"With the harness?" she asked, fingers already slipping under the blanket.

"Whatever feels right."

Julia's hand found the silicone still strapped to me. Her grip was confident. Possessive.

"My turn."

I wiggled out of the harness as gracefully as I could manage while Julia watched. Her expression was unreadable.

"Have you ever had sex with a man?" she asked.

I hesitated. "I, uh ... yeah."

Her smile was wry and knowing. "This won't be like that."

My eyes trailed down her body—those firm breasts, that tapered waist, the flush still painting her skin.

"I've no doubt."

Julia deftly separated the phallic toy from the harness. She lowered herself on the mattress until her warm breath tickled my stomach. The sound of silicone slapping against my upper thigh was obscene. My face flushed nearly the same color as the dildo in her hand.

"I'm going to fill you up," she murmured. She dragged her tongue slowly across my hip bones. "I'm going to suck your clit until you see stars. All the constellations," she solemnly vowed. "Every distant galaxy."

I could only release a long, shuddering breath.

Julia leaned closer, her lips brushing my lower abdomen. "Watch, darling. I'm going to split you open."

I felt Julia's hand between my legs, her fingers gently parting me. She teased me with the tip of the toy, circling, waiting until I was panting from the anticipation alone. Then, slowly, slowly, she began to slide in. Inch by inch.

The stretch was delicious—sharp and sweet. I exhaled a quiet noise as she pressed deeper.

"Look how pretty you are," she murmured, "wrapped around my cock."

She bent down and flicked her tongue over my clit, fast and featherlight.

"Oh my God," I moaned.

I gripped the fitted sheet as she began to fuck me with slow, deliberate thrusts. I could feel every inch as she slid in and out of me—deep, steady, relentless.

Her tongue didn't let up. She licked and sucked in a rhythm that left me gasping, my thighs shaking. The combination was overwhelming—too much and not enough. I could feel my orgasm coiling tight.

"That's it, darling," she said, her voice gentle and coaxing. "Let go."

My body shook as I came hard around the toy. Julia kept going, drawing my orgasm out, fucking me through it until I was boneless beneath her.

Finally, she pulled out. The dildo glistened with my arousal. She licked it, slow and greedy, then let out a soft, satisfied hum.

"How was that, my sweet girl?"

"Holy hell," I breathed out. My thighs were still shaking. My heart felt heavy in my chest.

Julia drew up on the bed and kissed me deeply, her tongue sweeping into my mouth. Her hand slid between my legs again, fingers teasing my oversensitive skin.

A fresh wave of desire hit me, dizzying in its return. I deepened the kiss, hungry now, ravenous. Our mouths moved in tandem, desperate and devouring.

Julia's touch was everywhere—fingers pinching my nipples, stroking down my stomach, finding me wet and aching all over again.

"I want to taste you again," she told me.

She kissed her way down my body, slow and reverent, until she settled between my thighs. Her tongue flicked out; I moaned as she began to lick me in slow, languid strokes. Her tongue was like velvet, her mouth unhurried. She knew exactly how to push me to the edge again.

Then her finger slid inside me—gentle, coaxing, perfectly in sync with her tongue. She stroked me from the inside out, and my body arched into her touch. This woman was hell-bent on wringing every last drop of pleasure from my body.

I felt wrecked in the best way, my body humming, my limbs heavy with satisfaction.

Julia stretched out beside me, propping herself up on one elbow. Her fingers traced idle patterns across my stomach.

"You look positively ruined, dear." Her soft voice was edged with smug satisfaction.

"I am," I admitted, letting out a breathless laugh. "Thoroughly ruined."

She pressed a kiss just beneath my collarbone. Then another, lower. "Good."

I sucked in a sharp breath. "I think you broke my legs."

"Mm," she hummed, dragging her nails gently down my inner thigh. "I think you'll recover."

∽

I woke up early the next morning to the scent of bacon. Like a cartoon carnivore, I followed my nose from the bedroom to the kitchen where I discovered Julia at the stovetop, a spatula in one hand. Her hair was messy. She wore no pants, only ankle-high wool socks and an oversized sweatshirt that looked like it had come from my side of the walk-in closet.

I cleared the sleep from my throat and croaked out a single word: "Bacon?"

Julia didn't normally keep indulgent food on hand. We weren't a junk food-free household or anything like that, but she also wasn't stocking the pantry with Oreos and animal byproducts.

"I had the building's concierge deliver it," she explained. "I thought you might have worked up an appetite during the night."

Julia let out a surprised noise, nearly a squeak, when I rushed toward her. My arms went around her waist and my face went into the crook of her neck. I moved with such momentum that I nearly lifted her off her feet. She momentarily stiffened from the near-tackle, but her body soon relaxed into mine.

"Good morning," she murmured. Her free hand, the one not tending to a frying pan of sizzling bacon, stroked the side of my face.

"How are you so perfect?" My question was rhetorical.

"Grab yourself some coffee and set the table," she instructed. "Breakfast will be ready soon."

I felt practically giddy grabbing plates and napkins and our designated coffee cups from the kitchen cabinets. I loved our quiet mornings in the breakfast nook. We'd savor cups of coffee and share the morning paper. Julia always gave me first crack at the sports and comics sections without judgment.

I found myself frowning at the thought of how those mornings might change with a baby in the condo, though. There would be nothing quiet or unhurried about our mornings then.

"Is everything okay, dear?"

I rattled my head, dashing the thought from my mind.

"Everything's perfect," I said, maybe a little too brightly.

I sat at the table for two just as Julia set down a plate of perfectly crisp bacon. My eyes grew even wider when a small, white bakery box joined the party.

"You didn't."

Julia sat down and crossed one leg over the other. "I did."

"Geez, babe. You don't have to bribe me to use the strap-on."

I heard her quiet scoff. She snapped the twine that secured the bakery box and lifted its top. "Just eat your donuts."

She didn't have to tell me twice.

I selected a maple-glazed donut and broke it in half. I offered Julia the segment with less icing but she shook her head.

She leaned her elbow on the table and tapped her fingers thoughtfully against her cheek. "I was thinking about your Sumner Field victims."

"Hopefully not while we were in bed," I quipped.

She coughed delicately. "*No.* I wasn't thinking much of anything when we were doing *that.*"

I couldn't help my cocky grin.

"*Anyway.* As I was saying," she re-directed the conversation. "The recovered remains. Has anyone considered doing DNA phenotyping?"

I took too large of a bite of my pastry. "I don't know what that is," I said around the aggressive mouthful.

"It came up with one of the cases my team might re-try —a potential wrongful conviction," she explained. "Police recovered DNA that wasn't in CODIS, and it didn't match their primary suspect either. One of my colleagues suggested phenotypic analysis. It's relatively new; it uses genetic information to predict physical traits, like a composite of what the person might have looked like."

"Like what a police sketch artist might draw?"

"Pretty much," Julia confirmed. "Only in this case, your eyewitness is DNA extracted from bones. Phenotyping can predict facial structure, eye and hair color, skin tone, even freckles. It's not perfect, and it's expensive," she noted, "but it might generate some leads."

I nodded, letting her idea sprout roots. "I love it. I'll talk to Ryan about it first thing Monday morning."

I reached across the table and lightly grasped Julia's hand. As much as I might have wanted to compartmentalize my life—to not bring work home with me—I loved these opportunities to talk over a case with her. I loved the way her brain worked.

Julia lifted our intertwined hands to her lips and sucked the last trace of frosting from my fingertips. "Oh. These donuts *are* good."

My nostrils flared.

Forget the bacon. Forget the donuts.

I wanted her back in bed.

Everything else could wait.

Chapter Thirteen

It was a long shot—and an expensive one—but once Julia had planted the idea in my head, I couldn't shake it.

I headed upstairs not long after arriving at the office Monday morning, timing it late enough to be sure Jason Ryan had already had his coffee. For some reason, I always pictured him sipping espresso from one of those tiny Italian cups, while the rest of us in the basement choked down whatever sludge happened to be in the communal pot.

Much like the Cold Case office, the Homicide division was a large open room. Unlike our basement digs, however, the detectives in Homicide had proper cubicles and office equipment from the 21st century. An oversized whiteboard that hung prominently from one wall. It listed the open cases the division was currently investigating. If the case remained on the board for too long, it would get kicked over to us in Cold Case.

I spotted Ryan right away at his desk. He looked crisply pressed like he hadn't been in the office for very long.

"Morning."

Ryan quirked an eyebrow. "So early today?" He leaned back in his office chair and lifted his arms and hands behind his head. "Don't tell me you missed me, Miller?"

I'd become accustomed to ignoring Detective Ryan's barbs and jabs. I launched directly into my reason for seeing him. "Does Homicide have a budget for the Sumner Field case?"

His face tightened and his feet returned to solid ground. "Why?"

"Phenotypic analysis. Ever heard of it?"

He didn't try to hide his scoff. "Of course. I work in Homicide, don't I?"

"Then why haven't you suggested it, Mr. Expert?"

"It's a couple thousand dollars."

"So? If we can find out what our victims looked like, maybe that will jog some of these former residents' memories. I've already spoken with a former resident and she gave me the name of a girl who went missing in the 1960s."

Ryan frowned. "This isn't a murder, Miller. Not in the conventional sense. No one shot anyone. No one poisoned someone's food. This wasn't premeditated, and it wasn't a crime of passion. This was just shitty luck to have been born with that skin color in that zip code."

"Bad luck doesn't get a person buried without a name in a housing project," I challenged.

Ryan ignored my reasoning. "We got the ground-penetrating radar results back this morning. I was actually just going to call you about it. Your Professor Washington says there's no more bodies in Sumner Field. And City Hall is eager to get the green light so those developers can resume construction."

I folded my arms across my chest. "You're gonna reclassify it."

Ryan nodded. "I'm recommending it be moved from homicide to death by natural causes."

"Just like that?"

"If you haven't noticed, no one is breathing down our neck to solve this thing—to bring some criminal to justice—they're leaning on us to *shut it down*," he emphasized. "There's a big difference there."

I stared at him, heart sinking. "But we still don't know who those kids were. Their names. What happened to them."

"We've found no more bodies. No foul play," Ryan ticked off. "Just some old-timey people who probably buried their dead kids in the backyard instead of a cemetery. If anything, we should be charging *them* with a crime. Inappropriate disposal of a body. Corpse mutilation."

Ryan's attitude—his dramatic change of heart—had me raising my voice. "Is this you talking or City Hall? Why even get Cold Case involved if you were just going to half-ass the investigation?"

Ryan spoke in a tone far more reserved than mine. "I know you've got some, like, hero complex or something, but the directive on this case has been crystal clear from day one." His look was severe. "We bury this thing."

I didn't go back downstairs. I couldn't. If I had to spend one more minute in that depressing basement office, breathing in Sarah's space-heater air and pretending not to hear the subtext in Ryan's orders, I'd lose it.

Normally, I'd hop on my motorcycle and head west with no destination in mind and too much throttle. But my Harley was still in storage, stowed away in a warehouse until the snow melted. So instead, I walked out the front doors of the Fourth Precinct. I shouldered past the buzzing entryway, pushed through the heavy doors, and flung myself into the cold.

The late winter air was an assault to the senses, but I didn't care. I welcomed it. Brisk, biting—it was exactly what I needed.

I started to walk. I didn't set out in any particular direction; I only wanted to put distance between me and the building. My strides were long and angry. I felt the tug on my hamstrings.

My walk soon turned into a jog. In dress slacks, boots, and a button-up, I was hardly dressed for a workout, but I just kept moving my legs. Just kept pumping my arms.

I'd always been more of a swimmer than a runner, but this would work.

I didn't stop until my lungs burned and my body begged for a break. I bent over, hands on my knees, and sucked in mouthfuls of dry, winter air.

"Miller?"

I lifted my head at the call of my name. Monica Hernandez sat perched on top of a frost-covered picnic table.

I immediately straightened. "Oh. Hey."

She looked perplexed. "A little far from the office, aren't you?"

It was only then that I inspected my surroundings. Trees, slush, park benches. I had no idea where I was. I hadn't thought about it. I'd just *run*.

"Trouble in paradise?" she posed.

I blew into my hands, my breath coming out in clouds. "Just a work thing."

"Wanna talk about it?"

"Nope."

"Okay." Her smile grew wider. "Wanna shoot at stuff?"

～

Afghanistan, 2012

The sun scorches the desert like it's trying to burn the whole world down. I wipe the sweat from my brow, but the gritty dust just sticks harder. Sand crunches underfoot, and every breath tastes like dry earth. Around us, the base buzzes—vehicles revving, radios chattering, distant gunfire rattling the horizon. But my focus is on the silhouette just a few feet away, sitting against the rough canvas of the tent flap.

I crouch down beside her, careful not to get too close—too obvious.

"Tough day?" I ask quietly.

She snorts, then exhales a long, slow breath. "Is there any other kind?"

I glance over my shoulder. Terrance Pensacola is across the way, chatting with a couple of guys near the mess tent. Pensacola's easy smile and smooth drawl are like an anchor for me—a reminder that there's still normal beyond this place.

I give him a quick nod. He grins and waves, but keeps his distance. He knows when to give us space.

Monica shifts, a little impatient. "How long will you be gone this time?"

I shrug. "As long as it takes, I guess."

I'll be gone in the morning. Intel has a key al-Qaeda operative in a vulnerable position. We're going to take him, quick and easy. Or at least that's what we're hoping for.

Her dark eyes soften, and for a heartbeat, the fierce edge fades. She reaches out, brushing a stray strand of blonde hair behind my ear. Her movements are cautious, like she's afraid someone might see.

My skin prickles under her touch.

"Be careful, okay?" she murmurs.

I want to say something—about how maybe we don't have to keep hiding, about how maybe it's okay to want more than stolen moments. But the hum of the base drowns me out.

Terrance calls from across the way, "Hey, Cass! Chow's up!"

I let my hand slide to her wrist, fingers curling lightly around it. It's a small act of rebellion. It's all that I'm capable of.

"Yeah," I yell back to Terrance, finally standing. "Coming."

Monica looks up at me, her gaze sharp but weary. "Do you ever think about what comes after this?"

"Only every damn day."

She laughs, a short, tired sound.

∼

I hadn't meant to say yes.

But there I was, shoving my badge into the glovebox of Monica's beat-up minivan, and letting her drag me away from work with nothing more than a wink and the promise of noise therapy.

The gun range was mostly empty at that hour except for some grizzled vets. The air smelled like oil and cordite, just the way I remembered.

"You still shoot like you're trying to impress a drill instructor," Monica snorted. She slid a loaded mag across the bench toward me.

I rolled my eyes and ignored the jab, but my fingers

remembered what to do. Grip. Breathe. Squeeze. The kick of the pistol felt good. Stupid good.

Monica leaned back on her heels, arms crossed and grinning. "There she is."

I didn't answer. I didn't smile. I just kept shooting.

Julia would have hated this place. It's too loud and too crude. Too many jokes about things that weren't funny outside of this world. I couldn't picture her here, not even in theory. And maybe that was the point.

"You ever miss it?" Monica asked casually.

"Sometimes," I admitted.

Monica's smile softened. "I missed you."

I didn't look at her. I didn't trust what my face would say if I did.

I set the pistol down and stepped back, wiping my palms on my work pants. "Not appropriate."

Monica shrugged like it didn't matter, but her eyes lingered on me for too long. "Relax, Miller. I'm just messing with you."

But that was the thing about Monica—she was never just messing.

I peeled off the ear protection and let the noise crash back around me, the steady bark of gunfire and the low rumble of laughter from the other firing range patrons.

I let out a breath and shook my head, more at myself than at her. Of course she'd find a way to push my buttons. It was practically a sport for Monica.

I didn't storm off or snap back. I only turned toward the benches like it had been my plan all along. Monica fell in step behind me, quiet for once, and I was oddly grateful for it.

We eventually sat, side by side. The heavy thud of gunfire filled the gaps in our conversation. Monica kicked a boot against mine, a playful nudge that felt too familiar for my liking.

"This used to be your happy place," she said after a while.

I hadn't been to a shooting range in a long while. Like the beach and like fireworks, it was a place I'd actively been avoiding for fear of triggering a flashback. Maybe I was so worked up about Homicide ditching the Sumner Field case that the echo of gunshots around me was more soothing than anything else.

But I had no desire to tell Monica any of that.

I shrugged instead. "People change."

"Yeah, well." She tipped her head back against the wall, her smile crooked. "Some of us are still stupid enough to miss the old days."

I didn't have an answer for that. I didn't have anything I could say without lying.

Instead, I pulled out my phone like it was a lifeline, thumbing through my messages. No new texts. No missed calls. Julia was probably buried under meetings or case notes, a world away from this place.

I typed *Love you* and hit send before I could overthink it.

Monica saw the motion and snorted. "Telling the missus you're out having a midlife crisis with your ex?"

I pocketed the phone and gave her a flat look. "I told her I love her."

"Real sweet," Monica retorted, voice too light. "Didn't know you were the type."

I met her gaze, steady and even. "First time I've wanted to be."

For once, she didn't have a comeback.

∽

I was later than usual getting home that night. Monica had given me a ride back to the Fourth Precinct since I'd left all of my things there. I'd taken the bus back to St. Paul. She'd offered to give me a ride home—well, she'd offered me a ride to wherever I wanted to go, unabashedly emphasizing the word *ride*—but I'd declined. More time in confined quarters with her seemed like a bad idea, and I'd rather she not know the location of Julia's condo.

It was quiet when I let myself into Julia's place. I silently hung up my leather jacket in the front coat closet and carefully removed my work boots to arrange them in the foyer among running shoes and rain boots.

My attention drifted to the hallway that led back to the primary bedroom when I heard footsteps on hardwood. Julia appeared, still in her clothes from work.

She leaned against the curved archway that separated the living room from the dining area. "I stopped by your office on my way home," she said. "I thought you might like a ride."

"Oh. I … I left early today."

"So I heard," she hummed. "Your co-worker, Sarah, told me she hadn't seen you all day."

"You spoke to Sarah?"

I racked my brain trying to remember if the two of them had ever met before. Julia knew Stanley, but I didn't think she'd ever met my other office co-worker. I tried to imagine a meeting between the two of them. Stanley could hardly complete his sentences around Julia. Sarah wouldn't be similarly intimidated. I imagined them sizing each other up in the basement office.

"Homicide is reclassifying the Sumner Field case," I told her. "I won't be working on it anymore."

The surprise was obvious on her features. "Who's taking the case?"

"No one. They're blaming the deaths on natural causes."

Julia took a moment to consider my news. "Do you want to talk about it?"

"Nah, I'm good," I breezed. "I went to the shooting range with Monica to blow things up."

"Oh?"

I just kept delivering the surprises.

"Yeah. We just ran into each other. Wild coincidence."

"Wild," she repeated. Her voice sounded off.

"I'm sorry," I immediately apologized. "I should have told you."

"I don't need to know your whereabouts at all times, Cassidy. I'm not your keeper."

My frown deepened. "I shouldn't have ditched work like that."

"Why did you?" Julia dropped gracefully onto the couch, one ankle tucked behind the other. She patted the space beside her. "Talk to me, dear."

I flopped down beside her and closed my eyes. "I thought we were getting somewhere. I recommended we try DNA phenotyping, but Jason Ryan in Homicide said it was too expensive. And then he dropped the bombshell that construction was resuming at Sumner Field."

"So MPD is just sweeping it under the rug."

"Yep."

"I'm sorry." Her voice was gentle and consoling. "I probably would have wanted to blow something up, too."

She leaned closer to me on the couch and stroked her fingers through my hair. Her blunt nails lightly scratched my scalp. All of the stress from the day seemed to vacate my body.

"Good?"

"You have no idea."

A question prodded my brain, desperate to be released along with the tension from the day. "Are you okay with me hanging out with Monica?"

The fingers in my hair noticeably stilled. "It's not my place to say whom you can and cannot spend time with."

"You're my fiancée," I pointed out. "Seems like that should come with a few privileges."

"Not this," she continued to deny. "And you must

know that I trust you. I've never given anyone my heart before."

I swallowed the newly formed lump in my throat.

"Me either."

"See?" Julia's tone turned bright. I couldn't tell if it was genuine or put on. "Then we've got nothing to worry about."

Chapter Fourteen

I slowed the car down as I approached the Sumner Field construction site. The machines were back at it —digging, hauling, laying foundations—as if nothing had ever been unearthed. Like they hadn't found bodies buried in the ground. A yellow excavator churned through dirt on the far end of the fenced-in lot, and a crane loomed over it all, swinging slow and deliberate like a pendulum counting down to something nobody wanted there.

Homicide had wrapped it up fast, reclassifying the deaths as "natural causes." Case closed.

I pulled the old Crown Vic to the curb, threw the car in park, and watched the drama through the front windshield. Protesters were clustered by the gate, a ragtag group of locals holding up cardboard signs with slogans written with black Sharpie markers.

Three uniformed police officers stood off to the side. They weren't in full riot gear, but they'd definitely bulked up—bulletproof vests over the powder blue uniform, batons swinging at their hips.

My blood pressure elevated a little when I realized I recognized one of them. FTO Mendez. My old partner from Precinct Four. The man who'd recommended I be taken off active duty and be chained to a desk. He didn't see me, but his posture told me everything. He stood loose, but ready, like how a boxer drops their shoulders before the bell rings.

The construction site hadn't ever had an assigned detail before. I thought it looked like intimidation dressed up as public safety. The message was clear: this was a construction site now, not a crime scene. Keep moving. Nothing to see here.

But I couldn't look away. Not when everything about it felt wrong.

I shut off the engine and rolled down the window a crack. The air smelled like dirt and diesel and something metallic. Somewhere across the street, someone was grilling—maybe a family still hanging on in the neighborhood before rents skyrocketed and everything became gentrified.

I watched as a cement truck eased onto the lot, its barrel spinning lazily. Reinforcements for the foundation, I assumed. I could almost hear the press release: *revitalization, mixed-income opportunities, long-overdue investment.* That's what they'd say when the luxury condos opened.

I watched the site for a few more minutes, letting the whole scene unfold. Letting myself get good and mad.

How many bodies needed to be under that dirt for someone to decide it mattered?

I reached over to the glove compartment and pulled out my notepad. The pages were worn from flipping, the top corner folded over from the last time I'd gone digging through it. I flipped past the cold cases I'd actually been assigned to: past the Jane Doe who might have poisoned herself with Botox to convince her girlfriend to leave her husband and take his money, past the scribbled notes where I'd obsessed over the location of Danika Laroque's body, and to the section I'd started for Sumner Field.

Names, addresses, hand-drawn building layouts from the old projects. Notes from interviews with former tenants. Questions in the margins for which I had no answers.

I looked back out at the site. The group of protesters was starting to thin out, a few people drifting away as the sun ducked behind a cloud and the temperatures began to dip. The police stayed put, watching like sentries. I wondered if any of them even knew what this place had been. What it had meant. Not just buildings, but lives. Not just crime statistics, but memories.

Someone had made a choice. Someone in City Hall—or maybe a few someones—had decided this land was worth more paved over than honored. And someone at a real estate developer's office had had enough pull or enough money to make the investigation disappear.

I didn't know who. But I knew I wasn't done.

I closed the notebook and shoved it back into the glove

Buried Promises

compartment. The engine turned over with a little whine and sputter. The heat kicked on, but I didn't drive away. I sat a little longer, watching the machines work, watching concrete being poured over the past.

Jason Ryan would be pissed. He'd say I was wasting time.

But I wasn't going to drop this thing until I knew who'd been buried under that dirt and who had decided they didn't matter.

~

Detective Jason Ryan had told me I was no longer on the case. But I didn't work for Jason Ryan. I didn't need his permission, not really.

It started with a map—a plain city zoning map from the early 1960s that I'd retrieved from the Hennepin County Library and had scanned with the help of a librarian who was either charmed or unnerved by my persistence.

Sumner Field, the former housing project, had been razed decades ago, but the ghost of Building Nine still lingered in old documents and former residents' memories. There was no CCTV to consult, no real digital trail to follow, just old city records that smelled suspiciously like mold.

I stared at the overlay of old maps and the current redevelopment plans. The stretch of grass beside Building Nine—the area Ms. Price and her friends had called "the Circle"—didn't overlap with where the bodies had been found. But Building Nine had backed onto a narrow alley that no longer existed—and *that* alley was exactly where the bodies had been discovered.

Back in the 1960s, it would have been a relatively private spot, which might explain why the remains had gone unnoticed for so long. Out of sight, out of mind. Or maybe someone had counted on that.

I imagined loud, boisterous parties happening in the Circle at night. Loud music and laughter that rose above the sound. All while someone slipped away into the shadows behind Building Nine, unnoticed. Maybe with a secret. Maybe with a body.

I followed that up with the missing person report for Linda Walker. It had been opened and closed all in 1964. She'd been labeled a runaway, filed away and forgotten.

Ms. Price had described what she remembered from that time, and the report corroborated just enough. MPD officers had come to the apartment building, interviewed a few tenants, wrote down a few sentences. No follow-up. No real effort.

I read the report twice. Then I read it again.

Linda Walker, age 11. Last seen at her mother's apartment. No mention of a father. According to neighbors, she'd been having trouble at home. I could read the subtext: it wasn't worth the effort. Just another troubled girl in a housing project nobody wanted to think about.

Except she hadn't just run away. Maybe she'd been killed and had been buried behind Building Nine.

Dental records would be the surest way to confirm.

Pediatric dental records, specifically. They were often more detailed due to the tracking of developing teeth, and if Linda Walker had had regular dental care—especially through a public health clinic or a school program—those records might still exist.

That was Step One.

Step Two was more complicated.

According to my initial research, Linda Walker had no living relatives. Her mother was deceased, and the man listed on her birth certificate had died as well. Census data pointed to her being an only child. No siblings. All of that made DNA confirmation tricky, but not impossible.

Forensic genetic genealogy had cracked tougher cases. If we could extract viable DNA from the remains—and that was a big if—then distant relatives might still light up a family tree. Even third or fourth cousins might be enough.

I picked up the phone. Stanley was babysitting the evidence warehouse on the other side of town that day. He picked up the landline like he'd been waiting on my call.

"Stanley, I've got a big job for you," I said.

He paused, like he was preparing to be asked to hack into federal servers.

"Let's not only focus on missing persons. I want to look at every police report related to Sumner Field in the 1960s, big and small. Complaints, domestic disturbances, misdemeanors, felonies."

"At the risk of sounding ignorant," Stanley said, "why?"

"A hunch?" I offered up.

Stanley made an affirming noise. "That's good enough for me."

∽

I found Gary alone in the exam suite, bent over a workstation that smelled faintly of antiseptic. Fluorescent lights buzzed overhead, throwing shadows across the silver table at the room's center. He looked up when I knocked on the open door frame.

"Detective Miller," he said, straightening. "I was surprised to get your call."

"I was hoping you had a few minutes."

He gestured to a stool near the wall. "Any friend of Stanley's …"

I'd become acquainted with the medical examiner through Stanley. They'd both gone to school together for that very purpose, although Stanley always described that he'd gotten distracted on his way to the morgue and had ended up with Cold Case.

I eased onto the stool. "I appreciate you taking the time."

Gary ran a hand through his full head of gray hair. He looked like a man who never quite slept—his long face drawn tight, wide-set blue eyes swimming in soft bags. He leaned against the counter, arms folded.

"What's this about?"

"Those remains from Sumner Field," I started. "I saw the report. No signs of trauma. Natural causes."

He nodded. "Correct."

"But is that really the end of it?" I pressed. "We're talking about half a dozen bodies buried in unmarked graves. You're telling me every single one of them just died naturally and no one reported it?"

"I didn't say it made sense," Gary amended. "I said there was no evidence of foul play."

"There's a difference," I muttered.

He gave me a small, sympathetic smile. "Detective, I've been doing this job for close to two decades. I know when someone wants me to see more than what's there."

"I don't want you to make something up," I made clear. "I want to know if we could be missing something. You said no trauma, but what about asphyxiation? Poisoning? Neglect? Can you even tell after this long?"

"Some things, yes. Others, no. We can detect heavy metal poisoning in bones, but nothing turned up," he said. "No fractures, no knife nicks, no gunshot wounds, no ligature marks on cervical vertebrae. The skeletons are remarkably intact for being buried that long. That tells me no one was trying to hide a violent crime."

"But they were trying to hide *something*," I challenged.

Gary tilted his head, considering. "I won't argue with that."

"I get that this might not fall under Homicide's purview anymore," I said, "but I'm not convinced we should just close the door. These people didn't get proper burials. No names. No records. Just dumped like garbage under what used to be public housing."

"That's not my call," he said cautiously. "But if you want my opinion ... I don't think they all died of the same thing."

My throat tightened. "Can you help me keep looking?"

"I'll re-run the toxicology screen with a broader panel," he said after a moment. "Dig a little deeper on mineral deficiencies, environmental exposures. It might not tell us anything new, but it won't hurt."

"Thank you, Gary."

"Don't thank me yet," he said. "This won't be solved in a lab."

"I know," I said, standing. "But I appreciate the extra effort."

It was a hell lot more than what Detective Jason Ryan had been willing to do.

Chapter Fifteen

The waiting room at Julia's doctor's office looked like a kindergarten classroom had exploded inside of it. Construction-paper hearts in every shade of red and pink covered the reception desk. A giant Cupid cutout with googly eyes hovered over the sign-in sheet. Even the receptionist was wearing a headband with tiny, glittery hearts bobbing on springs as she greeted us.

"Happy Valentine's Day!"

Julia merely nodded, her expression a masterclass in restraint.

I leaned into her. "Pretty romantic, huh? Nothing says 'love' like a medical procedure."

She shot me a look, but the corner of her mouth twitched.

The home injections had come to an end, culminating with a final shot designed to trigger the timed release of Julia's eggs. Her doctor had described the out-patient procedure as minimally invasive and remarkably routine, but the drive from Julia's condo that morning had been tense and quiet.

I hadn't even been tempted to make a joke about it being the wrong holiday for an egg hunt.

Julia hadn't been very forthcoming when I'd asked her about the details of the procedure, so I'd had to do my own research, late at night after she'd fallen asleep. I'd never pictured myself searching on my phone's web browser for more information about *oocyte retrieval*, yet here we were.

I'd learned that the doctor would administer a local anesthetic to numb the pelvic area, along with intravenous sedation. Using ultrasound guidance, the doctor would remove the eggs from the follicles. Julia would feel no pain, and she probably wouldn't remember the procedure either.

Julia signed in at the reception desk and made polite small talk with the woman wearing heart-shaped antennae. Once she'd finished the requisite paperwork, I rested my hand in the small of her back and guided her toward an empty row of stiff chairs.

She exhaled, a soft, barely-there sound, and sat down with the practiced grace of someone used to being observed. I sat beside her, stretching my legs out in front of me while she kept her posture perfect, hands folded in her lap. I resisted the urge to reach for one.

The room was empty except ourselves and the receptionist. That thought somewhat eased my nerves. Julia would get the staff's undivided attention that morning instead of her procedure being squeezed in between multiple appointments like she was just getting her hair cut and colored.

Not long after our arrival, a nurse in pale pink scrubs entered the waiting room. She smiled warmly in our direction. "We're ready for you."

Julia immediately stood. I caught her fingers, just for a second, before she could walk away.

"I'll be right here," I told her.

Something flickered in her expression, too fast for me to name, but she gave a small nod before following the nurse.

The waiting room television played some home renovation show at a respectable volume, but my attention drifted. It wasn't Julia who hated hospitals—it was me. I'd spent too much time in places like this while doctors had stitched me back together, reminding me how lucky I was to still have my spine intact.

Lucky.

Like surviving the blast that killed my whole squad, took Pensacola's legs, and left me with a mangled back and PTSD was some kind of miracle.

I forced myself to take a breath, to unclench my jaw, to relax my shoulders. This wasn't about me. Julia wasn't in danger. This was a routine procedure, and I was here to make sure she got home safely.

I tried to lose myself in the glossy pages of outdated gossip magazines, but every little sound, every little movement I spotted in my peripheral vision, had me jumping out of my skin with worry. I consulted my cell phone over and over again to gauge how much time had passed. I wished I'd asked more questions. What was too much time? When should I start to really spiral out?

Eventually, a different hospital staffer emerged, asking if I was there for Julia Desjardin. She, too, wore pink scrubs, making me wonder if the uniform was holiday specific or typical for the day.

I jumped to my feet, my heart lodged in my throat. "Yeah. Is she okay?"

"She's fine," the nurse assured me with a practiced smile. "She's just in recovery. You can come back now."

I followed the woman down the hall, past somber, closed doors labeled with neat, sterile plaques. She stopped and knocked lightly on one of the doors before entering. I tentatively entered the room as well, trailing a few steps behind.

The room was awash with soft sunlight. Julia sat in a reclining chair, a blanket draped over her lower body. She looked far too elegant for someone who had just been sedated. Her gaze was a little unfocused, but when she spotted me, her lips curled up at the edges.

"Cassidy," she murmured, her voice thick and groggy. "You're my ride."

I stepped closer and cleared my throat. "Damn right I am. I give the best rides."

I tried to be charming and cheeky, but the words got caught.

She made a soft sound—something between a chuckle and a sigh. I reached for her hand, and this time, she let me hold it. The tips of her fingers were a little cold, but they curled around mine.

"Let's go home," she mumbled.

I squeezed her hand gently. "Yeah, babe. Let's go home."

~

When we returned to the condo, I helped Julia get settled into bed. I wrapped her up in her favorite silk robe, arranged a mountain of pillows against the headboard, and draped a knitted afghan over her lap. The blinds were half-drawn, letting in soft winter light that spilled across the bedroom's minimalist furniture.

I stepped in from the kitchen, carefully balancing a tray with a teapot, two mugs, and a small heart-shaped box of assorted chocolates I'd picked up in anticipation of the Hallmark holiday.

"Tea time," I announced, setting the tray down on a bedside table.

Julia gave me a faint smile, her movements slow as she adjusted the blanket. "You didn't have to fuss."

I took my time pouring the tea into the mugs, deliberate with my movements so as to not spill. "Fussing is part of the deal." I handed her a mug. "How are you feeling?"

"Tired," she admitted, taking the tea with both hands. "And a little sore. Nothing unbearable though."

"You're handling this like a champ." I sat on the edge of

the mattress, close enough to feel the warmth of her against my side. "Though I'm not surprised."

Julia let out a sigh. Her fingers brushed the edge of the box of chocolates, but she didn't open it. "I'm sorry this is the least sexy Valentine's Day you've ever had," she said quietly. Her voice was soft with a tinge of regret. Her gaze flicked over to me, but she didn't quite meet my eyes. "I know you were probably hoping for ... well, something a little different than this."

I put my mug down and moved closer on the bed, close enough that our shoulders pressed together. She was so composed, but I could see the weight in her posture, the exhaustion still lingering in her eyes. She was beating herself up over something that wasn't her fault.

"You don't have to apologize." I tilted my head so I could catch her gaze. "This is perfect. I wouldn't want it any other way."

Her lips parted, and I could see her working through the words she wanted to say. But she didn't say anything; she let the silence hang between us for a moment.

"You've been through a lot today," I continued, my hand finding hers and gently squeezing. "This," I said, gestured to the cozy, low-key atmosphere around us, "is what I need. Just you, here. Safe. Relaxing and recovering. That's the best Valentine's Day I could ever ask for."

Julia's eyes softened and her fingers tightened around mine. "I guess I just feel like I should've done more for you. Valentine's Day is supposed to be about new lingerie and all the bells and whistles."

"And here I thought it was about candy," I smirked. "I've been doing this holiday all wrong."

Julia's stare took on a look of concern. "Are you satisfied? Are you happy? Everything lately has been about me and *my* wants and desires—whatever is best for me. But what does *Cassidy* want?"

"You've given me more than I could ever hope for."

Julia wet her lips. "I don't want to be presumptuous, but it seems like you're warming to the idea of a baby."

I exhaled. "I-I think I am," I agreed. "When you first told me about wanting to freeze your eggs, I was hurt that you hadn't thought to involve me in that decision. It was something you wanted, so you did it. And after that, I got scared," I admitted. "A baby? What did I know about raising a baby?"

I took a break from my soliloquy. I ran my thumb over the diamond-decorated ring on my left ring finger, causing it to spin.

"Do you know the history behind the ring finger?" Julia saved me from my spiraling thoughts. "Why engagement rings go on that particular finger?"

"No, but something tells me you do," I smiled.

"It's from the ancient Romans. They believed that the fourth finger on the left hand possessed a vein that connected directly to the heart." She took my left hand in hers. She stroked a single finger the length of my ring finger. "They called it *vena amoris*. The vein of love."

"That's ... that's really sweet," I decided. "Who knew the Romans were such romantics?"

"And who knew all of those Classics classes in college would come in handy someday?" Julia continued to stroke her fingers across my left palm. "Are you still scared?"

"Not like I should be. This ring—maybe it's all in my head, like these things usually are—but I feel a little invincible. I'm not naive; I know whenever this baby happens it's going to feel impossible."

I swallowed, feeling myself getting choked up.

God, where were these emotions coming from? It's not like I was the one who'd had the hormone shots.

I took a sharp breath. "But you make the impossible feel possible."

Julia rewarded my mini soliloquy with a melting smile. "The Romans have nothing on you, darling."

"I know this isn't a traditional holiday," I announced, "but I did get you something."

I opened the slim drawer of the bedside table and pulled out a small, neatly wrapped gift.

Julia's eyes narrowed. "You didn't need to do that, Cassidy."

I shrugged, placing the present on her lap. "It's nothing extravagant. Just something I thought you'd like."

She unwrapped the gift with meticulous care, unfolding the paper rather than tearing it. Inside was a slim, leather-bound notebook embossed with her initials in gold.

"I thought you deserved a proper notebook for all of your plans," I explained, watching her run her fingers over the cover. "Now you won't forget about diapers."

She chuckled softly, shaking her head. "You're impossible, you know that?"

"But you like it?"

She set the notebook aside and reached for my hand. "I love it. And you."

I leaned in, pressing a gentle kiss to her forehead. "I love you, too. Even when you act like you don't need spoiling."

She hummed and drew me in for a proper kiss. "Maybe I'll allow it. Just this once."

Chapter Sixteen

It was sleeting. It was the kind of wet, slushy mix that coated the roads and made everyone drive like someone had cut their brakes. Julia had made the decision to work from home that day so she offered up her car so I didn't have to take the bus.

I was proud of her for taking things easy after her egg retrieval procedure. She insisted that she was fine, but I was happy she was taking the time and space to acknowledge that she'd just been through something both physically and emotionally taxing.

She'd handed me the keys to her Mercedes with a kiss and a stern warning: "Don't eat in it."

"I would never," I grinned.

It was taking longer than what was typical to get to work. The rotten weather had teamed up with morning rush hour, slowing downtown traffic to a negligible crawl. I tried to save time by cutting through side streets but still managed to hit every red light.

I was stopped at one of those red lights when I saw her. Her hood was drawn over her head, but I still recognized her. There was something about her posture—her aura. I'd recognize it in a crowded room.

Her hands were bare and she held a cardboard sign that was already disintegrating in the cold, wet weather.

Homeless Vet. Anything Helps.

I could have looked away. I could have pretended that I hadn't seen her.

But I didn't.

I pulled up to the concrete median and rolled down my window. "You lose a bet or something?"

Monica squinted into the sleet. Her mouth curled, almost a smile. "Cassidy Miller in a Mercedes. Hell must have frozen over."

"Get in before you do, too."

She hesitated like she might actually say no. The light had turned green and cars behind me were starting to lay on their horns. I didn't move though. I heard Monica swear under her breath before she yanked open the passenger side door and slid in.

Her jeans were soaked up to the knees and she smelled like cigarettes. But somehow, she looked better than the last time I'd seen her.

I shifted the car into drive. I didn't have a plan beyond

that. We were only a few blocks from the police station, but I didn't really want to go in yet.

We drove in silence for a while, with only the windshield wipers filling the void.

Monica pointed at a food truck parked near the edge of Webber Park. "Pull over. My treat."

"You have money?"

It was the first time I'd vaguely made reference to her precarious situation.

"It was a lucrative morning," she said simply.

I waited in the car, the engine still on, while Monica braved the elements once more. I watched her through the freezing rain and past the furiously moving windshield wipers as she presumably ordered breakfast from the taco truck.

The passenger door opened and quickly closed, blasting the interior of the car with frigid wind and rain.

"Jesus," Monica complained. "You Minnesotans are fucking crazy for living here."

Her observation tempted me to ask her how long she was planning on being in town for, but I didn't want to upset her. Instead, I acted interested in the food she'd purchased.

"What'd you get?"

"Breakfast burritos," she said with a quick smile. "But don't worry, I didn't have them put hot sauce on yours. I know your *gringa* ass thinks mayonnaise is spicy."

"Funny," I huffed.

Monica handed me a massive burrito wrapped in

aluminum foil. The scent hit me fast—grease, onions, cheap beef. I could already feel it sinking into Julia's leather seats, but I had no other options. It wasn't like we could eat outside.

Monica took a massive bite and groaned. "Goddamn. This is better than sex."

"You'd know?"

She grinned at me with her mouth full. "You tell me."

I kept my eyes on the windshield. Too close. Too warm. Too much.

We didn't talk much after that, just chewed and listened to the freezing rain pelting the roof. Every once in a while, I'd feel her eyes on me like she was waiting for something.

Eventually, all that remained of our breakfast was the aluminum foil the burritos had been wrapped in. The windows had fogged up enough to draw shapes on. Monica leaned back in the passenger seat and patted at her stomach with satisfaction.

I saw so much of myself in her mannerisms, it was uncanny. Was it something we'd gleaned from each other? Or something our time in the military had manifested?

She broke into my thoughts: "You remember Camp Leatherneck? That first dust storm?"

I nodded without looking at her. "They told us to stay inside. You decided it was the perfect time for a jog."

"Couldn't breathe by the time I got back," she snorted. "Spent the night coughing up sand like a cat with a furball."

"You scared the hell out of me," I admitted.

Monica glanced at me. "You didn't show it."

"That was the job."

"No," she said quietly, "that was you."

I didn't have an answer for that.

She leaned her head back against the seat, staring up through the fogged windshield. "I do miss it sometimes. The quiet after the mortars. That weird, buzzing calm when we knew the worst had already happened and everything was going to be okay."

I swallowed hard. "Yeah."

"I don't miss the heat, though," she added. "Or the smell. Jesus. Everything smelled like plastic and shit and gunpowder."

"And sweat," I said. "God, the sweat."

Monica barked out a laugh. "You used to stink worse than the guys."

"Occupational hazard."

"Nah. You were just a purist." She finally turned toward me. "Didn't want anyone to think you got special treatment."

"I didn't."

She raised an eyebrow. "You *did*," she rejected. "But you worked twice as hard to pretend you didn't."

I stared down at my lap. "I don't want to do this."

"Do what?" she asked.

"This. The memory lane bullshit."

"Fine." Monica wiped her fingers on a thin paper napkin and crumpled it in her fist. "Let's talk about something else. Like your girlfriend. She let you drive this thing, or did you steal it?"

I wondered at her word choice. She'd already commented on my engagement ring. It made me wonder if she'd deliberately chosen the word *girlfriend* instead of *fiancée* to see if I'd correct her.

I didn't.

"She let me."

Monica made a noise between a grunt and a snort. "And she knows you're out here picking up stray dogs like me?"

"She knows I have a soft spot for lost causes."

That one hit a little too close, and we both knew it.

She didn't say anything for a while. She silently stared out the window, her reflection blurry in the glass. Then, like she couldn't help herself, she looked back at me and effortlessly smiled.

"Three dates in and still no action?" she smirked. "You're slipping, Miller."

I shook my head and started the engine again. "This isn't a date."

"No? Coffee, gun range, and now breakfast burritos in a car during a sleet storm? That's romance, babe," she taunted. "That's practically *The Notebook*."

I didn't have a response. I stared out into the freezing rain, wishing I'd kept driving.

By the time I pulled into the underground garage, the smell of onions and guilt was still heavy in Julia's car. I'd cracked a window on the drive home even though it was still sleeting, but the evidence of my indiscretion still clung to the leather interior.

I parked, shut off the engine, and sat in the car for a minute with my hands on the steering wheel. The leather was warm under my palms, buttery soft. Fancier than anything I'd ever driven.

Upstairs, the condo was quiet. A few lamps scattered around the living room cast a soft glow over the furniture. Julia was curled up on the couch in an oversized sweater and those reading glasses that I had always found strangely alluring, tapping on her laptop. Her bare feet were tucked under a throw blanket. She looked like a goddamn revelation.

I closed the door harder than I meant to. She looked up.

"How were the roads?" she asked.

"I saw Monica."

The confession tumbled out before I'd even taken off my boots.

Julia blinked slowly. "Again?"

"She was on the street, holding a sign. It was freezing." I rubbed the back of my neck. "So I gave her a ride, and we grabbed some food."

"In my car."

I sighed. "In your car."

She set her laptop aside and folded her arms. "Are you okay?"

I admired her poise—and how she never led with jealousy.

"I'm fine," I said.

Julia gave me a long, unreadable look, then nodded once, like she was filing it away.

I stepped deeper into the room. "She made a joke. About it being our third date."

Julia's mouth tightened.

"She was kidding," I said.

"Was she?"

I shrugged. "Doesn't matter. Nothing happened."

Julia stood from the couch and walked to the kitchen where she poured herself a glass of water. Her movements were precise, almost too casual. I watched the muscles in her back shift under the thin sweater.

"To be clear: I'm not worried about what happened," she said, not turning around. "But I *am* a little worried about why you keep letting it happen."

I didn't have an answer for that.

She turned back to face me, her expression calm. "It's fine if you're friends," she insisted. "But I hope you don't think you owe her something."

I looked down at the floor. My boots were still wet. "I know."

Julia walked to me and laid her hand on my cheek. Her fingers were warm and grounding.

"I've never minded your ghosts, Cassidy," she said

gently. "But I need to know you're not still trying to live with them."

∼

Dr. Susan Warren had a way of making silence feel intentional and not awkward. She didn't fill the space with mundane small talk or soften her questions with smiles. She just waited, pen hovering over her yellow legal pad like she already knew what I didn't want to say.

I shifted uncomfortably on the gray upholstered couch. My neck and lower back were feeling stiff from having slept on Julia's couch the previous night. She hadn't banished me to the living room; it had been self-imposed. Guilt gnawed at my consciousness. I'd been relieved when I'd called Dr. Warren's office and she'd been able to accommodate me on such short notice.

"So," she said, flipping a page. "What would you like to talk about?"

"I don't know."

We started every session with this song and dance until she finally coaxed something out of me.

I sighed. "I've been spending time with someone who was over there with me."

I didn't need to elaborate on the location of *there*.

"And how has that been for you? Triggering? Any nightmares?" she anticipated.

I scratched at the back of my neck. "Not exactly."

I saw her small frown. "You know you'll have to be more specific, Cassidy."

"She and I—this *friend*—we used to, like, hang out over there. We didn't date, but we, uh, had fun."

"I see."

Did she?

"She was on the corner near my work," I explained. "Holding a sign. It was cold as hell out so I gave her a ride."

Dr. Warren didn't say anything, but she made a note.

"We got food," I added. "Breakfast burritos. Sat in the car for too long."

Another pause. I hated that it made me feel like a kid getting caught, instead of a grown ass woman who happened to have a soft spot for people she used to sleep next to in a war zone.

"She made a joke," I said finally. "Said it was our third date. You know—'third date rules.' Like it was funny."

Dr. Warren didn't smile. "Did you think it was funny?"

"No." I shifted on the couch. "I mean ... maybe a little. Monica has always had that way of poking at things. Seeing what bleeds."

Dr. Warren sat back in her high-backed chair. "And you?"

I knew what she meant. I looked down at my hands, thumb grazing the raw edge of my thumbnail. "I keep telling myself that I'm helping. That I don't want anything from her. But maybe part of me likes that she still wants something from me."

I swallowed. It sounded worse out loud.

Dr. Warren wrote that down, too.

"I just mean ... Julia doesn't *need* me." The words came out quieter than I meant. "She's got her whole life figured out. A career. A condo. A plan for the future. Even her grief is organized."

Dr. Warren's voice remained even and nonjudgmental. "So you feel more important in Monica's world?"

"That's messed up, right? I *love* Julia. Like, so much I forget to breathe when I'm looking at her," I emphasized. "But sometimes ..." I swallowed. "Sometimes I feel like a guest in her life."

Dr. Warren leaned forward. "Does Julia know you feel this way?"

I laughed even though nothing about this was funny. I'd originally started going to Dr. Warren to treat my PTSD. But that day's session felt more like marriage counseling.

I cleared my throat in avoidance. "I just keep thinking about the version of me that Monica knew. And the version that Julia sees."

"And which one feels more like you?" Dr. Warren pressed.

I didn't answer. Not right away, at least. Mostly because I didn't know. And that scared the hell out of me.

Chapter Seventeen

Detective Jason Ryan stood in front of my desk. "Who's Linda Walker?"

"An eleven year old girl who went missing in 1964. Why?"

Ryan dropped a manila envelope onto my desktop. "The crime lab must have mixed up where these dental records were supposed to go."

I grabbed the open envelope and pulled out the papers inside. My eyes scanned over the results.

"It's not a match, Miller."

My heart sank as my own eyes confirmed his words. Linda Walker's pediatric dental records hadn't matched those from the recovered remains. It wasn't her.

I flicked my gaze up to Ryan's face. His mouth was tight. "Mind telling me why you're still poking around Sumner Field?"

I stood from my chair, not willing to let him tower over me. "I was following up on a lead."

"That case was DOA, Miller. And it was never yours in the first place. Stay in your lane."

I didn't move. I didn't sit. I let his words hang between us.

"My lane?" I repeated. My voice sounded far more calm than I felt. "Is that the one where we close a file because it might ruffle a few politicians' feathers?"

"You think you're the only one who cares around here?" he challenged.

"No. But I might be the only one acting like they care."

Ryan's eyes narrowed. "You want to play hero, go join a nonprofit. What we do around here is triage. And this?" He jabbed his fingers into the documents on my desk. "This is a waste of police resources."

"Tell that to Linda Walker's mom."

"She's dead," he snapped back.

"That doesn't mean we shouldn't do everything we can to find out what happened to her daughter."

"You're really pissin' away your good will here, Miller. I'll only say this one more time—stay out of it."

As I watched Jason Ryan stalk away to return to his cushy, above ground office, a quiet fury pulsed through my limbs. I wanted to throw something. Smash a coffee mug. Put my fist through drywall. Do something stupid and reckless—something Monica Hernandez might have done.

She wouldn't sit with this kind of anger. She'd slam the

door on her way out, grab a beer, a bottle of whiskey, or someone to kiss just for the mess of it. And for a second, I wanted to be that person. Not the by-the-book Girl Scout cop. Not the quiet Marine trying to hold it all together. I wanted the explosion.

But I wasn't Monica. I didn't want a bottle or a fight. I wanted to *win*.

By the time I left the precinct, my heart was still jackhammering in my chest, but my head was clear. This case deserved more than police indifference and half-closed files. It deserved someone who would wield the law like a scalpel.

Traffic blurred past the windshield of the second-hand Crown Vic as I made the short drive to her office. I parked in the visitor lot without checking if I was crooked in the white lines.

Alice noticed me and my aggressive stride. She popped up from her cubicle. "Cassidy, hi. Ms. Desjardin's—"

"I won't be long," I said, waving her off.

I gave the office door a perfunctory knock, more of a courtesy than a request, and pushed it open.

Julia looked up from the open files on her desk, surprise flashing across her face, brief but unmistakable. I shut the door behind me.

"I've got a proposal," I announced.

"I thought I'd already done that, dear."

I ran the pad of my thumb over the platinum band that encircled my left ring finger. "Are you working on any cases right now? Defending anyone?"

"Not actively, no. I'm still reviewing a few cases—potential Brady violations where the prosecution withheld exculpatory evidence, leading to the defendant's conviction."

I nodded, although I wasn't fully listening. "What do you think about a class action suit?"

Julia pursed her lips. "Who are we suing?"

"The City of Minneapolis."

She released a sharp breath. "Your unmarked graves."

"Uh huh."

Julia sat with my suggestion. She chewed on her lower lip and tapped a pen against her desktop.

Finally, she spoke.

"What you're considering is career suicide, Cassidy. I can imagine no scenario where the city police would continue to employ you if it gets out that you turned me on to this case."

"It's a viable case though, right? We could get money—reparations—for these families and their descendants."

"Grisham & Stein specializes in criminal defense," she pragmatically noted. "I was brought on to help with wrongful convictions, not class action litigation."

"No one was wrongly convicted," I conceded, "but isn't this the very definition of restorative justice? You get the city to admit they were complicit and award the impacted families with money that they can use to improve their lives."

Julia continued to hesitate. "I'm not sure I want to comment."

"Will you ask the partners?" I wasn't above begging. "The worst thing they can do is say no, right?"

"I'm not worried about the partners, Cassidy. I'm worried about *you*."

"I took an oath to *Protect and Serve*. And that didn't mean protect the city from scrutiny or serve these greedy real estate developers."

Julia was slow with her response. "I will speak to the partners," she eventually vowed. "But Cassidy, I'm serious—it was one thing for me to defend Landon Tauer. This is on a whole other level."

I steeled myself. "It's the right thing to do."

∽

The conference room at Julia's law firm had floor-to-ceiling windows that framed the city in dusk. It was after normal working hours, but the long table was still cluttered with open laptops, legal pads, and half-finished coffee cups.

I checked my phone again—no texts or calls from the office. I wasn't expecting one, but I was still anxious. I wasn't doing anything illegal, I hadn't given Julia access to documentation she shouldn't have in her possession, but my nerves were still fraught. I was used to cold cases and chain-of-custody procedures, not civil litigation.

Julia sat at the head of the table, poised in her usual controlled, elegant way. She introduced the group to me with a crisp nod. "You already know Alice," she said, gesturing to the pretty woman seated beside her. "And these are our new paralegals—Anthony and Ann."

Anthony offered a brief nod. He was a slim, serious-looking young Black man. Ann, a young Asian woman with blunt bangs, smiled politely.

"Cool," I said, settling into one of the open chairs. "The A-Team."

My attempt at a joke was met with silence.

Okay then.

"God, you're all young," I muttered, mostly to myself.

Julia's voice sharpened slightly, cutting through the awkward pause. "As I was saying..."

She turned her attention to the woman sitting across from her.

"I want to thank Professor Charlotte Cunningham for joining us tonight," Julia said. "And for agreeing to be an expert witness, should this lawsuit go to trial. Her historical expertise and ability to contextualize systemic patterns of neglect will be invaluable to our case."

Professor Cunningham nodded once, folding her hands on the table. She, like myself, looked a little nervous. But unlike myself, she had the advanced degrees that indicated she belonged.

Julia launched into the legal strategy with razor-sharp precision. "We're still in the early stages, but we're building a case around the city's long-term negligence—

what amounts to institutional abandonment. Sumner Field wasn't just a failed housing project. It was a death trap born out of disinvestment, redlining, and racial covenants. This case isn't about a single policy—it's about the systemic stripping away of resources and human dignity over decades."

She paused to let the words settle before continuing. "We won't need to collect every claimant's name until we file the suit officially. But we will need a lead plaintiff. Someone to represent the class. Cassidy, any suggestions?"

I hesitated. Ms. Price came to mind, but I didn't feel comfortable offering her name without her consent. Not yet.

"Not at the moment," I said. "But Melody's been speaking with more former residents than I have. I'll loop her in and ask for recommendations."

"Good," Julia said. "We need someone with an impeccable reputation. No skeletons in the closet that will shift the focus off the city's failure."

"Like Rosa Parks," Professor Cunningham added, her tone gently academic. "Did you know she wasn't the first to refuse to give up her seat? She was actually the thirtieth. But she had a spotless record. That's why the NAACP chose her. She couldn't be discredited."

"Most of the former residents who might remember anything are in their sixties at least?" Alice asked.

"Seventies and eighties, more likely," Julia replied. "And the city officials who signed off on the neglect are probably the same age or older. Some might be gone already. That's why we need to move fast."

She glanced down at her notes. "The biggest hurdle we face right now is that we can't positively identify any of the remains found on the property. We can talk about health disparities, infant mortality, unsafe conditions—but the city will argue we can't prove the bodies were residents. Without names, we focus on the living. The people who made it out."

I nodded slowly. I'd spent so much time obsessing over the identities of the children buried behind those buildings that I hadn't considered how critical survivor testimony would be.

"The crime we're alleging is negligence," Julia said. "Not physical abuse, but deliberate abandonment. We're talking about unsafe structures, no pest control, poor ventilation, and failure to maintain fire safety codes. Add to that the lack of public services—transportation, healthcare access, under-resourced schools."

"Divestment of community infrastructure," Charlotte chimed in. "I'm sure we'll find documentation showing the city knowingly cut funding to inner-city neighborhoods while maintaining full services in white suburbs."

"And don't forget the housing covenants," she added. "The city concentrated poverty by design. We can prove it with zoning maps and historical ordinances."

Alice cleared her throat. "What about the development company building on the site now? Should we investigate them, too?"

"Yes," Julia said instantly. "What's the name of that company?"

"Greenrock," Alice supplied.

"Right." Julia's voice tightened. "I want to know everything about that deal. Did the city sell the land at market value? Were there tax incentives? Who negotiated the contract?"

She turned to Charlotte. "Let's find out how long Greenrock has operated in the city. What projects they've been tied to. If I find so much as a *suggestion* that they pressured city officials to demolish Sumner Field instead of rehabilitating it, they're getting added to the suit."

Charlotte made a note. "I'll look into potential ties to past housing policies or political donations."

Julia's focus returned to the table at large. "This isn't just about damages. The survivors' stories matter. Cassidy, I want full transcripts from Melody's oral history project. Even if they're still raw audio files."

She turned to the two paralegals. "Ann, Anthony—you'll start reviewing those testimonies. Pull out anything useful. Patterns, timelines, quotes. We're not expecting a smoking gun, but resident narratives will be the soul of this case. I want the D.A.'s office drowning in discovery before we go to court."

"Got it," Ann said, already typing.

"And Cassidy," Julia added, meeting my eyes again. "I'm not giving up on the remains, either. Once we have access to the police records, we'll send out the DNA for phenotypic analysis. The lab can generate facial composites. I want to see if former residents recognize those children."

"I can circulate the sketches," I said. "Melody gave me a long list of contacts to follow up with."

Julia nodded. "Good. Every piece counts."

There was a beat of silence as people turned back to their laptops and notepads. Despite the gravity of the work, I felt strangely hopeful. The stakes were enormous, but Julia was a force. Calm, clear-eyed, and relentless—if anyone could push this case forward, it was her.

"We should leak this to the press," Anthony suggested.

"No," Julia refused. "Media is leverage. We don't give that up until we're ready."

"Melody's already mentioned the Sumner Field bodies on her podcast," I noted. "But not the lawsuit. I'll make sure she doesn't spill the beans on air."

Anthony raised an eyebrow. "Wait. Melody as in Melody Sternbridge? From the *Lost Girls* podcast?"

"Yeah," I said.

Ann suddenly looked up. "That's where I know you from. You were the detective on that case about the missing Native American girl."

I winced. "That was me."

Julia gave me a sideways glance, sensing my discomfort but choosing not to comment. Instead, she tapped her pen on the table and changed the subject.

"We'll reconvene next Monday. Anthony and Ann, expect a mountain of paperwork. Alice, track city council records, zoning meetings, and any planning commission files tied to that development. If there's a paper trail, I want it."

I clasped the professor's hand. "Thank you. For everything."

"Of course." Charlotte Cunningham's smile was gentle. The corners of her eyes crinkled behind her tortoiseshell glasses. "And thank *you* for pushing me out of my comfort zone—for getting me out of the university library."

We stepped into the corridor, the heavy conference room door clicking shut behind us. The law office was nearly empty, most of the other attorneys and paralegals already gone. I matched Dr. Cunningham's pace as we headed toward the bank of elevators.

"I wasn't sure you'd show up today," I admitted.

Charlotte looked straight ahead. "I wasn't sure either. I'm sorry if it seemed like I was ghosting you."

"It's okay," I allowed. "You were."

"Yes." She winced. "I was."

She slowed and turned toward me. "I got scared," she explained. "I've spent most of my career writing books and articles no one reads. I didn't sign up for cameras. Or police. Or angry community members protesting at construction sites."

"What changed?" I asked.

"The housing covenant database we've been creating only has value if it spurs meaningful change." She let out a slow breath. "I spent years thinking the only responsibility I had was to the past. But this lawsuit—it's forcing me to reckon with the present. And the living."

Charlotte reached for the elevator button, but paused. "I'm still nervous," she admitted. "But I'm here."

I pressed the button for her. "That's what matters."

Everyone had cleared out. Laptops closed. Chairs pushed back under the table. The conference room was quiet, lit only by the glow of the city beyond the windows. Minneapolis at night always looked colder than it was—steel and glass and a thousand tiny lights reflected in the river.

Julia stood near the windows, her arms folded loosely across her chest. I admired her for a second before crossing the room. I wrapped my arms around her from behind and rested my chin lightly on her shoulder.

"Thank you," I said quietly.

She didn't ask what for. She let out a soft breath and leaned back into me.

"I know this case isn't your usual," I said. "And you've got a full plate already. You didn't have to take it."

"No," she agreed. "But I wanted to."

I held her a little tighter. "You didn't have to," I said again, softer this time. "But you did."

Her fingers traced over mine where they were clasped at her waist. "Someone had to. And you wanted it so badly. That was enough for me." She turned her head slightly.

"Besides," she added, "it felt good to scare the interns a little."

I smiled against her shoulder. "Yeah. You were terrifying."

She quietly chuckled. "*A-Team*. Why would you ever think they'd get that reference? How do *you* even know that reference? You're far too young."

I brushed my lips against her cheek. "I pity the fool."

Chapter Eighteen

Melody balanced a pastry box in one hand and knocked with the other. "Hey. Can old people have sugar?" she whispered.

I gave her a look. "You're asking *now*?"

"I know, I know." She let out a frustrated huff. "But it just hit me. What if we spike her blood sugar or something? I should have brought fruit."

"Ms. Price isn't opening the door for a banana."

Melody didn't look convinced. "Okay. But if she starts jittering, I'm blaming you."

I sighed and knocked on the door myself. I didn't want to regret inviting Melody along—without her, I never would have discovered Ms. Price—but she made it so hard sometimes. It was like she was programmed to annoy me.

After a moment, I heard the rattle of a chain and the deadbolt disengage.

Ms. Price cracked open the door. "Well, well," she murmured. "If it isn't the Bobbsey Twins."

I smiled, a fondness for this woman overcoming me. "Good morning, ma'am. Thank you for agreeing to see us again."

"Come in, the both of you," she tutted. "And if that box smells the way I think it does, I hope there's raspberry."

We followed Ms. Price inside. The third-floor unit hadn't changed since our initial visit—walls lined with black-and-white photos, vinyl records stacked on a polished buffet, and a living room that smelled faintly of peppermint oil.

"I made tea," she said, nodding to the ceramic pot on the coffee table. "Hope you don't take it with cream."

"Only oat milk," I grinned.

Melody hesitated near the entryway, still holding the bakery box.

"Don't stand there like a coat rack, honey. Sit down." Ms. Price motioned Melody towards the living room furniture. "You didn't drive all the way here just to hold those poor donuts hostage."

Melody smiled and sat down on the flower-patterned loveseat. I took up the spot on the couch closest to Ms. Price's recliner. Melody set the pastry box on the coffee table and lifted the lid.

Ms. Price's eyes lit up. "Raspberry," she announced with some satisfaction. "See? The world isn't completely broken." She gingerly lifted a jelly-filled donut to her mouth. "Now. To what do I owe this unexpected sugar-bribery?"

I pulled a manila envelope from my bag and pulled out a few glossy prints. I laid them out, side by side, on the coffee table. "We're hoping you'll look at some photos for us. See if anyone looks familiar."

"These aren't real photos," she said. It wasn't a question, but I could understand her confusion.

"No, they're not," I confirmed. "They're based on DNA retrieved from those bodies at Sumner Field. It's a new technology," I told her. "It's probably as close as we're going to get to what those children may have looked like."

Ms. Price made a noise, not quite critical, but not quite impressed. "What will they think up next?"

Melody and I stayed quiet as she scanned the first two images. Her brow furrowed on the third. She paused for longer on the fourth.

"Take your time," I said gently.

"I don't need time," she muttered. "I need certainty. Which I don't have."

Ms. Price laid one of the composites on her lap and tapped the edge. The image was of a young girl with dark brown skin and a strong jawline. Her dark eyes were haunting—a little too symmetrical, a little too smooth. The uncanny valley effect of AI trying too hard to be human.

"This one," Ms. Price said. "She's familiar. Not her face—not entirely. But the set of her mouth. The way her chin sits too forward. It reminds me of someone."

I stayed quiet, not wanting to rush her or break her train of thought.

"Was she one of my daughter's friends? Did they go to the same school? Did *I* go to school with her?" She tapped the image again, more insistently. "Her name might have started with a K. Or a hard G. But I can't place it."

She sounded frustrated with herself.

"It's okay," I said gently. "This is more than we had before."

Ms. Price looked up from the images scattered on her coffee table. "This is all for your podcast?"

I exchanged a look with Melody. She shrugged and I hesitated.

"No, ma'am. It's for a lawsuit," I eventually revealed. "The city of Minneapolis needs to be held accountable for what happened to you all."

"For what happened," she echoed.

I wish I'd brought Julia to this meeting. She would have been much better at articulating the details of the lawsuit.

"There's still going to be a podcast series," Melody added. "But we're also pursuing a class-action suit. You and your friends could get money if we win."

Ms. Price hummed. "I see."

Something had shifted. I could see it in Ms. Price's body language and hear it in her tone. Even the intake of air or the way she held her cup of tea had changed. And I didn't think it had anything to do with sugar.

. . .

The walk to the parking lot wasn't far, but it felt longer.

We left Ms. Price's building after exchanging assurances that we'd be in touch and that she should reach out if she remembered anything else about the faces in the digital photos. I wasn't going to hold my breath that she'd be in contact with us, however.

I'd arrived that morning feeling hopeful that Ms. Price might recognize at least one of the individuals from the composite sketches, but I should have known it wouldn't be that easy. Instead, an unsavory emotion that felt a lot like dread had settled in the pit of my stomach.

Melody silently matched my pace until she couldn't keep her peace any longer.

"She doesn't believe us," she vocalized. "She doesn't think we're trying to help."

Something my Cold Case colleague, Sarah, had once said to me stuck in my brain.

"White savior."

"Huh?"

I exhaled. "I think we messed up. I don't think we should have mentioned the lawsuit yet." I stared back at the brick complex as if expecting to see Ms. Price watching us from one of the windows. "That woman has experienced a lifetime of empty promises. She has no reason to believe this is any different."

"She'll see," Melody remarked. I wondered if she'd heard anything I'd said. "I'll show those composites to the others. Someone will recognize one of them. And if they don't, I can always post them on my socials."

"It won't be enough." My voice came out harder than I meant it to. "We've got DNA and bones and reconstructed guesses," I lamented. "And the people who *might* know something are living on borrowed time and scrambled memories. By the time we piece this thing together, the ones who did this—if they're even still alive—will be dead." I thought about Jason Ryan and his missive from City Hall. "Or they'll be protected."

Melody didn't say anything.

"You know what kills me?" I continued. "It's not just the bones or the names we don't have. It's that there's whole buildings in this city, full of people like Ms. Price."

"It's not just Minneapolis," Melody tried to appease. "You'd find that anywhere."

"That doesn't mean it's right or somehow permissible," I challenged.

I stopped walking just short of the division's Crown Vic. "We're going to need a whole lot more than composites," I decided.

Melody regarded me from across the hood of the car. "Then let's find more."

Chapter Nineteen

Charlotte Cunningham was the kind of woman who wore wool skirts and sharp blazers, even on a Saturday. The archival room in City Hall was a windowless, stuffy box that smelled like mildew and old library books. Stacked cabinets lined the walls, and the hum of an old HVAC unit filled the silence between us.

I was grateful she'd agreed to accompany me, especially over a weekend. My badge would have gotten me laughed out of the building if I'd come alone, but walking in behind Professor Charlotte Cunningham had meant the city clerks held the door open.

"I feel like I'm trespassing," I admitted. I felt like I needed to whisper, so as to not disrupt the dust.

"You are," Charlotte confirmed. "That's why you brought me."

She handed me a notepad and a Ticonderoga Number 2 pencil that reminded me of those standardized tests I'd dreaded in high school. When I'd asked about needing gloves to handle the aging documents, she'd waved off my concerns. People mishandled manuscripts more easily if they wore ill-fitting archival gloves, she'd told me.

"We're looking for minutes from the Housing Subcommittee," she said, "especially if they mention the Sumner Field redevelopment or the Sumner-Glenwood neighborhood."

I went to the first cabinet, top drawer. The metal shrieked as it opened. Inside were yellowed folders marked in a spidery hand. Committee Reports. Public Testimony. Budget Oversight. It felt like rifling through someone else's attic, albeit a boring one.

"I don't suppose any of this is digitized," I remarked. "I'd kill for a keyword search about now."

"You sound like one of my students," Professor Cunningham lightly scolded. "This is where real historians prove their mettle, Detective. Paper cuts and dusty documents."

I opened another squeaky cabinet drawer. "And tetanus," I mumbled.

We didn't speak for a while. We spent hours sorting through endless file folders and fading typewritten pages. My lower back started to ache from standing for so long.

I took periodic breaks to check my cell phone for texts from Julia, but Charlotte's shrewd eyes always shamed me into putting my phone away. I nearly felt like one of her aforementioned students. She was a formidable woman who I could easy see being in control of a classroom of early twenty-somethings.

Just when I thought my eyes were starting to cross from scrutinizing illegible handwriting for the better part of the day, Charlotte spoke.

"I think I found something," she said quietly.

She laid a document on top of the filing cabinet closest to me. The memo was dated June 1984 from the Office of Urban Development. I silently read over the details of a plan to "expedite relocation of residents deemed 'non-compliant'" from the projects to make way for a new mixed-use development.

"'Non-compliant'?" I asked.

Charlotte's mouth twisted. "A euphemism. It usually meant tenants who challenged maintenance violations or asked for legal counsel."

There was more. A list of private developers invited to bid on parcels before public notice had been given. Some company names I recognized as still being in operation.

"They used the guise of progress to force displacement," Charlotte observed. "And the city kept the public out of the loop while promising 'revitalization.'"

"Here's something else," she continued. "Documentation about shutting down a fire station in 1972 that would have served the projects." She tapped her finger on the typewritten document. "They claim they're consolidating city resources, but the supporting documentation acknowledges it will put Sumner Field residents at risk."

I looked over the second set of documents to confirm her discovery. "We can use this, right?"

Charlotte's gaze was razor sharp behind her glasses. "This doesn't just support the case. This builds a foundation. Pattern, intent, institutional complicity."

I leaned back against the cabinet, my breath catching a little. Julia had asked for a smoking gun. This wasn't the weapon, but it might have been the bullet.

Charlotte calmly gathered the documents, taking photos of each page with her phone before filing them back exactly as we had found them.

"Careful," I cautioned. "If you keep being this useful, I might get you indicted."

She smiled mildly. "It's not about usefulness, Detective Miller. It's about telling the truth while we're still here to tell it."

We left the room without fanfare, walking back through City Hall like we belonged. No one stopped or questioned us.

We pushed open the heavy glass doors of City Hall. The late afternoon chill was in sharp contrast to the temperature-controlled environment of the archives. Charlotte pulled her wool coat tighter and glanced around, her breath visible in the cold.

"I don't envy the clerk who has to come in on a Saturday," she said with a smile.

"I don't envy *us* having to come in on a Saturday

either," I countered. "You must have a very understanding husband and kids."

Charlotte said something in response, but my attention had drifted to a figure across the plaza. The woman was sitting on a low stone wall, bundled in a threadbare coat. A faded cardboard sign rested in front of her.

Anything helps. God Bless.

Charlotte must have noticed my pause and followed my gaze. "Do you know her?"

I swallowed and took an instinctive step forward. "Yeah. It's complicated."

Monica's gaze snapped up the moment she spotted me. Her eyes flicked quickly over to Charlotte, then back to me. A half-smile, more challenge than warmth, curved her lips.

"Fancy meeting you here," she said.

I forced my voice steady. "Monica."

She arched an eyebrow. "Are you following me?"

I involuntarily stiffened, not expecting the presumptive question. "What? No. I just came to City Hall for some research."

Monica narrowed her eyes. "Research, huh? Funny how we keep running into each other. What are the odds?"

"I didn't know you'd be here," I insisted, trying to sound sincere. "I swear."

Before I could say more, Monica's gaze shifted and landed on Charlotte. She silently studied the professor like she was measuring up a rival.

"You're not the fiancée," she accused.

Charlotte blinked, caught off guard. "I'm sorry?"

Monica's eyes narrowed. "Didn't she tell you? Cass is engaged. Seems like she keeps a lot of secrets these days."

"Charlotte's a colleague," I said quickly.

Monica shrugged and gave me a crooked smile. "Whatever, Miller. If you want to step out on your girl, that's none of my business."

Charlotte looked confused but polite, clearly unsure how to respond. "I'll-I'll meet you by the car."

I watched Charlotte walk briskly in the direction of where I knew she'd parked her SUV. I turned my attention back to Monica.

"We don't have to do this," she said before I could speak.

"Do what?"

"The pity talk," she said. "The 'how'd-you-end-up-like-this?' speech."

I exhaled hard through my nose. I didn't know how to fix this. Maybe I never had.

"I'm not offering a speech." I pulled a business card from my wallet and scribbled my cell phone number on the back with the Ticonderoga Number 2 pencil. "If you need anything, seriously, just call. Please."

Monica curled her lip. "Cassidy Miller, still doing the hero thing."

I continued to hold out the card like a peace offering. "It's just a phone number, Monica."

She took it anyway, holding the card between two

fingers like a cigarette. "Is she single?" she asked, jerking her chin toward Charlotte's retreating figure.

"I didn't realize that middle-aged midwestern moms were your type."

I tried to make a joke, tried to give her a hard time like we might have ribbed each other out in the desert, but the words felt tight and foreign in my throat.

Monica tucked my business card into her coat, deep enough that I wasn't sure she'd find it again.

When I got back to the car, Charlotte didn't ask any questions. I was a little afraid she'd gotten spooked off the case all over again. Protesters at the construction site had caused her to ghost me once. How would she react to getting accosted by a transient former Marine?

I didn't know how to explain the situation without making it awkward.

Luckily, she broke the silence with a low chuckle. "Well, that was unexpected."

I nodded and exhaled. "Yep. Life's never boring."

～

Afghanistan, 2010

The cards in my hand are garbage.

I've got a two of hearts, a five of clubs, a queen of spades, and two mismatched tens. Across from me,

Terrance Pensacola—Detroit's finest shit-talker—is grinning like he already knows he's got me beat.

"You gonna fold or bluff like you did last night, Miller?" he taunts.

I snort and toss a peanut shell at him. It misses and lands in the dust, which is basically everything out here: dust, sweat, and sarcasm. The plywood table we're playing on is uneven, the legs shimmed with cut-up MRE boxes. Everything creaks when we move.

"Just for that, I'm staying in," I say, setting a ten on the table.

Pensacola has this laugh that starts in his chest and rises like a drumroll. "Girl, I love when you make bad decisions. You know it makes my job easier."

A dry breeze kicks up through the open side of the tent, carrying in the scent of diesel and sand and something faintly burnt. I glance past Pensacola's shoulder and see her.

She's leaning against the support beam outside of the tent, arms folded, boot heel propped up like she's just killing time. But I know better. She's watching me. Watching *us*.

Her face is a mask of indifference, but there's tension in her jaw, a tightness around her mouth I've seen a hundred times before. Monica Hernandez doesn't get jealous often—she's too cocky for that—but when she does, it shows in slivers, sharp and silver like shrapnel.

Terrance follows my gaze.

"You know Hernandez has been eyeballing you this whole game," he says casually.

I raise an eyebrow, keeping my tone neutral. "Oh, yeah?"

"Uh-huh," he says, tossing down his cards. Full house. *Of course.* "If I didn't know better, I'd say somebody's got a little crush."

I bark a laugh that sounds real enough. "You think everybody's in love with me."

He shrugs. "I'm just saying. She's fine. Real fine. Even with that stick up her ass."

I give him a mock-scandalized look. "Disrespecting a fellow Marine? That's bold, Pense."

He waves it off. "I'd let her clear a building with me anytime."

I slide my cards into the discard pile and glance over at Monica again. She's still there, pretending not to care, even though I know she does. The way she looks at me sometimes makes my throat ache.

"You hungry?" Terrance asks, leaning back in his chair and stretching until his spine pops.

I look at Monica, and it comes out before I can think better of it.

"Starved."

The path behind the motor pool is dusty and narrow, tucked between a concrete T-wall and the rusted shell of a supply shed. It's where we go when we don't want to be seen. It's where I go when I can't stand not touching her anymore.

Monica's already there, boots planted wide, arms crossed under her vest. Her jaw works like she's been chewing on a bad taste.

"You looked real cozy with Pensacola," she says without greeting.

I sigh. "Not this again."

She steps close, the anger shimmering off her. She's shorter than me, smaller, but I'd never point that out to her. "Don't play dumb. He was practically undressing you with his mouth."

I press a hand to my forehead and feel the sweat and sand there. "Pensacola flirts with everyone. He'd hit on a sandbag if it had curves."

"Yeah, well," she says, eyes flashing, "maybe I don't like the way you laugh at his jokes."

I close the distance between us before I can think better of it. "Are you jealous?"

"No," she lies.

She grabs me by the collar of my t-shirt and pulls me into her. Her mouth crashes against mine, rough and demanding, all heat and teeth. It's not gentle; it never is. There's no time for gentle here.

My back hits the concrete wall. I kiss her back, fiercely, trying to breathe her in, trying to remember this in pieces I can hold onto later, when it's finally quiet and I'm pretending none of it ever happened.

Her fingers dive beneath my shirt, tracing fire along my

ribs. I grip her vest and tug her closer until our bodies are flush, every inch of her pressed against me like a secret I'll never get to say out loud.

"Don't hold back," she whispers against my mouth.

"You wish," I bite back.

She smirks, that wild glint in her eyes sparking brighter. "What, you don't like the thrill of it?"

I groan as her lips trace the line of my throat. "Not when the thrill could get us court-martialed."

She's fearless, like a wildfire, and I'm the cautious ember trying not to get burned.

Her hand is already sliding into my waistband, reckless and sure. "Then stop moaning like that."

I bite my lip and try to keep quiet, my fingers buried in her dark, sweat-damp hair. I'm trembling now, caught between caution and craving. I want to tell her to slow down. I want to ask her to wait. But I never do. Because this is the only way we get to exist: hurried, hidden, and desperate.

I hate how much I love it.

She kisses me like she's drowning and I'm the last breath she'll ever get. The world shrinks to just this: the scrape of her belt buckle against mine, the grit of sand and dirt under my boots, the low thud of my heartbeat in my ears.

Then it's over.

Too fast. Always too fast.

We stand there, pressed together in the shadow of the wall, both of us breathing like we've just finished the

Crucible. She rests her forehead against mine, her fingers still tangled in the fabric at my waist.

"I hate not being able to touch you in daylight," she murmurs.

"I know."

She leans back and looks at me. Her face is flushed, mouth swollen, eyes soft in a way she'll never let anyone else see.

"I think about you," she says. "Even when I'm cleaning my rifle. Even when I'm kicking in doors. I think about you."

The silence stretches. It's not awkward, just heavy with everything we don't say.

I clear my throat. "We should get back."

"Yeah." She doesn't move.

"Someone's gonna notice we're both gone."

She sighs and finally steps away. "Let them."

"Monica ..."

"I know," she says. "I know. Just ..."

She reaches out and brushes a thumb across my bottom lip. It's the softest thing she's done all week.

"Just kiss me one more time like you mean it."

I do.

And then I walk away first, because if I don't, I'll never leave.

Chapter Twenty

Mrs. Geraldine Carter sat in her recliner, a folded blanket across her lap. Her fingers curved around the armrests, knuckles knotted from arthritis. I sat across from her, notebook on my knee, recorder running on the coffee table. She'd already offered me sweet tea twice and had told me I looked too thin.

"You know, some people don't like to admit they grew up there." She tipped her chin toward the black and white photo on the coffee table—one of the Sumner Field buildings, before the city tore them down like they were doing the neighborhood a favor.

"I'd never deny it, though," she said. "It was tough living, but some of the best days of my life."

"Thank you for agreeing to this meeting, Mrs. Carter," I started. "I've spent the past few weeks reading everything I can about the Sumner Field housing development.

Records, inspections, zoning applications. I saw your name come up time and again in neighborhood meetings going back decades."

The archival field trip to City Hall had produced a windfall of evidence for Julia and her team to sift through. In the meantime, it was my task to continue to track down former residents who might serve as our primary party to represent the claimants on the lawsuit.

She gave a dry chuckle. "You mean the ones they never listened to?"

I nodded, smiling despite the circumstances. "Exactly those."

Mrs. Carter leaned back with a sigh. "We weren't asking for luxuries. Just heat in the winter. Clean water. For the elevator to work more than twice a week. They always said they'd fix it, but when they did send notices, it wasn't for repairs—it was for evictions."

"Where did you go after they tore the buildings down?"

"They said they'd relocate us," she said. "But they gave us a list of apartment complexes that were too expensive or had five-year waitlists. I had to move in with my sister on the south-side for eight months." She frowned at the memory. "I lost my job during that time. I couldn't get to the daycare I worked at anymore."

"Did the Housing Authority ever offer any compensation?" I asked.

"A $200 grocery card and a bus pass," she huffed.

"That's what forty years in that building was worth to them."

My jaw tightened. "I'm sorry," I said quietly. "No one should be treated that way."

Mrs. Carter gave me a long look. "What's your angle, Detective?"

"A class action suit," I told her. "I'm working with a lawyer at a firm downtown." I was purposefully vague with the details. I didn't know how the name Grisham & Stein might land yet. "She thinks we can get the city to admit corners were knowingly cut to the detriment of former residents."

Mrs. Carter continued to look skeptical. "I thought you said you were the police?"

"I-I am," I admitted haltingly. "But I'm trying to do the right thing."

"Well," she said, her fingers tapping against the armrest again, "if you're serious about this lawsuit, I'll talk. Lord knows I've got stories. So do a lot of others. And we've been waiting a long damn time for someone to listen."

～

My second stop of the day wasn't to a former Sumner Field resident, but rather someone whose job it had been to oversee the housing project itself. Dan Yates had retired years ago after decades of employment with the Minneapolis Housing Authority.

I met him at his single-family, middle-class dwelling in

the south Minneapolis neighborhood of Diamond Lake. The community had a sparse suburban feel where most residents owned their own homes and the public schools were above average. It was similar to the kind of neighborhood in St. Cloud where I'd grown up, worlds away from the projects of Sumner Field.

Yates' home office was cluttered with a wall of framed certificates that tried too hard to look official. I took note of the framed photographs of him shaking hands with important-looking individuals. One photo in particular caught my eye. I leaned in closer and squinted.

"Is that you with Jesse Ventura?"

"You betcha," he proudly confirmed. "Greatest governor our state has ever had if you ask me."

I hadn't asked.

He motioned me to a chair across from his desk. I didn't bother pulling out the recorder yet.

"You said you're with the city?" he questioned.

"MPD, yeah," I confirmed.

I was working under the assumption that Yates would be more forthcoming if I was coming to him as a representative of the city police department rather than someone pulling evidence together for a civil lawsuit.

It was morally gray, admittedly, but I went with it.

"We're gathering information about the demolition of the Sumner Field housing development," I said. "You were Deputy Director of Housing Policy when that process started, correct?"

He leaned forward in his chair and clasped his hands

on the desktop. "I was part of the task force, yes. But I transferred jobs before the actual tear-down."

"Convenient."

I couldn't help myself.

Yates made a face like he'd tasted something sour. "Is this a fishing expedition or do you have real questions?"

"You signed off on the inspection reports that claimed the units were structurally unsound."

"They were," he said flatly.

I slid a photocopy of a document across the desk. Charlotte had discovered it after a second archival trip to City Hall.

"That's odd. The engineering assessment from just four months earlier concluded that with proper maintenance, the buildings had a twenty-year lifespan."

He didn't touch the paper. "Different firms have different standards."

"Sure," I said. "But you chose the firm with financial ties to Greenrock Development, which only recently bought that land for pennies on the dollar."

He chuckled, but there was no humor in the sound. "You've done your homework."

"That's my job."

Yates finally looked at the paper, but more for show than anything else. "The truth is, those buildings were a mess. Everyone knew that. Mold, rats, plumbing issues. No sane person wanted to live there."

"No sane person had a choice," I countered.

His gaze narrowed. "We were trying to break the

cycle," he said. "Make space for mixed-income housing, economic opportunity. You call it displacement. I call it revitalization."

I raised an eyebrow. "Revitalization for whom?"

He folded his arms across his chest. "People always want a villain. Maybe that helps you sleep. But I was trying to solve an impossible problem with limited tools."

"Was one of those tools kicking out Black families and replacing them with high-priced condos?"

He didn't answer. But he didn't deny it either.

I let the silence hang.

"We'll be subpoenaing documents," I said eventually. "Emails. Memos. Personal notes if they're relevant. You can get ahead of that." I shrugged. "Or not."

He smiled, but it didn't reach his eyes. "Be careful where you dig, Detective. This city has a long memory."

I stood from my chair, the meeting now over. "Luckily, so do I."

∼

It was dark by the time I got to Julia's office; the building's occupants had thinned to the custodial crew. The only light in her office came from a floor lamp by the bookshelf and the glow of the computer monitor reflecting off of her glasses.

She looked up when I knocked and waved me in. She slipped off her readers and rubbed the bridge of her nose.

"I know, I know," she sighed. "I should be at home."

I settled into a chair. "That makes two of us."

"Did you have dinner?" she asked.

"A gas station sandwich, does that count?"

Her red painted lips curved into a frown. "No, it does not, Miss Miller."

My stomach twisted at the formality. *Jesus*, this woman had a hold on me. A simple honorific or title and I was putty in her hands.

"I talked to Geraldine Carter this morning," I told her. "She lived in the projects for forty years. The city offered her a grocery card and a bus pass when they kicked her out."

Julia's eyes narrowed. "How charitable of them."

"She's sharp," I noted. "Still has documentation—photocopies of letters from the housing authority, maintenance request forms they ignored for years. She kept *everything*. I think she could be the cornerstone."

Julia nodded slowly, picking up her pen. "Good. A credible lead plaintiff with lived experience and records to back it up."

"And I met with Don Yates this afternoon."

Her eyebrows lifted. "From the Housing Authority? You've been busy."

And MIA from the Cold Case office all day. My PTO was coming to a reckless end.

"Uh huh."

Julia leaned forward. "What did he have to say?"

"Nothing special, but he didn't deny my allegations," I

said. "He tried to spin displacement as revitalization. He claimed he was solving an impossible problem."

"God," she muttered, jotting down more notes.

"We'll need to subpoena everything from his tenure," I observed. "Emails, memos, meeting notes, internal assessments. I don't trust a single document to be handed over voluntarily."

"Neither do I," she agreed, tapping her pen. "And we'll want a discovery motion early. Get ahead of any so-called 'lost' documentation."

I nodded. "Also, Geraldine mentioned that some folks who were displaced wound up homeless for a stretch. We could track down others willing to speak to build a pattern."

Julia's eyes lit up. "Exactly. That's how we demonstrate systemic harm. You don't just prove that they did it—you prove they knew it would hurt people and they did it anyway."

I watched her brain go into litigation mode. "You're really good at this," I admired.

She smiled warmly. "So are you, Detective."

"We're gonna piss off a lot of people," I anticipated.

"Good." She flipped her legal pad to a fresh page. "Let them squirm."

"Is that the reason you got into law?"

I knew she'd started out as a Classics major in college but had eventually switched to law to appease her father. I'd never asked about her particular brand of law, however.

"I got into law," she said, "because of people in power

who make the rules and then decide when they do or don't want to follow them. I want to make them regret that."

There was something beautiful and brutal about her when she said things like that.

I leaned forward, elbows on my knees. "Do you want me to keep doing interviews with former residents?"

She nodded. "Please. The more firsthand accounts, the stronger our case. See if Mrs. Carter will introduce you to others. We'll need a handful of plaintiffs to get class certification."

"Already ahead of you. She gave me three names."

"We'll also want a civil rights angle—Equal Protections violations, maybe a Fair Housing Act claim," Julia added. "I'll loop in Dan and Sofia from the firm. I know they've handled federal filings."

"Sounds good," I approved. "The more the merrier."

Julia looked suddenly pensive. "Cassidy—this is big. Are you *sure* you want to go through with it?"

I held her gaze. "More than anything."

She nodded, appeased for the moment. "Okay, then. Full speed ahead."

Chapter Twenty-One

The Number 6 bus wheezed as it rounded the curve, a low mechanical sigh that reminded me of my own joints these days. I sat near the back of the bus, with my leather jacket zipped to my chin. My thumb ran circles around the edge of my badge in my pocket.

The other passengers—mostly college students and senior citizens—kept to themselves. I didn't blame them. There was something humbling about riding the bus with the same people, day in and day out.

A plastic bag was stuffed under the seat in front of me—someone's forgotten lunch, perhaps. It made me second-guess my decision to show up at Ms. Price's apartment empty handed. I should have brought something. A box of pastries. A peace offering. But I hadn't. It was just me and a folded printout of a new DNA reconstruction photo in my coat pocket.

The bus hissed to a stop two blocks from the senior living complex, its brakes groaning. I stepped off into the chill of a gray morning, stuffing my gloveless hands deeper into my jacket pockets.

Three flights of stairs bought me time to reconsider the whole thing. I'd spent weeks pretending to be someone I wasn't with Ms. Price, sitting across from her in her living room with Melody grinning beside me. I'd told myself it was harmless. Tactical, even.

Now it just felt like cowardice.

By the time I reached the third floor, I'd gone over the speech in my head four different ways and hated all of them. I knocked on the apartment door before I could over-think it anymore.

The door creaked open. Ms. Price blinked at me, wrapped in a forest green cardigan.

"You again," she said. "Forgot the donuts?"

"I did," I admitted. "And the podcaster, too."

Ms. Price continued to stand in the doorway, neither inviting me in nor sending me away.

"I was hoping I might bother you for a cup of coffee," I tried. "I've been hankering for some oat milk."

Her mouth twitched. "I'll see what I've got."

I sat in my usual place in Ms. Price's living room while she tinkered about in the kitchenette. I looked around while I waited—sun-faded family photos, crocheted blankets, a calendar from a local church with Bible verses written in cursive. The view beyond the living room window looked out over the leafless trees behind the building. An empty bird feeder swung gently in the wind.

Ms. Price returned with coffee in two mismatched mugs. She added a dash of oat milk to mine from a carton she'd pulled from the fridge. It looked almost empty.

I murmured my thanks and took a sip. The oat milk had gone a little sour, but I didn't mention it. It felt like I deserved it.

Ms. Price took her time settling into her recliner. "All right, then. Let's have it."

I set my cup on a coaster on the coffee table. "I'm not a podcaster."

"No kidding," she snorted. "You and that redheaded girl made a strange pair. She had too many opinions and too much energy to be a journalist."

"She's a real podcaster," I admitted. "But I'm a detective. Cold Case. Minneapolis PD."

Ms. Price didn't flinch or react right away. She lifted her mug to her lips, took a sip, and looked at me over the rim.

"So you've come to arrest me," she said, bone-dry.

"No, ma'am." An ill-timed church giggle bubbled up my throat, but I managed to push it down. "I was hoping I could come clean. And maybe earn another conversation."

"At least you didn't bring donuts as a bribe."

I smiled sheepishly. "It crossed my mind."

Ms. Price leaned back in her chair, studying me. I tried not to squirm.

"I figured something was off," she said after a moment. "You sat too straight. Asked too many questions without taking notes. And that one, the redhead. She had no poker face."

"She thought it would go better if we didn't lead with the badge."

"Better for you," she said. It wasn't cruel, just true.

I nodded. "Yes."

Ms. Price sighed through her nose. "Well, I appreciate the honesty. Eventually."

"I'm sorry," I said, and I meant it.

She turned from me and looked out the window. "I've lived through enough of this city lying to me. It's nice when someone admits it."

Ms. Price tapped her fingers against her mug, quiet for a long moment. Then she nodded as if she'd made up her mind.

"I was born in South Minneapolis," she started. "Near 38th. My mother was a teacher, my father was a janitor. When I was ten, the city declared our neighborhood 'blighted' and bought up our block. Forced relocation, they called it. We ended up in Sumner Field. It was a brand new housing project—the first in the city—but with the same old racism."

Her mug clinked as she set it down.

"I remember the first time we walked into the unit. Concrete floors. Cold as hell. My mama cried when she saw the mold in the corner of the kitchen."

"What year was that?" I asked.

"1940. Just before the war."

I made a mental note.

"Did you like living there?" I asked. "Besides the mold."

"Sometimes," she said, head bobbing slowly. "It wasn't perfect, but there was community. We didn't have much, but we had each other. And music. Always music coming through the walls." A small smile played on her thin lips. "And the kids playing outside until the streetlights buzzed on."

I leaned forward on the thin couch cushion. "I looked into Linda Walker, but none of the recovered bodies were a match. We had a new composite done on one of the bodies, though. I was hoping you might recognize her. She would have been about fourteen."

I pulled the printout from my coat pocket. It was folded twice, a soft crease running right through the girl's eyes. I laid it on the table and tried to smooth it out.

Ms. Price leaned in, squinting.

"She looks familiar," she said. "But that could be my memory playing tricks. There were so many girls. Some came and went. Some didn't come back at all."

Her thin lips twisted in thought. "She might've been in the building next to ours. Name might've been Sharonda or Shauna, something like that. She had a green coat with fur around the hood. Always wore it, even in spring."

My adrenaline kicked up a notch. "Anything else you remember?"

"Her hair was natural. Big halo around her face."

I nodded, committing every detail to memory. Every thread mattered.

Ms. Price looked out the window again for a long moment. "There's always been a cost to being poor and Black in this city," she said. "They just hide it better now."

She turned back to me. "Did I ever tell you about my husband, Henry?"

I shook my head. "No, ma'am."

Ms. Price pointed at the polished buffet along one wall, the one stacked high with vinyl records. "Bring me that photo."

I stood and did as I was told. Among the John Coltrane and Miles Davis and Billie Holiday, I found a gilded frame that contained a black-and-white snapshot.

A tall Black man stood beside a younger version of Ms. Price. His hand rested lightly on her waist; both of them squinted into the sun. She was wearing a church dress and kitten heels. He wore rolled-up sleeves and a tie a little too skinny for his broad frame.

I held it up for Ms. Price to see.

"That's the one," she confirmed.

I brought the framed photo back to Ms. Price's recliner. She cradled the image as though it was precious—because it was.

"Henry," she said fondly. "When we first met, he promised to take me away from Sumner Field. Said we'd get a little place with a porch, a garden, and a big kitchen so my mama could cook Sunday dinners properly."

"He kept that promise," she said. "Eventually. We

stayed in Sumner Field for a few years after we married. Couldn't just leave my parents behind. He worked two jobs—nights, weekends. And I took in people's mending. We scrimped and saved every penny. Finally got us a place in Shingle Creek just before our second son was born."

Her eyes lingered on the photo.

"He passed ten years ago. Stroke. I still talk to him every day, though. And we listen to our records."

"Sounds like he was a good man." My voice was creaky with emotion.

She smiled. "The best man I ever knew."

She set the framed photo on the end table beside her, and then tilted her head, looking at me a little differently. Her gaze dropped to my left hand.

"You're engaged," she observed. "What does your beau think about all of this?"

"I, uh, I actually have a *belle*," I stumbled on the admittance.

I'd kept the truth from Ms. Price once; there was no use in doing it again.

Ms. Price's smile widened. "Well, now. That's lovely."

"She's a lawyer," I added, still a little shaky. "*The* lawyer, in fact, handling the Sumner Field lawsuit. Her office should be reaching out to you soon if you don't mind."

Ms. Price was quiet for a time before delivering her response. "I suppose it can't hurt."

A clock on a shelf chimed with the hour. I was late to work.

I stood reluctantly. "I've got to get to the precinct," I apologized. "I'm late already."

She waved me off. "Don't let me keep you."

"I'll be back," I said. "And if that name ever comes to you, or anything else, I hope you'll let me know."

"I'll let it rise," she said, tapping her temple. "Like dough. Sometimes memory takes its sweet time."

I hesitated at the door. "Thank you for the coffee. And for trusting me."

"Bring your redheaded friend next time," she allowed. "But not without something with frosting."

I smiled. "I will. Thank you again, Ms. Price."

"And be honest next time," she said, her voice firm but not unkind. She shook a weathered finger in my direction.

I bobbed my head. "Yes, ma'am."

∽

Captain Forrester's office smelled like mothballs and deer antlers. I didn't know if the latter actually had a scent, but whatever it was, it hung in the stale air. Forrester didn't look up when I entered his office. He continued fiddling with a glue gun and what looked like a half-stuffed ferret on the filing cabinet behind his desk.

"You wanted to see me, sir?" I asked.

There'd been a barely legible note from him awaiting my arrival that morning, admittedly over an hour late because of my prolonged visit with Ms. Price.

"Sit," he said, finally turning around. He gestured

toward the cracked leather chair in front of his desk, the one where people usually landed when they'd either screwed up or solved something big. Judging by the flatness in his expression, I knew which one this was.

"You've been ghosting this place more than you've been in it, Miller," he accused.

"Sir, I've been out interviewing witnesses—"

"For what?" he interrupted. "The Laroque case is already with the D.A., and that case from Homicide's been reclassified." He leaned back in his chair, which groaned in protest. "What the hell are you working on?"

I hesitated, not because I didn't know what to say, but because I couldn't say it. Not all of it. Not the late-night strategy sessions with Julia or the weekends in libraries and archives, or the hours spent tracking down displaced residents from a torn-down housing project the city would rather forget.

"Some of it's off-the-books. It's still in early stages," I said carefully.

"For who?" he pressed. "Because unless there's a cold case with a badge on it, that's not your jurisdiction."

"I'm following leads that could intersect with our department's history," I offered. Technically, it wasn't a lie.

Forrester snorted. "Cut the crap. I know you're playing freelance detective on someone else's agenda."

Defiance flared in my chest, hot and dull. "I'm doing my job."

"You're not a private investigator, Miller. You're a detective. Cold Case. Get cold or get gone."

He dismissed me with an aggressive wave and picked up his glue gun again like he hadn't just gutted me with five words.

Sarah greeted me when I returned to our shared office space. "You good?"

"Just peachy," I said.

She offered a sympathetic look. "Forrester pulled your file. He said you've been logging fewer hours than a beat cop on half-pay."

I worked the muscles in my jaw. "He's one to talk."

It was well known in the building that Forrester was counting down the days until he could retire with his full pension. He stayed cloistered in his private office most days, caring for his taxidermy collection. The only time he tended to leave his office was to obstruct our progress on a case or shut it down altogether.

I slumped at my desk, feeling like a teenager who'd just lost their driving privileges. *What now?* How was I supposed to balance my desk job with the lawsuit? I couldn't just stop; I was in too deep.

Stanley hovered by my desk with his laptop tucked under one arm. He tapped anxious fingers against the lid of his personal computer.

"Something I can help you with, Stanley?"

"I know it's probably too late, but I compiled all those reports you asked for."

I pinched at the bridge of my nose, only half listening. "I asked for reports?"

"Sumner Field," he said. "Police reports from the Sixties."

I exhaled. "Shit, right. I'm sorry. I forgot you were doing that."

Stanley set his laptop onto my desk and lifted the lid. "It was a lot of data, so I plugged it into this text analysis tool to look for patterns. Words or phrases that come up a lot. Popular dates. Response times."

Stanley's ingenuity never failed to impress.

"Did anything interesting pop up?"

Stanley pointed at some multicolored squiggles on the program he had open on his computer's desktop.

"Between '63 and '66, calls from Sumner Field averaged almost triple the response rate of any other neighborhood in the city. But the reports almost never resulted in arrests, or even follow-up investigations."

He clicked into one example. "This one—domestic disturbance, May 1965. Officers logged the address, but no narrative, no action taken. Same for this noise complaint. And this assault. Nothing. It's like they showed up, scribbled something down, and left."

"Or didn't show up at all," I said.

Stanley nodded grimly. "There's a pattern. The more calls that came from Sumner Field, the shorter the narratives became. By '65, most reports from Black residents are just timestamps and addresses. Compare that to similar calls from white neighborhoods in North Minneapolis—

pages of narrative, follow-ups, even patrols scheduled afterward."

"Shit," I cursed. "Shit, shit, shit."

"What's wrong?" Stanley asked.

I stared at Stanley's laptop screen. "I think I'm going to get myself fired."

∼

The conference room at Grisham & Stein looked like it had been designed with one purpose in mind: intimidation. A polished walnut table, leather chairs, and walls lined with art and law books all came together to complete the expertly curated look. The blinds were drawn against a rare sunny day, casting long shadows across the faces of the city of Minneapolis' attorneys as they settled in across from Julia and her team.

I took a seat in one corner of the room, not even at the table. I wasn't there to talk, only to listen and observe.

Julia sat upright, still and calm, her hands folded neatly in front of a yellow legal pad. She didn't need notes, though. She had the facts locked away, neatly catalogued in her impressive mind.

It was a little surreal watching her—seated across the negotiating table from a team of city prosecutors. Back in Embarrass, it had been her job to defend the city from lawsuits. Now, however, she was on the other side, bringing suit against the city that employed me.

"Intentional divestment of city services in Sumner

Field wasn't an oversight," she began. "It was a policy choice. One that produced multi-generational harm."

An older man with thinning hair and a pinstripe suit adjusted his tie. "Ms. Desjardin, our team has thoroughly reviewed your complaint. But it's difficult to prove intent from administrative records dating back over sixty years."

Julia's lips barely twitched as though expecting that exact defense.

"It's not difficult when the records show police response times markedly slower than other precincts. Or the closing of local fire stations. Or public schools that received less funding per pupil. The housing wasn't just neglected," she accused, "it was structured to fail."

I looked at her fingers, resting calmly beside her pen. Not even tapping.

A younger attorney across from her—a man with slicked-back hair that he probably thought made him look like Gordon Gekko—spoke up next. "It's a stretch to link that to liability. We're not saying these communities didn't face challenges, but systemic issues aren't always actionable in court."

Julia's eyes landed on him like a spotlight. "Systemic issues are *exactly* what make this actionable. The Fair Housing Act doesn't stop protecting people just because a few decades have passed. The city made promises. They broke them."

Julia flicked a subtle glance towards Alice who, anticipating her boss's needs, handed over a thick stack of documents. I knew what the records contained—Stanley's data,

Charlotte's archival finds, interviews I'd helped chase down in the narrow kitchens of former Sumner Field residents.

The city's attorneys flipped through the pages but looked neither surprised nor impressed. They'd seen the evidence. They just didn't want to acknowledge it.

"The City has no interest in pursuing a settlement at this time," the older man said eventually. "We see no grounds for financial responsibility."

Julia nodded once, and I caught the faintest flicker of emotion behind her eyes. Not disappointment, but recalibration. Like someone moving a chess piece three turns ahead.

"I understand," she said smoothly. "But I'll remind you that my clients have so far chosen not to engage with the media. When we do go public, I imagine City Hall will find itself scrambling to explain why underserved Black families were herded into housing the city had already given up on." She wet her painted lips. "I wonder how that will land in the court of public opinion."

The silence that followed was chillier than the late winter temperatures.

The city's legal team left soon after. Julia thanked and dismissed her paralegals. She gathered her untouched legal pad, and we walked silently from the conference room back to her private office.

I exhaled when I closed the door behind us. I felt

simultaneously calm, but also like I could run through a wall for this woman.

I reached for her hand. She didn't pull away.

"You were incredible," I admired. "You could've stared down a whole firing squad."

She smiled knowingly. "You just think competence is sexy."

"I think *you're* sexy," I corrected. "The rest is just confirmation bias."

The fight wasn't over. Hell, it was barely beginning. But with Julia at the helm, I knew we were going to make them answer for what they'd done.

Chapter Twenty-Two

It had been weeks since we'd had a real date, just the two of us—no work stress, no cold cases, no fertility shots, no ex-girlfriends materializing out of thin air.

I'd been sitting at my desk in the basement of the Fourth Precinct during the workday and spending most evenings in the kitchens and living rooms of potential persons to add to the class-action suit. It was exhausting work, physically and mentally, with little time for anything else.

I slept just enough to keep me functioning. I couldn't complain, though. Julia and her team were working just as long of hours with greater urgency to pull the details of the case together. The construction crews had returned to Sumner Field and the former residents and their descendants weren't getting any younger.

Julia had made dinner reservations at some trendy new place where the waitstaff wore black button-ups and every cocktail had a puny name and an elaborate garnish. Julia nursed a glass of red wine while I'd ordered an Old Fashioned.

Her fingers skimmed over the rim of her wine glass. "I've been thinking about next steps with the fertility treatment."

I sat up a little, alert despite my lingering fatigue. "Already?"

She nodded. "My doctor said it's best not to wait too long between retrievals. I'll take a short break, let my body reset, and then we'll start the shots all over again."

I blinked. "Oh. I didn't realize there'd be a second round."

"For a woman my age, one round isn't usually enough," she said. "My doctor wants to freeze as many viable eggs as possible to increase our chances for a live birth."

Our chances.

Intellectually, I knew I was part of that 'our.' But I still felt like a bystander sometimes, like Julia was the one with the plan and I was just following her lead, afraid to mess it up. I only had myself to blame though. I needed to take the initiative and ask more questions if I didn't want to be left in the dark.

"That makes sense," I said. "Are you ... okay? Like, physically? After the first procedure?"

She gave me a small but weary smile. "Bloated. Tired. A little moodier than I'd like to admit. But yes, I'm okay."

I reached across the table and laced our fingers together. I was mindful not to spill our drinks on the white linen tablecloth or accidentally knock the heavier-than-necessary silverware onto the floor.

"Do you want me there for the second procedure? I can take the day off," I offered. "Or more than that."

Julia squeezed my hand and smiled. "I'd like that."

She drew her hand back and reached for her wine glass. She toyed with the stem, turning it in slow half-circles on the linen.

"Have you seen Monica lately?"

I let out a short laugh before I could stop myself. "Have I seen Monica?" I repeated. "Julia, I've barely seen my own bed this week."

She tilted her head, half-apologetic. "I wasn't accusing you of anything. I was only asking."

"No, I haven't seen her," I said, quieter this time. "And if I did, I'd tell you."

Julia continued to fidget with the base of her wine glass.

"I'm not proud of it," she said, "but I think about her sometimes. Not in the jealous sense," she qualified, "but wondering what she meant to you."

I ran a hand over the back of my neck. "She meant something once. But not like this. Not like you."

That seemed to settle things—for the moment, at least.

Our waiter stopped by our table to refill our water glasses with a flourish. I forced a smile at him and picked up my menu to decide on an entree.

The table next to us clinked champagne flutes. A birthday, maybe. A celebration. Or just rich people celebrating another Tuesday.

It wasn't unusual for me to feel out of place in Julia's refined circle, but no more so than in that moment. I knew she'd chosen this place to make the evening special. But I'd spent the better part of a month in old kitchens and cramped apartments, recording the memories of people on fixed incomes who'd grown up in abject poverty.

The contrast between that and foie gras on tiny plates felt almost violent.

"Do you think we could order and take it to go?" I asked.

Julia's features crumpled in concern. "Is everything okay?"

I closed the oversized menu and set it on the table. "I'm not ... I'm not feeling my best."

To her credit, Julia didn't push. She just nodded and flagged down the waiter.

I stepped out into the cool night air with a paper bag in hand. The scent of steak au poivre and French fries followed us onto the sidewalk. Julia's heels clicked softly beside me.

"Are you sure you're okay, dear?" she asked, looping her arm through mine. Her fingers curled affectionately around my bicep.

"Uh huh," I assured her. "Just feeling a little tired."

She hummed. "You've been burning the candle at both ends."

"I know," I sighed. "But it's not like I have a choice."

"There's always a choice," she gently challenged.

"You mean quit Cold Case and work with you."

She leaned into me with a quiet chuckle. "I didn't say it."

"And you say *I'm* the bad influence," I tried to joke.

I was prepared to go the distance with the Sumner Field case, but I was well aware that something had to give. More than likely, I'd have to take a step back and force Julia to finally hire a private investigator to complete her team. It made the most sense even if I was reluctant to have someone else following up on leads that I'd discovered. I made a mental note to follow up with Rich about the job. He was a good cop, and he had a big heart. He would do a good job.

We crossed the plaza toward the public parking structure where Julia had left her Mercedes. The air outside was colder than expected, biting at my cheeks and neck. Spring would be just around the corner, however, if that underground rodent's prediction had been right.

"I had a good visit with my mother this morning," she revealed. "She was lucid for the entire visit."

"That's really great, babe."

I made a second mental note to call my own mom. These unintentional reminders from Julia had made me realize how much I took my own parents for granted—how much I assumed they'd always be there.

"There are so many milestones I'd like for her to be a part of," Julia observed, "but it feels like I'm running an impossible race against time. I've been so focused on my biological clock as of late, I didn't give myself the headspace to think about having her at our wedding."

I held up a hand, fingers closed in a fist, but Julia had never been in the military before; she kept talking.

"I know I've been hesitant to tell her about you in the past, but I think I'm finally ready to do it. I want her to know you and to be a part of our life for as long as she's able."

Julia frowned when she realized I was no longer participating in the conversation.

"Cassidy—did you hear me?"

I shook my head, my mind elsewhere.

"Someone's following us."

A million scenarios, each worse than the next, sprung into my head. We'd forgotten our packed-up dessert at the table and a hostess was chasing us down. Or maybe Monica had been observing us from afar but had had enough of the voyeurism. Or maybe some bigot who didn't like the look of two women holding hands and speaking to each other with such fondness had decided to confront us.

I reached for Julia's hand. "Keep walking," I murmured.

When we reached the parking structure, I angled us toward the stairwell instead of the elevator. My boots were nearly silent on the concrete steps. Julia stayed close, thankfully silent and accommodating.

I slowed at the third level even though Julia's car was on the fourth. I turned sharply, catching movement in my peripheral. A white man, mid-thirties, brown hair, medium build, hoodie pulled low over dark eyes.

"Hey!" I barked, stepping forward. "You got a problem, buddy?"

He hesitated, and that was enough.

I surged forward, caught the man by the collar, and slammed him against the concrete wall. I pressed my forearm across his chest; my other hand pinned his shoulder.

His breath hitched, and I caught the scent of sweat and cheap cologne.

"You got something to say?" I growled, low and even.

The man squirmed, trying to push back. We were about the same build, but I had anger and leverage on my side.

"Get off me," he snapped, twisting under my grip.

"Not until you tell me why you've been following us."

"I don't know what you're talking about."

Wrong answer. I shoved him harder against the wall.

His jaw clenched. "You're making a mistake."

"Try me," I said, shifting my weight just enough to cut off his wiggle room. "Who are you?"

"Nobody."

"That's funny," I huffed. "You don't look like nobody."

Behind me, I heard Julia's heels pause a few feet away. "Cassidy."

I didn't take my eyes off the man.

"You've got about ten seconds before I start getting creative."

"Tell your girlfriend to stop poking around where she doesn't belong," he hissed.

My forearm dug harder into his sternum. "What the hell does that mean?"

Julia moved behind me, her phone already in hand. "I'm calling the police."

The threat of the police must have spooked the man. He jerked hard before I could stop him; the fabric of his jacket slipped through my fingers. He broke into a run down the stairwell, his boots pounding on the concrete steps.

I cursed under my breath and debated chasing him, but Julia's hand on my arm stopped me.

"Cassidy." Her voice was steady but quiet.

I nodded, breathing hard. "Yeah. Okay."

We stood there a moment, our To-Go containers cooling in a paper bag at her feet. I looked down the stairwell and then back at her.

She touched my elbow. "Let's go home."

Neither of us spoke on the drive back home. Julia parked her Mercedes in the underground parking structure and we rode the elevator up to her condo. She silently let us inside, paused long enough to slip out of her heels, before walking back to the kitchen with our uneaten dinners.

I followed her into the kitchen, even though I had no

desire to eat. After what had happened in the public parking garage, I'd lost my appetite.

I continued to silently regard her. She pulled two plates from one of the upper cabinets and turned on the oven to preheat.

"I can't keep you safe."

Julia paused her activities.

"I thought you did an admirable job tonight," she observed.

"Tonight, sure," I conceded, "But what if that guy had been waiting outside of your office building?"

"I'll have security escort me to the parking garage."

Julia resumed prepping for a dinner that I still had no interest in. She pulled silverware from a drawer and produced napkins from another cabinet. I couldn't continue having this half conversation where she robotically multitasked. I gently wrapped my fingers around her wrists, compelling her to stop.

"Cassidy."

She said my name so carefully, so softly. I braced myself for words I didn't want to hear.

"It's going to be like this," she said. "It was one of the considerations I had to make before accepting the job. What I'm doing won't be popular with a lot of people," she noted, "except the ones that matter."

I stroked the pad of my thumbs across the fine bones of her inner wrists. "Only if you're sure."

Her caramel eyes bore into mine. "I'm sure."

She cupped my jaw with cool fingers and drew me to

her mouth. Our lips connected in a kiss that started slow but didn't stay that way. It deepened, heat curling between us, her hands slipping beneath my jacket, mine finding the zipper of her dress.

"Bedroom," she whispered against my lips, but I was already lifting her, already pressing her against the closest surface.

I knew we weren't making it to the bedroom anytime soon.

Julia's breath caught in her throat when I pressed her back against the cool edge of the kitchen counter. I kissed her again, deeper this time, tasting the wine on her lips, the softness of her mouth turning hungrier with every pass of her tongue against mine.

"I missed you," she murmured.

"I'm right here," I promised.

I knew what she meant, though. We hadn't had sex since before Valentine's Day, but I'd tried not to read into it. Her body had been recovering, and I'd been fucking things up by spending too much time with Monica.

Her hands fumbled with my jacket, pushing it from my shoulders, her fingers moving with urgency; she'd waited long enough. I tugged the zipper of her dress the rest of the way down and slipped a hand beneath the fabric, finding her warm and flushed underneath, goosebumps rising as my palm skimmed her bare back.

I kissed the hollow of her throat, then lower, until her dress slipped past her shoulders and gathered around her waist. I traced the edge of her lacy bra with my thumb, watching the way her eyes fluttered closed at the touch.

There was something sacred about this—about her. About the way she let go just for me.

I hooked my fingers in the waistband of her underwear and pulled them down slowly, savoring how the expensive material slid down her smooth skin. Julia bit down on her lip. She watched me from beneath half-lidded eyes, like she couldn't look away, like she didn't want to.

I didn't rush. I kissed my way down her stomach, held her steady as she shifted closer to the edge of the counter, knees falling apart for me with something like surrender. Her breath was already uneven when I slipped my fingers between her thighs and found her soaked, ready, and waiting.

Her hips lifted to meet my hand.

"God, Cassidy," she gasped.

"I've got you."

I meant it in every way.

Her body arched when I slid two fingers inside her, slow at first, curling deep until I found the place that made her fall apart. She gripped the edge of the counter, her head fell back, mouth open in a silent moan, as I set a rhythm she couldn't resist.

And I watched her—watched the flush rise on her exposed chest, the way her breath shortened, the way she broke apart for me. I felt it when she came, sudden and sharp, her whole body trembling against me, around me.

I held her through the aftershocks, forehead pressed to

hers, my hand still gentle inside her, like I couldn't quite bear to let her go.

When she finally caught her breath, she worried her teeth into her lower lip. "Are you scared?"

"Of?"

There were too many options.

Telling her mom about us? Getting married? Starting a family? Me sabotaging this perfect thing?

A creep in a parking lot was barely the tip of the iceberg.

"The man in the garage," she said.

I rested my hand on her lower back. "No. I'm not scared of him. He made a mistake going after you. I'll pull the CCTV from the parking structure first thing tomorrow. We'll find him."

"There will be others."

"And I'll find all of them, too."

She reached up and brushed her fingers along my jaw. "I know."

And then she kissed me again—like she believed it.

Chapter Twenty-Three

I knew I was toeing a fine line with Captain Forrester, so over the next few days, I became a model employee. But just because I was back in the Cold Case office full time, that didn't mean I couldn't also keep working the Sumner Field case.

When Homicide had reclassified the Sumner Field remains as a natural death, it was like watching the truth get buried twice. The evidence folder would be moved from Homicide to Records, stamped with whatever code they used for *no longer our problem.* The logs would show the case as closed, not solved—a subtle but important difference. No justice, no closure. Only a bureaucratic shrug.

Reclassifying a death didn't just change the paperwork; it changed the entire trajectory of what got remembered and what became forgotten. It closed doors that might have otherwise led to hard questions and real answers. And if someone had made those remains disappear in life, they'd probably be relieved to see us doing the same thing in death.

The physical evidence—bone fragments, soil samples, disintegrated remnants of clothing—would get boxed up and shelved in the evidence warehouse. Eventually, some desk sergeant would flag it for destruction. Budget cuts. Storage limits. New priorities.

And the remains themselves? If they were still in the medical examiner's custody, they might be released for cremation. With no family members to claim them, they would be buried in a pauper's grave, a thin metal tag instead of a name. That was assuming they hadn't already been returned to some overgrown lot or unmarked municipal cemetery plot.

I found the original case files boxed in the evidence closet on the first floor. I knelt down and pulled the top box toward me, the cardboard edges giving a little groan like they didn't want to be disturbed.

I thumbed over the multiple folders—documents, photographs, bagged evidence from the scene. Jason Ryan had collected and organized most of it. He was thorough, to his credit. But thorough didn't mean persistent, not in the way it mattered.

The first folder held the standard reports. I found excavation photos from behind what had been Building Nine, the inventory of physical remains, and the medical examiner's initial findings. I flipped through them, my eyes scanning over the familiar language.

Child. Female. Approximate age: 10-12 years old. No match.

Child. Male. Approximate age: 8-9 years old. No match.

Child. Female. Approximate age: 13-14 years old. No match.

Halfway through the list, something caught my eye.

Item 12: One (1) metal chain with heart-shaped pendant. Partial engraving visible.

I stopped. I hadn't remembered that detail from before. Maybe I'd skimmed the documents too quickly the first time through and had moved on, like Detective Ryan probably had. Maybe I'd been too caught up in the bigger picture to see what was dangling right in front of me.

I turned the page. The chain had been photographed, tagged, and sealed. I found the print—an overhead shot of the necklace on a plain white background, its thin silver links tangled, a heart charm oxidized and dulled from time. The engraving was faint, but visible. *M—*

I stared at the photograph like it might reveal the rest of the name. Michelle? Mary? Marie? Was this the name of the victim? A detail, perhaps, that didn't show up in dental records or in CODIS.

It could also mean nothing, I realized. The initial could have belonged to the person who'd given the necklace as a present. I wasn't a big jewelry person, but I could imagine myself wearing something with Julia's initials engraved on it.

Back at my desk, I pulled up the database that Stanley had quietly pulled together. I typed in a few key phrases: *Sumner Field*, *missing person*, and most importantly, *names beginning with M*—girls, mostly, around ten to twelve. I narrowed the timeline, then added the word *necklace* just in case it had ever been mentioned before.

The search took a few seconds. I watched the little spinning wheel.

Six matches. All girls. All missing between 1960 and 1970. All names beginning with M.

Margaret Richards. Monica T. Hill. Missy Williams. Mary Dandridge. Michelle White. Molly Fox.

I opened each file and read.

Most of the police reports were a few pages long, written in faded ink or scanned typewriter text. The girls had gone missing from corners of the city that had long since been bulldozed or renamed. Some had families who never gave up. Others had only a single report, never revisited.

But Mary Dandridge's report stood out.

Reported missing in September of 1966, Mary Dandridge had last been seen near the housing project's laundry facility. Ten years old. The note in the margin had been scrawled by a patrol officer: *Wearing pink sweater, denim jeans. Necklace—heart charm. Gift from grandmother.*

My chest tightened.

I pulled the folder with the necklace again and stared at the photo. The charm wasn't fancy. It was the kind of thing a grandma might pick out from a department store for a birthday or first communion. *M—*

It wasn't a confirmation. Not yet. But for the first time in a while, I felt a flicker of hope.

∽

I didn't head straight to Julia's office. I stopped off at the precinct bathroom first, splashed water on my face, and stared at my reflection. I still looked like someone who hadn't slept enough but was too wired to rest.

Julia's office door was open when I got there. Alice saw me and stood to intercept, but I shook my head and gave her a look.

"I'll just be a minute," I promised, not slowing down.

Julia was on the phone, pacing behind her desk with one hand resting on her lower back. Her shoes were off. I spotted them on one side of her desk, red lacquered bottoms abandoned like she'd kicked them off mid-thought.

When she saw me, her eyes narrowed with the faintest trace of concern. She said something to whomever was on the other end of the call, and then hung up.

"Everything okay?" she asked.

I held up the folder. "I think I found something."

She motioned me to take a seat. I closed the door behind me.

"This isn't a smoking gun," I qualified before handing over the folder. "But it's the closest we've had."

She opened the folder and stared at the image. Her eyebrows lifted and then drew together.

"The engraving?"

"It matches a missing person report from 1966," I said. "Mary Dandridge. Ten years old. Her file mentioned a necklace with a heart charm. It had been a gift from her grandmother."

Julia looked up at me. "You found her."

"It still might not be a match," I cautioned. "I'll need dental records or DNA from a relative."

My words were pragmatic, but my gut told me that this was her. And if we could positively identify her, maybe that might lead to identifying the others.

"How does this affect the lawsuit?" I asked.

Julia leaned back, her fingers threading together as she stared at the file on her desk.

"If we can confirm the remains belong to this girl, and if we can prove she was buried beneath a city-owned property," she said, thinking it through out loud, "then the case shifts from historical injustice to something with names and timelines. A death that was never investigated," she noted. She paused and wet her lips. "It changes everything."

She reached for a pen and clicked it once. Her brain was already moving the chess pieces.

"We'll need to amend the filing. Add her estate as a party. Notify her family, if any are still living. And we'll have to brace for the city fighting us harder than ever. If that's really Mary Dandridge, this case is no longer systemic neglect. It's concealment. It's potential liability for wrongful death."

"Will it stand up?" I asked. "Legally?"

"If we're careful. If we document everything. And if we're willing to let this girl become the face of what happened there."

I stood, but my hand lingered on the edge of her desk. "I'll put in a request for dental records. I'll ask Stanley and Sarah to help track down a living relative."

She nodded. "Keep me posted."

I didn't say goodbye. I just gave her a look that said I would see her later. I had one more stop to make.

～

Spencer's bar wasn't the kind of place I expected to find someone like Detective Jason Ryan. It was too rough around the edges and too sticky underfoot. Spencer's was where beat cops nursed cheap beer and swapped tall tales. It wasn't where polished detectives went to brood.

And yet there he was.

I'd tried Homicide first, but the desk sergeant on duty had told me to try the popular cop bar. I found Ryan sitting alone in a booth near the back, drink in hand, the sleeves of his normally crisply starched dress shirt rolled up to his elbows. His suit jacket hung limply over the back of the booth seating.

He didn't see me until I was standing at the edge of his table.

"Didn't think this was your vibe," I said, eyebrows raised.

"I'm a cop, aren't I?" he shot back.

I slid into the empty booth seating across from him. "That stands to be seen."

Ryan studied me for a second, then let out a breath. "Are you here to bust my balls or to drink?"

I didn't answer him. I reached into my coat and pulled out a printout of the photo—of the necklace—and set it on the table between us.

Ryan's eyes dropped to the creased printout. "Dropping hints for the holidays or something?"

"It was in one of the Sumner Field evidence boxes," I told him.

"God damn it, Miller," Ryan scowled. "You're like a dog with a bone."

"Look at it, will you?" I said, frustration mounting.

Ryan made a disgruntled noise of his own and grabbed the piece of paper. "What am I supposed to be looking at?"

"Do you see the engraving?"

He squinted. "Is that an *M*?"

I nodded. "Mary Dandridge, 10 years old. Missing since 1966. Last seen in the Sumner Field projects. Her police report mentions a necklace—a heart charm. It was apparently a gift from her grandmother."

Ryan exhaled hard. "You're not supposed to keep working a case once it's closed, Miller."

"And you're not supposed to close a case just because City Hall tells you to," I countered.

Ryan's jaw tensed. "I saw the charm in the file. But I didn't connect it."

"You were under a lot of pressure," I said, even though we both knew it was a flimsy excuse.

"Still," he muttered. "I should've caught it."

I leaned forward in the booth and lowered my voice. I doubted anyone was listening to our conversation, but I cautiously continued.

"There's a class-action suit," I told him. "Julia's law firm filed it on behalf of former Sumner Field residents."

Ryan had come to know Julia through her defense of a young man, Landon Tauer, who Ryan had blindly believed was guilty of homicide. I couldn't be sure if mentioning her name would cause him to become even more defensive. Our differing policing styles had been on full display back then. Ryan prioritized clearing cases over getting it right. Ryan assumed people were guilty until proven innocent. Someone wouldn't be arrested unless they'd done something to deserve it in his opinion.

Ryan looked surprised. "Julia? I thought she was a public defender."

"She's with Grisham & Stein now."

"Jesus. Those soulless bottom feeders?"

I grimaced at the description. Julia's role as a lawyer had long been a touchy subject for myself, my co-workers, and my cop friends. That she was now employed at the high-profile criminal defense firm was sure to make that worse, even if her new position was about wrongful convictions and reparative justice.

I let his judgement slide. "She's been building the case around environmental damage and systemic neglect. If we can confirm this girl was buried under city property and was an un- or under-investigated death—"

"Neglect turns into liability," Ryan finished for me. "Maybe even criminal concealment."

"Julia thinks so."

Detective Ryan stroked his chin. "You always were a pain in the ass."

"You're welcome."

For the first time, he gave me a ghost of a smile. "You want help tracking a relative?"

"I won't say no."

He nodded. "I'll make a few calls."

I stood from the booth. "Thanks. You know how to reach me."

Ryan picked up the copy of the photo again. He silently studied it, jaw working.

"I should've caught it," he said softly.

"We all miss things," I pacified. I'd missed it the first time, too. "But we don't always get the chance to make it right."

I quietly let myself in. The condo's lights were dim, except for the recessed lights above the stove that Julia left on when she knew I'd be late. I slipped out of my boots and hung my jacket on a hook in the foyer, listening for her. The TV was off. I heard no sounds of typing. Only the faint clink of a spoon against ceramic led me to her.

I found her in the kitchen, wearing an oversized hoodie and yoga pants. She sat on the countertop with a bowl of ice cream perched on her lap. Butter pecan—the kind she pretended she bought for me even though rocky road was more my style.

She looked up as I stepped into the kitchen; she made no effort to hide the ice cream. "Hi."

"Hey," I said, eyeballing the oversized bowl. "You good?"

Julia shrugged. Her eyes followed me closely as I crossed the room. I stood between her knees and let my hands settle on her upper thighs.

She held out the spoon, and I took it. The ice cream was soft, slightly melted around the edges.

"I've got Jason Ryan hunting down family members," I said, "and I put in a request for dental records."

Julia took the spoon back and stabbed it into the bowl. "We don't have to talk about it tonight. You can clock out."

I nodded and wrapped my arms around her waist. My cheek pressed into her shoulder and I slowly exhaled against her. We didn't move for a long moment.

"I keep thinking about her family," I vocalized. "About someone out there who thought she ran away, or disappeared, or just vanished. And they never got answers."

"If we're lucky," she said, "we might finally give them some."

We stood like that for a while, quiet and connected, until Julia nudged the bowl of ice cream toward me again. "Finish this so I don't," she instructed me. "Then come to bed."

I took the spoon back with a faint smile. "Yes, ma'am."

Chapter Twenty-Four

It was a quiet Sunday afternoon when Julia and I pulled up to the residence of Derrick Dandridge. The man, now in his mid-70s, lived in the home with his daughter and her family. The house sat on a tidy lot in North Minneapolis—two-story, white vinyl siding, a well-kept American flag mounted near the porch.

A concrete goose still dressed up for Valentine's Day was perched on the wrap-around porch, close to the front door. I wondered if it had a St. Patrick's Day outfit or if it would only get changed for Easter.

Julia adjusted the strap of her leather work bag, which held the plastic evidence envelope and the composite sketch. I glanced at her, trying to read her emotions. Her world was typically a courtroom or a conference room, not necessarily someone's living room. I had more experience with that, especially as of late.

"Ready?" I asked.

She nodded once, eyes serious. "Are you?"

I didn't have an answer. This wasn't the kind of house call I thought anyone could really be prepared for. I opened the gate and started toward the front door.

Julia had called ahead, so when we walked up the steps, the front door opened before we could knock.

A woman in her late forties stepped onto the front porch. She had short, natural hair and a calm expression. Behind her stood a man about the same age—her husband, I assumed—tall, salt-and-pepper beard, arms crossed over his chest.

"Ms. Desjardin?" the woman guessed.

Julia stepped forward and offered her hand. "Julia is just fine. Thank you for having us, Mrs. Whitaker."

"Courtney," she adjusted. She gestured to the man behind her. "And this is my husband, Tim."

"It's nice to meet you both," Julia greeted. She turned to me next. "This is Detective Cassidy Miller. She's with MPD's Cold Case division."

"Cassidy is fine," I amended.

"Well, since we're all good friends now," Courtney Whitaker laughed, "why don't we go inside."

Courtney and Tim Whitaker stepped back to let us inside. The house smelled like something was baking—warm nutmeg or cinnamon. A child's voice echoed faintly from somewhere deeper in the house, but they didn't make an appearance.

Julia slipped out of her heels, leaving them in the front foyer. I followed suit, removing my boots so as to not spoil the freshly vacuumed carpet with old snow and rock salt.

"Dad's in his den," Courtney explained, closing the front door. She gestured to the living room. "Why don't you have a seat, and I'll go grab him."

Julia and I silently entered the living room and sat next to each other on the navy blue upholstered couch. The living room was full but not cluttered. A bookcase filled with framed photos and paperbacks lined one wall, and an upright piano stood against the other. On top of it sat a series of elementary school pictures in plain black frames.

My attention stopped on a worn leather recliner. It made me think about Ms. Price and her bad hip. I hadn't been back to visit since I'd revealed myself as a police detective. I would have to make good on my promise to see her soon and bring a baker's dozen with me.

I noticed next the military branch-themed throw blanket over the back of the recliner. My eyes stopped on a shadow box on another bookshelf. It could have belonged to either Courtney or Tim Whitaker, but my gut told me that Derrick Dandridge was a veteran—Vietnam if I'd had to guess.

Tim Whitaker hovered anxiously in the archway, obviously uncomfortable with the situation. He rocked back on his heels.

"This weather, eh?" he said conversationally.

I bobbed my head. "It might be summer before the snow is gone."

I turned my head toward the sound of heavy footsteps,

punctuated by the tap of a sturdy cane. Julia and I both rose to our feet when Derrick Dandridge entered the room.

He was a tall man, slim in the way older men often get. I might have expected a curved back or rounded shoulders to go with the wooden cane, but Derrick Dandridge stood like he had a steel rod for a spine.

"Mr. Dandridge," I said, offering my hand. "Thank you for meeting with us today."

He took my hand, his grip firm, but his face remained neutral, curious and cautious about the strangers in his daughter's living room.

"And thank you for your service, sir," I added.

His eyebrows lifted on his lined forehead. "Were you military as well?"

"Eight years in Afghanistan," I confirmed.

He gave a low whistle and stepped back slightly to look me over. "Afghanistan, huh? I should be saluting *you*."

I shook my head. "I think you've got me beat on seniority, sir."

Mr. Dandridge looked between Julia and me. "My daughter said you might know something about Mary."

"Yes," Julia said gently. "Why don't we all have a seat?"

Mr. Dandridge sat in the corner armchair. His daughter sat next to him on a loveseat. Julia and I returned to the couch, the coffee table between us, empty except for a coaster and a remote.

Tim Whitaker continued to hover in the archway. "Sorry," he apologized. "I've got snickerdoodles in the oven. There's a school bake sale tomorrow."

Julia opened her work bag and pulled out the items slowly, carefully. She started with the manila envelope that held the computer-generated image—the composite sketch based on DNA recovered from one of the young girl's bones. She set it on the table, turned it toward them, and slid it forward.

Mr. Dandridge didn't react right away. His eyes scanned the image with a soldier's discipline, looking for accuracy, for something he could verify. It was Courtney who made the first sound—a sharp breath, not quite a sob.

She stood abruptly and crossed the room. "Hang on," she said, voice thick with emotion. She pulled one of the framed photos from the top of the piano and brought it back. She set it down beside the composite.

My throat tightened. It wasn't just a resemblance. It was *her*.

Same bone structure, same eyes, same mouth. The phenotype model wasn't perfect, but it was eerily close.

Mr. Dandridge swallowed hard, still staring at the two images side by side. Courtney leaned forward, looking between them, still quiet herself. No one rushed to speak.

After a long pause, Mr. Dandridge nodded. "That's Mary."

"H-how do you have that?" Courtney asked.

Julia folded her hands in her lap before answering. "We recovered DNA from remains unearthed at the former Sumner Field projects. It's a process called forensic phenotyping. It analyzes genetic markers to predict physical traits—eye color, hair color, facial structure. It's not an exact science," she noted, "but it's one of the tools we can use when we don't have a name."

She paused, glancing at the photo Courtney had placed beside the composite. "We had hoped someone might recognize her. I'm so sorry it had to be you."

"Sumner Field," Mr. Dandridge spoke up. "She ... she was there the whole time?"

I cleared my throat. "Yes, sir. We believe she died not long after she went missing."

Something passed over the man's face. A reckoning or realization. "I shipped out to South Vietnam not long after she went missing. I figured she'd be back by the time I got home." His lips trembled. "I told myself that for years. That she'd show up one day, full of stories."

I reached into my jacket pocket and pulled out my notebook. "We're going to find out who did this to your sister," I told him. "I can't promise when. But I promise we won't stop."

He met my eyes. "You think someone killed her."

"I do."

"Because she didn't run away," he said.

"No," I said. "She didn't."

Julia didn't offer additional condolences. She didn't say "we're so sorry for your loss" or anything that sounded rehearsed. Instead, she opened the smaller evidence bag with the pendant inside and laid it down next to the pictures.

"I believe this belonged to her," she said. "It was recovered with the remains. It's been cleaned and cataloged, but I wanted you to see it for yourself."

The pendant was heart-shaped with a cursive *M* in the center. Time had dulled it, but it still caught the afternoon light.

Mr. Dandridge reached forward and picked up the pendant through the plastic. He looked at it for a long time before passing it to his daughter.

"This was hers," he said, voice low. "Our grandmother gave it to her for her ninth birthday. She said it stood for 'Mary' and 'mighty' at the same time."

No one spoke for a while. The only sound was the muted tick of a cuckoo clock on the wall. From elsewhere in the house, a timer went off. Tim Whitaker quietly cursed before rushing off to attend to his snickerdoodles.

"I know this is difficult," Julia said, finally. "And I know there's nothing we can say to undo the time that's passed. But we'd like to include Mary in a civil suit we're filing against the city. We're representing the families of those who were displaced or experienced hardships while living there. We'd like Mary to be the face of that effort, but only with your permission."

Mr. Dandridge leaned back, still holding the bag with the pendant.

"We'll take every precaution to protect your family's privacy outside of what's necessary," Julia emphasized. "But the truth is, we think the public will respond if they can *see* who this happened to. If they see the injustice done to a real child, not just a case number."

Mr. Dandridge looked at his daughter. They remained silent until Courtney nodded. "If it helps other families, I think it's worth it."

Mr. Dandridge turned his eyes back to us. "You have our permission. Do what you need to do."

"Thank you," Julia said, inclining her head graciously. "We'll send everything over in writing, of course. There's no pressure to move quickly."

Courtney wiped her eyes and reached over to squeeze her father's hand. "Will there be a funeral?" she asked. "A real one?"

"We'll work with the medical examiner's office to get the remains released to your family," I said. "You can decide the kind of service you want after that."

"I want her buried next to our mother," Mr. Dandridge decided. "She always missed her."

"We'll make that happen," I vowed.

Mr. Dandridge leaned back in his chair. His daughter rested a hand on his shoulder. I could only imagine the thoughts and emotions they were both experiencing.

The patter of small feet thundered down the hallway, and a small girl came barreling into the living room.

"Granddad!" she hollered, arms flung wide. She was all skinny limbs and puffball braids, oblivious to the heaviness in the room.

"Inside voice," Courtney gently corrected.

Mr. Dandridge's face broke into something close to a smile. "There's my girl." he said.

"This is Mary," Courtney introduced. She smoothed a

hand over the girl's back as she climbed up into her grandfather's lap. "She's named after her Great Aunt."

The little girl beamed at us, unaware of the name she carried, or maybe too young to know its significance. Still, something about the timing made my throat tighten.

"Hi, Mary," I said gently.

She waved, already halfway distracted by the buttons on her grandfather's cardigan.

We stayed for another twenty minutes. Julia explained the civil process in clear, calm terms—no legalese, no drama, just the facts. What they'd be asked to sign. How Mary's image might be used. What protections would be in place. The family asked a few more questions, mostly logistical. By the time we stood to leave, the mood had shifted from grief to resolve.

Julia and I stepped out into the cold. March hadn't thawed yet—just dirty snowbanks and the sound of meltwater trickling into storm drains. As we stepped out into the cool air, I heard the piano behind us. Mary, maybe, plunking out a tune.

Julia's heels clicked neatly on the concrete, the only other sound in the otherwise quiet neighborhood. She didn't look over at me, and I didn't say anything either. There wasn't much left to say.

She waited until we were halfway down the front walk before speaking. "That went about as well as it could have."

I hummed, but made no other comment.

Julia didn't say anything else as we walked to the car. She moved like she had somewhere else to be, even though I knew we were only headed home.

She unlocked the Mercedes without a word. I got in and so did she.

She didn't look at me. She started the engine and pulled away from the curb.

I didn't ask what was on her mind.

∽

"Are you hungry?" Julia asked.

"Sure."

I wasn't starving, but I could always eat. Julia surprised me by turning on her blinker and pulling into the parking lot of a fast food chain. She didn't stop in the lot, however, but kept driving towards the drive-thru lane.

She turned to me briefly before her car reached the exterior speaker box to place our order. "Cheeseburger, no onions?"

"Yeah," I approved, still taken aback.

I remained silent while Julia ordered for the both of us from the disembodied voice coming out of a worn metal speaker. I was surprised when she ordered a cheeseburger for herself as well.

She smoothly pulled the Mercedes around the corner and paid for the meal. She was kind to the teenager at the second window and collected the To-Go bag. She handed me the white paper sack and continued to coast to the end of the drive-thru lane.

I expected her to turn back onto the road—she rarely ate this kind of stuff, and definitely not in her car—but instead she selected a spot in the restaurant's parking lot. She cracked the front windows and turned off the ignition.

"Are you sure about this?" I teased.

She gave me a look, faintly amused. "Desperate times."

I took over the task of digging through the fast food bag and of handing her a burger while balancing mine on my lap. We were quiet in the car with only the crinkle of fast food wrappers as our soundtrack. We shared a container of French fries from the center console.

"Jonathan's death was a surprise," she said eventually, her voice low and even. "But at least my family got closure. We didn't have to wonder what happened to him, even though no one ever found a note."

I never forgot that Julia had lost her younger brother to suicide, but sometimes it slipped my mind. I hadn't thought about what kind of memories or emotions might get stirred up visiting the brother of someone whose life had also prematurely ended.

Her fingers tightened briefly around the remnants of her burger. "Hearing that man talk about his sister—it brought it all back. Not just the end, but the confusion in the months before when he wasn't really himself anymore. I thought I was smart enough to see everything. But I wasn't."

There was a bitterness in her voice she didn't bother

hiding. Julia was always harder on herself than anyone else ever could be.

"I'm sorry," I said. The words felt small and inadequate. "The grief doesn't ever go away, does it?"

"No," she agreed. "It only changes shape."

She gave a small, humorless laugh. "And now I've turned a cheeseburger into a therapy session." She shook her head. "I'm sorry."

"Don't be."

I reached into the bag and passed her a napkin. She took it from me without looking, wiping her fingers methodically, like the act alone could help her keep control.

Julia's gaze softened. "I can't believe I let you eat this in here."

That finally made me smile.

She picked at the cooling French fries in their conical container. "We really need to get you a vehicle with four wheels."

I grimaced, knowing she was right, but hating it.

"You want me to sell my bike?"

"I never said that, darling. I only think it would make things easier if we both had more reliable transportation."

"But you *do* want me to sell the bike," I guessed, plucking a few limp fries from the center console. "It's not very practical."

"Not everything needs to make sense, darling," she replied. "Besides, maybe I'd like another ride."

I choked a little, coughing around a half-swallowed fry.

She didn't blink; she only turned toward me like she hadn't just detonated a memory.

The memory surged in my mind's eye—of her straddling my Harley inside of the storage unit, the echo of her low moan as I'd opened the throttle beneath us. I'd barely touched her and she'd come undone. Not even a month later, she'd gifted me vibrating underwear for my birthday. She'd controlled the remote in her pocket while we were out drinking with my closest friends and had acted like she wasn't toying with me while I turned to liquid in the middle of a crowded brewery.

I squirmed in my seat, thighs pressing together against the phantom buzz.

"That wasn't really a *ride*," I said once I'd recovered.

Julia delicately shrugged. "It worked just fine for me."

She plucked the last fry from the container and licked the salt off her fingers, eyes on me the whole time.

My face burned hot.

"Still hungry?" she asked.

God help me.

Chapter Twenty Five

J ulia delicately pierced a piece of romaine lettuce with a plastic takeout fork.

I'd been spending my lunch breaks at her law office over the past several days. The recent connection between Mary Dandridge and one of the bodies recovered from Sumner Field had bought me a little leeway with Captain Forrester, but I still felt under his microscope having to account for all of my time away from my desk.

I hadn't felt so heavily monitored since high school and needing a hall pass to use the bathroom. Lunches were on my own time, however; Forrester had no say over where I stopped on my midday break.

I wasn't uncomfortable at the Cold Case office, per say, but I did feel a little guilty about asking Julia to take over the Sumner Field case without talking it over with my co-workers first. I had no doubt Sarah and Stanley, and maybe even Jason Ryan, would have supported the decision, but it was too late now. It would all come out eventually, especially if the lawsuit ended up going to court. It wasn't everyday someone sued the city for millions of dollars, after all.

I bit into my deli sandwich and brushed the crumbs from my chest.

"When you're pregnant," I asked, "are you going to eat real food, or will you continue to stick to rabbit food?"

"If memory serves me correctly, wasn't I the one who bought fast food just the other day?" she mused.

I raised my eyebrow. "I have serious doubts about you sneaking Cheetos in your briefcase."

"I'd rather not jinx it," she cautioned. "You know there's a high probability that I won't ever get pregnant."

"I'm choosing to think positive thoughts," I smiled.

"Positive?" she echoed. "Like me being as big as a house?"

"There will only be more of you to love," I easily returned.

Julia chuckled. "You should write a book, darling. *One-Liners to Appease Your Self-critical Fiancée.*"

I took another bite of my sandwich. "Sounds like a mouthful," I teased.

She shook her fork at me. "I'll give *you* a mouthful."

I grinned, enjoying the rare moment of levity and banter. It had been too long, and with not enough frequency, that we'd allowed ourselves this playfulness. We'd dealt with long stretches of seriousness sneaking into our lives before, especially after the death of her father and having to rehome her mother. And now with fertility treatments and this lawsuit, we'd been denying ourselves permission to have fun and be unserious. I would have to make it my mission to make her laugh more.

I wondered how she felt about bounce parks or batting cages.

"I'll start up shots again soon," she said. "My doctor said my body responded well to the hormones the first time around, so he's optimistic that this second egg retrieval could be the final one."

I wiggled my eyebrows suggestively. "I have no complaints about how your body responded to those hormones either."

Julia made a noise, something between a cough and clearing her throat. She stabbed another lettuce leaf.

"What's the science behind orgasms and egg production?" I wondered aloud. "Any correlation?"

"I actually asked my doctor about that," she quietly revealed. She stared at her salad rather than meet my eye. "He said that orgasms themselves don't directly increase egg follicles or improve ovarian reserve."

I watched the blush creep up her neck. I couldn't recall if I'd ever seen her so obviously embarrassed.

"It can't hurt though, right?"

"I guess we'll have to see," she said evenly.

"Whatever you want to do, babe. I'm at your service."

A quiet knock on Julia's partially closed office door had us turning toward the sound. Alice stood in the entryway.

There was no way of knowing what or if Alice had overheard our unorthodox conversation, but she was probably used to it by now.

"Ms. Desjardin? I've got the Mayor's office on the line for you."

I watched a rolodex of emotions flicker across Julia's features until she settled on indifferent.

"Thank you, Alice."

The office door closed with Alice's departure, but I didn't know if I should remain.

I started to stand and jerked my thumb towards the door. "Want me to go? Give you some privacy?"

"No. Stay. Sit," she instructed.

I didn't take offense to the canine commands. I imagined the chaotic swirl of scenarios churning through Julia's thoughts. *What was the Mayor's office calling about? Would they try to intimidate her? Were they going to court?*

I settled back into the too-comfortable office chair across from her desk.

Julia cleared her throat and exhaled a long, calming breath before picking up the office landline.

"Mr. Mayor," she warmly greeted. "What can I do for you?"

I leaned forward, but tried to be an unobtrusive observer. Julia hummed and said phrases like "I see," and "of course," but I couldn't make out anything being said on the other end of the call.

Finally, after too long and too tense of a moment, Julia ended the call. "Yes, I'll be in touch."

She gently set the receiver back into its cradle. She straightened her shoulders, but her features gave nothing away. Had it been a good call or no?

Julia wet her lips before speaking: "We're not going to court. They're ready to settle."

I blinked. "Just like that?"

"Just like that," she echoed. She stared down at her silent office phone. "They weren't ready to negotiate before, but once you discovered Mary Dandridge ..." She trailed off. "They probably want to avoid the bad publicity," she observed, continuing to think aloud. "It's an election year, after all."

∽

I'd received a text message from a number I hadn't recognized. At first I thought it might have been from someone related to the Sumner Field lawsuit, but I eventually recognized the address where my anonymous texter wanted to meet. It was the same coffee shop where I'd met up with Monica weeks ago after our paths had crossed.

The message had given a time and date when she wanted to meet. I made sure not to be late, but I knew that this would be the last time. Julia might not have given me an ultimatum, but she had been right about my ghosts. I wasn't that girl in the desert anymore. And I didn't want to be.

I spotted Monica right away at the same table where we'd originally sat. She looked a little more cleaned up. She wore the same hoodie and thin, inadequate jacket, but she looked more like herself than the past few times I'd seen her.

I slid into the empty chair across from where she sat. "Hey."

"Hey yourself,' she returned.

Her dark eyes inspected me for a moment before she returned her attention to what looked like an apple cinnamon muffin. She picked at the crumble topping and popped each bit into her mouth.

"So what's up?" I pressed. Her text message hadn't been forthcoming except that she'd wanted to meet up. "Do you need anything?" I asked, keeping my voice low, almost casual. "A place to stay, some cash?"

"I didn't come here to wreck anything for you, Miller. I swear. I just ... I don't know," she struggled. "I guess I just needed to see that at least one of us made it out."

She stared at me, her fingers shredding the muffin wrapper.

"I'm sorry," she added. "For showing up like this. For digging up shit you probably buried a long time ago."

I swallowed against the lump in my throat. I hadn't buried it—not really. Some scars just went quiet for a while.

"I'm getting married," I said. "And we're going to have a baby. Not right away," I clarified, "but eventually."

"Shit, Miller."

I exhaled. "I know."

"I'm ... I'm really happy for you." She smiled, but it looked more wistful than anything. "If one of us was going to land on their feet after that fucked up experience, I'm glad it was you."

I could have told her about the marbled scar tissue down my back or about the night terrors and flashbacks, but it didn't feel necessary.

"Thank you," I said instead. "What about you? What's next for Monica Hernandez?"

"I'm going home to Texas," she said. "I've put my folks through hell this past year. It's time I make it up to them." Her head tilted, thoughtful. "Do you still talk with your parents?"

"It was rough when I first got back, but it's getting better," I revealed. "My mom actually helped Julia pick out my engagement ring."

Monica's gaze dropped to my hands. "Julia—that's the lucky lady's name?"

Lucky? Who was to say which of the two of us had lucked out.

When Monica finally stood up, the chair scraping against the cafe floor, she looked down at me and gave a short, almost shy nod.

"Take care of yourself, Cass."

She pulled her jacket tighter around her torso and walked out of the coffee shop without looking back.

I stayed seated for a long time after she was gone, the deconstructed muffin a mess and a reminder on the table.

Chapter Twenty-Six

The box was small and flat, neatly wrapped with no frills—just crisp edges and a folded note resting on top. Julia's handwriting was sharp and deliberate, like everything else about her. No hearts, no unnecessary punctuation, only an instruction she expected me to follow.

Wear me

My heart lodged in my throat. The last time something had appeared in a box that she'd wanted me to wear, I'd been gifted a strap-on.

I held my breath as I tore off the wrapping paper, but my apprehension dissipated the moment I saw what was inside.

A maroon sweatshirt, the fabric worn soft with age. The phrase *University of Minnesota Law* stretched across the front in faded gold. I ran my fingertips over the screen-printed lettering.

I pulled the sweatshirt over my head. The material was thick and slightly oversized. It smelled clean, but underneath the laundry detergent, there was something distinctly Julia—faint traces of her perfume and the fancy lotions she used.

When I stepped out of the bedroom, I caught the scent of something buttery and rich. Julia stood at the stove, one hand on her hip, the other stirring something in a pot. She must have heard me because she turned slightly, catching my reflection in the window over the kitchen sink.

She hummed her approval. "You take instructions so well."

I crossed my arms, feeling the way the sleeves bunched at my elbows. "Where's this been hiding?"

I didn't have her entire wardrobe memorized, but I'd never seen the sweatshirt before.

"It was boxed up with some other things at my parents' house," she said. "I brought it back after our last trip to Embarrass."

I huffed a quiet laugh. "Didn't think you were the sentimental type."

"I'm not," she said, turning back to the stove. "Dinner's almost ready."

I stepped closer, catching sight of two plates and a steaming pot of soup.

I raised an eyebrow. "Grilled cheese and tomato soup?"

We didn't have fancy, elaborate meals every night, but I couldn't recall her ever making something so pedestrian.

I reached for a plate and took an impulsive bite. The

bread crunched under my teeth, perfectly crisp, and the cheese pulled apart in strands. It reminded me of grilled cheese my mom would make when I wasn't feeling well, or the grilled cheese sandwich my dad used to buy me when we'd go to the State Fair.

I exhaled through my nose. "Damn."

Julia's lips twitched. "Eager, dear?"

Instead of answering, I grabbed a bowl and dunked the sandwich into the soup. The first spoonful was rich, creamy, and slightly tangy—exactly how it should be.

"Dang. You really *can* cook," I muttered.

Julia hummed. "You're easy to impress, darling." She nudged me toward the living room. "Go sit. I'll bring the food."

"I can do it," I insisted. "You're the one going through medical treatments," I pointed out. "I should be pampering *you*."

"Nonsense," she rejected. "Everyone deserves a little pampering. And you've been the most supportive partner I could ever dream of."

"How about we call it a tie," I negotiated.

"That will be satisfactory," she agreed with a smile.

I grabbed the remote while Julia carried everything over on a cutting board. She set the makeshift tray on the coffee table before settling in beside me. It was rare that we ate in the living room in front of the television. Julia usually insisted we eat at the dining room table or breakfast nook like civilized humans.

The prospect of spilling tomato soup on the couch or carpet made me a little anxious.

"I might also be reassuring myself that I'm not a bad partner," she unexpectedly added. "I come with a lot of baggage."

"At least it's designer," I quipped.

She knocked her shoulder against mine. "Hush."

I considered telling Julia that Monica was leaving town, but I didn't want to disrupt the cozy evening she'd orchestrated. We would talk about that later.

I tried to hand Julia the remote, but she shook her head. "Your pick."

I raised my eyebrows. "Are you *sure?*"

Julia wrinkled her nose. "Just nothing horror or gory. I'd rather not consume tomato soup while a sorority house gets massacred."

I laughed, feeling lighter. "Stupid comedy is it."

I took another bite of my sandwich and leaned back into the couch. I let the moment settle around us. The nostalgic warmth of the food, the comforting weight of Julia's sweatshirt, the way she let herself totally relax beside me.

Yeah. It was a good night.

Julia had fallen asleep on my shoulder sometime during the latter half of the movie. I didn't attempt to wake her up until the movie's final credits scrolled across the screen.

We'd both been working overtime, and her body more than usual.

"It's over?" Her voice sounded soft and a little groggy, like she was still halfway between sleep and waking.

"Don't worry." I fondly brushed some hair away from her forehead. "You didn't miss anything Oscar-worthy."

"That's a relief."

I pressed an input button on the remote, bringing the television back to our cable subscription. The late night news was on.

Headlines from the day's events and breaking news scrolled across the bottom of the screen. One chyron in particular caught my attention: *Officials acknowledge failures at Sumner Field site.*

I sat up and turned up the volume.

The news broadcast switched over to coverage of a press conference the Mayor had apparently held earlier that day. I recognized the background. It was the construction site for the new luxury condo development at Sumner Field.

"Did you know about this?" I asked.

Julia yawned and stretched her arms over her head. "Someone from the Mayor's office emailed me about it, but it was very last minute. Even if I had left the office immediately, I doubt I would have made it in time."

The Mayor stood behind a podium, flanked by a number of individuals who I didn't recognize. Everyone wore hard hats and smiles. A banner had been strung up in the background: *Owning the Past. Building the Future.*

"Today," the Mayor began, "starts a new chapter in this great city's story."

He looked down for a moment and then back up at the cameras.

"What happened here at the Sumner Field housing project is part of our shared history—one that hasn't always been acknowledged. We can't undo the past. But we can choose what we do with it."

The banner behind him fluttered gently in the breeze.

"I'm proud to stand here and say we're taking that responsibility seriously. We've reached a historic settlement with the families connected to this site. The living descendants will receive direct financial reparations, not just in recognition of what was lost, but as a commitment to equity moving forward."

He gestured toward a poster on an easel that resembled blueprints.

"We've also amended the development plans for this property. Twenty-five percent of the new housing units will be reserved for low- and fixed-income households so that longtime residents, seniors, and families who've been here for generations are not pushed out by progress, but included in it."

He cleared his throat, the words more practiced now.

"And I'm pleased to share that this space will also include a permanent memorial to those who lived here. It will be visible, intentional, and lasting—a space for reflection, for remembrance, and for truth."

Julia's shoulder pressed into mine. "You did that."

My attention didn't stray from the glossy printed banner behind the Mayor as he fielded questions from the press.

"They turned it into a damn campaign slogan." I couldn't help my scowl.

"The living descendants get reparations. A memorial to those buried at the site is going up at the location. *And* they've changed the design plan for the new condominiums to accommodate low and fixed income households. That seems like an awfully big victory, darling."

I was familiar with the parameters of the settlement, but watching it unfold on the evening news had made something twist in my gut.

"No one got arrested."

I felt the couch cushions shift beneath me as Julia repositioned herself closer.

"Is that your litmus test for success?" she asked.

"I guess."

Julia trailed a single, tapered finger down my arm. "We can find better uses for your handcuffs if that's what's gotten you so upset," she smoothly flirted.

I must have been *really* distracted to have not taken the bait, although my brain did reward me with a mental image of Julia's naked, prone figure, her smooth muscles straining as I licked her to completion.

I waved my hand at the television. "It's all performative," I complained. "I didn't recognize a single person on that platform with the Mayor. Where was Mary

Dandridge's family? Or Mrs. Carter? Or Ruby, Earl, Leon, or Ms. Price?" I continued to fume.

"Let them have their little publicity stunt," Julia soothed. "You were able to get those people far more than 10 seconds of screen time on the local news."

"And what about the guy from the parking garage?" The loose ends had me unraveling as well. "He's got to be connected to someone at City Hall or Greenrock."

"You'll find him. I know you will."

Julia turned off the television and stood from the couch.

"Will you help me with my next shot?" she asked.

I continued to stare at the television even though the screen had faded to black.

"Yeah," I sighed. "I'll poke you."

Julia sat on the edge of the bed, her bare feet flexing into the area rug while she waited for me. She passed me the syringe, already prepped and capped. I knelt on the floor in front of her and pushed up the expensive fabric of her nightgown to expose more of her upper thigh. Her skin was warm under my hand.

She tensed slightly when I swabbed the injection site with alcohol.

"I'll be quick," I said.

"It's not the pain."

I paused. "What is it, then?"

Julia softly exhaled. "It's the reminder, I think. That

my body needs help doing something it should just know how to do."

I rested my free hand on her knee. "There's no shame in needing help. You taught me that."

She nodded, just once.

I held the syringe at the correct angle and pushed it into her thigh with clinical precision. Julia inhaled but didn't flinch. I pressed the plunger slowly, giving the solution time to settle into her muscle. I pulled the needle free and pressed gauze to the site with the flat of my thumb.

"All done," I said. "Minimal carnage."

"Thank you, dear," she said quietly.

I tossed the syringe into the sharps container on the dresser—nothing but net. I waited for Julia to scold me for being so haphazard with needles, but she didn't say a word.

I rubbed the pad of my thumb over her kneecap in a gesture meant to be soothing.

"Are you okay?"

She tilted her head down just enough for her eyes to meet mine. "I hate that I'm not in control of this. I hate needing things."

"I know." I dropped my gaze and continued to rub her knee. "In my last session with Dr. Warren, I might have told her you don't need me."

Julia's caramel eyes widened. "I hope you don't honestly believe that."

I made a noise. "Eh."

"Cassidy. Darling. You're the *one thing* I need. And I'm not talking about helping with hormone shots or rides to the doctor or even an extra hand when I can't get to my mother right away."

"You know I'll do whatever you need from me."

"I *need you t*o believe that you're my everything," she emphasized.

I swallowed and let her words blanket me. "Okay."

"Don't 'okay' me," she scolded. "This is a very serious thing."

I looked down at my hands. I'd never been proficient with serious things. I typically used humor to deflect or defuse the situation. I kept the punchlines contained for the moment.

I wanted to say something, anything that would make the moment feel less intense, but the truth was, I didn't know what to say. Instead, I let the silence stretch between us.

Eventually, Julia gently tilted my head back up so my gaze met hers.

"Come to bed?"

I swallowed thickly. "Okay."

I followed her under the covers without hesitation. She laid down on her side, facing away. For a second, I wasn't sure if she wanted space. But then she shifted backwards, just enough that her back met my chest. It felt like an invitation. A request.

I curved my body to fit against hers. My arm hovered and then settled around her waist. She caught my hand and brought it close, tucking it under her own like it belonged there.

Maybe it did.

I brushed her dark hair out of the way. I kissed the top of her shoulder and then her neck, letting my lips linger just under her ear.

"Will you let me take care of you a little longer tonight?"

I heard her quiet exhale. "Please."

I ran my palm over her hip, bunching up the lower hem of her sheer nightgown. Her skin was warm and smooth beneath my hand.

My fingers fluttered over her breast, coaxing her nipple through the satin fabric. I skimmed my fingertips against the hardening bud and felt her press her backside more firmly against my front.

I eased the skinny nightgown strap down her shoulder and kissed the newly exposed skin. I marked a slow path with my mouth down the center of her back.

Julia sighed, hip pressing into the mattress, as I slid my hand between her breasts, over her abdomen, and between her thighs. Her breath hitched when I brushed my fingertips over her clit.

"Cassidy," she murmured, reaching back to touch me. "Don't make me wait."

I didn't.

I nudged her leg forward with my own. My top arm went around her waist while the other slid between her thighs from the back. I pressed my middle finger against her entrance. I teased her opening and luxuriated in the slick arousal that collected on my fingertips. We seemed to release a collective breath as I eased my finger into her.

My shallow thrusts grew deeper until I could replace one finger with two. Julia released a soft, unguarded moan. Her back arched into me as her body opened and she pulsed around my fingers.

I cupped her breast with my free hand and kissed behind her ear.

"You feel so good like this," I quietly praised. "So fucking perfect."

Her breath came in shallow pants. "Harder."

I gave her what she needed, curling my fingers inside of her and alternating between pinching her nipple and grinding my palm against her clit. I nudged my leg between her knees, opening her wider to my efforts. She rocked back into me, meeting every thrust.

Her short, polished fingernails dug into my upper thigh. "There. Right there, yes," she encouraged.

I bit down on the top of her exposed shoulder when something feral unfurled in my chest. I heard her surprised intake of air but it only seemed to propel her hips back faster to meet my thrusting fingers.

"Don't stop," she urged me.

I tightened my arm around her waist. Her fingers fisted the sheets.

"I'll fuck you all night," I promised.

Julia arched her back and looped her arm around my neck. I heard the noises she made—the quiet but desperate whimpers. She pushed back against my fingers, again and again.

When her orgasm hit, she went still and then gasped, high and strangled.

I slowly withdrew my fingers and wrapped both arms around her. I held her through the first wave. "I've got you, I've got you," I soothed.

I shut my eyes tight and worked to match the measured pace of each inhale and exhale until we seemed to breathe as one.

When she finally caught her breath, she turned over. Her fingers went to my sternum and she pushed me onto my back.

"My turn."

Julia rose from the mattress to straddle me, her thighs resting on either side of my torso. She removed a hair band that I hadn't noticed before from her wrist. Anticipation coiled in my chest as I watched her pull her hair into a high ponytail.

I reached for her, but she caught my wrists and pinned them above my head.

"I *said* my turn," she repeated.

I swallowed hard. "Yes, ma'am."

Julia stroked the sides of my face; she bent down to kiss me tenderly, sweetly. Her mouth turned hot and greedy as she kissed down my neck and then lower. She tugged up the front of my t-shirt and her tongue circled my nipple. I hissed, hips rising to meet her, when she gently bit down.

She licked and sucked until I was a whimpering mess beneath her.

She didn't tease.

She pushed me into the mattress, her hands rough on my hips, her mouth trailing fire down my stomach. She pulled off my boxers in one practiced move.

"I need this," she said, voice low and urgent. "I need *you* like this."

Her fingers gripped my thighs, spreading me with a kind of hunger that stole my breath. When her mouth found me again, it wasn't soft. It was feral. Possessive. Like she needed to mark me with every flick of her tongue, every moan she dragged out of me.

Julia went down on me like she needed it, like the only thing sustaining her was the sound of my moans and the way my thighs quivered under her grip. Her mouth was wet and insistent, her tongue moving with precision and purpose, until I was a breath away from coming.

"I'm gonna—"

She didn't stop; she didn't even slow down. She just looked up at me through those dark eyelashes, her mouth working me until I fell off that cliff.

It wasn't gentle. It was everything. Her name tore up my throat as my body practically levitated off the bed. She held me down, riding out the orgasm with me, until I collapsed back against the mattress.

"Holy shit," I wheezed.

When Julia finally came up for air, her lips were shiny

and her cheeks were flushed. She looked devastatingly proud of herself.

"Now what was that you said about fucking me all night?"

Epilogue

The parking lot outside of the senior co-op was half ice, half slush, and entirely miserable. It was one of those March days that still felt like December. Melody was already there, leaning against the dented hatch of her Subaru, bundled in a massive puffy winter jacket that made her look like a fashionable sleeping bag. She saw me first and waved with both arms like she was directing air traffic control.

Julia pulled in beside the old Crown Vic, easing her Mercedes into the narrow space. She stepped out in her perfectly tailored camel coat, her dark hair pulled away from her face, sunglasses pushed to the top of her head. Always composed. Always breathtaking.

Melody's eyebrows jumped. "Jesus Christ. Is that her?" she asked me in a stage whisper.

"Play nice," I muttered.

Julia strode over to where we stood. She extended her hand in greeting.

Melody grabbed Julia's hand and gave it a few too many enthusiastic shakes. "Julia Desjardin. The woman who spooked City Hall."

Julia's smile was tight, but not unfriendly. She diplomatically extricated her hand from Melody's exuberant grip. "I don't know about all of that," she said smoothly. "It was a team effort."

Melody gave me a sidelong smirk. "Sure. A team of sharks in expensive heels."

I coughed into my hand to hide a laugh, but Julia only arched an eyebrow.

Inside, the senior living facility was warm and filled with the scent of radiator steam and something vaguely floral. Ms. Price's apartment was on the third floor, and Melody practically bounded up the stairs like she couldn't get there fast enough.

Julia slipped her arm into mine as we mounted the stairs at a more even, measured pace.

Julia nodded in the direction of Melody, who'd started to take the steps two at a time. "Is she always like this?"

"Sometimes worse," I smiled.

Ms. Price met us at her door, wearing a burgundy sweater and her usual suspicious expression. She eyed Julia and Melody, and then me. "Three of you today?" She sighed, sounding weary from the bother of it. "I'll put on the kettle."

Melody gave her a grin that showed all her teeth. "Let's talk first. And then we can have tea. You might want to sit down for this, Ms. Price."

Melody's suggestion earned a skeptical eyebrow. Still, Ms. Price stepped back to let us in.

Her living room was small but tidy, everything in it arranged with care. She lowered herself into her recliner, the one that helped ease the stiffness in her bad hip, and motioned for us to take the couch and loveseat across from her.

Melody didn't sit. She crouched down next to Ms. Price and pulled a piece of paper from a thick envelope. She unfolded the paper with deliberate care.

"This isn't symbolic," she began. "This is real. You're getting the first disbursement from the city's reparations fund for former Sumner Field residents. There's more to come," she noted, "but this ..." She pressed the check into Ms. Price's weathered hands. "This is just the beginning."

Ms. Price looked down at the slim piece of paper, her fingers visibly trembling. Her eyes scanned the check as if to ascertain its legitimacy.

"Well," she said, her voice very soft. "I'll be damned."

She didn't cry. Ms. Price didn't seem like someone who'd let you see her cry.

"People have been promising things to this neighborhood for years," she murmured. "Nice to see someone finally follow through."

Julia had been silent since we'd entered the apartment. I felt her hand in the small of my back before she leaned closer on the couch. Her words were low, intended only for me. "Better than an arrest?"

I hummed an affirming sound as I continued to observe Ms. Price and Melody interact. I could see the disbelief, but also the hint of joy in the older woman's features.

"Doesn't suck."

Julia's touch moved from my lower back to my waist. Hidden beneath my leather jacket, her fingers tugged affectionately on the fabric of my button-up shirt. "You could have this feeling all the time, working with me."

I nearly, reflexively, denied her again. But instead of immediately repeating my well-practiced rejection, I exhaled and let her offer swim around in my brain. My badge felt heavy at my hip. It was a weight I'd carried for so long that I'd stopped noticing it. But recently, it had felt like being laden down with bricks.

Shit. Was I seriously considering leaving MPD? Could I actually be a private investigator for a criminal defense firm?

There was still the unresolved business of our stalker from the parking structure. CCTV hadn't been able to provide a clear image of his face. His features had been obscured by his hood. But every atom in my body knew that if I could find him, I could follow the money back to City Hall. And then there was the business of Greenrock Construction and how they'd come to win the contract for the Sumner Field development project.

And what about the murder of Mary Dandridge and those other children behind Building Nine? If I left Cold Case for Julia's office, would anyone still care?

I could feel Julia's eyes on me. I hadn't said no.

I had never *not* said no before.

"Cassidy?"

I cleared my throat.

"Let's ... let's go home."

∼

I didn't make a big plan. No dinner reservations. No dramatic speeches. Just a Saturday morning, gray and still, with new snow dusting the edges of the windows and the smell of coffee and maple syrup lingering in the kitchen.

Julia was curled up on the couch in leggings and one of my old Marine Corps hoodies, her laptop balanced on her knees. She had her reading glasses on, the ones that I insisted were sexy instead of matronly.

She didn't look up. "You're hovering."

"I'm not hovering," I refused, even though I definitely was.

She still didn't look away from her computer. "You only hover when you're about to say something difficult."

I snorted. "Okay, that's fair."

I sat beside her, holding the small box in my pocket like it might burn a hole in my sweatpants if I waited any longer.

She finally turned to me, pulling off her readers. "What is it, dear?"

I didn't say anything. I pulled the box from my pocket and held it out.

Julia's breath caught, so quiet I almost missed it.

"A little anticlimactic since you beat me to the punch," I said, reflectively going on the defense.

"You've never had an issue with climaxes, darling."

It was a joke, but her face was so serious it made me worry.

Julia wet her lips. "I have to admit. I'm … I'm a little surprised. I thought with Monica—"

"Uh uh," I cut her off.

Julia regarded me, her caramel eyes still guarded and unsure. "I thought maybe you were getting cold feet."

"Monica was the past," I said. "You're my future. And I'm so sorry if I ever made you feel anything different. I'm prepared to spend the rest of our lives proving it."

I opened the box. It was nothing flashy. A platinum band that shone, simple and elegant in a way that reminded me of her. I'd nearly had a panic attack trying to pick out a ring. Luckily I'd had Grace Kelly Donovan to talk me through it, even if it was only on video chat.

"I know you already did this," I noted, "but I wanted to make sure you knew I was choosing you right back."

Julia swallowed, and I could see the way her throat worked, the way her fingers shook just slightly as she closed her laptop and set it aside.

"I don't want a big wedding," I added. "I don't want monogrammed anything or a venue with a waitlist. I just want you. However this works. However we make it ours."

I stood from the couch, but only so I could get down on one knee. My heart pounded in my ears. I'd never been more nervous about anything in my life.

I watched her face for some indication of what she was thinking—what she was feeling. There was a stillness about her, the way she always processed things in full before reacting.

Then, she smiled. It wasn't the polite smile she wore in public; it was the real one. The one that made my chest explode.

"You're really doing this?"

"I am." I exhaled. "Unless you're about to say no, in which case I'm going to make a run for it and claim I was tying my shoe."

She laughed, and it hit me how badly I wanted to hear that sound every day for the rest of my life.

"Cassidy Miller." She leaned forward and cupped my cheek with one hand. "Yes."

The relief was physical, like something in my chest unlocked and let me breathe all the way for the first time in years.

She kissed me, slow and deliberate, her fingers sliding into my hair. I felt her say yes all over again without words. *Yes.* Yes to me. Yes to us. Yes to this wildly unlikely thing we'd built together.

It wasn't the dramatic moment people wrote love songs about. No spotlight. No crowd. It was just the two of us on a Saturday morning at home.

Julia stroked her thumbs over the apples of my cheeks. "Took you long enough."

I grinned. "Worth the wait."

About the Author

Eliza Lentzski is the author of sapphic fiction, romance, and erotica including the best-selling *Winter Jacket* and *Don't Call Me Hero* series. Although a historian by day, Eliza is passionate about fiction. She was born and raised in the upper Midwest, which is often the setting for her novels. She lives in Boston with her wife and their cat, Charley.

Follow Eliza on Instagram, Threads, or BlueSky @ElizaLentzski, and Like her on Facebook for updates and exclusive previews of future original releases.

http://www.elizalentzski.com

Printed in Dunstable, United Kingdom